Chase Me

by LAURA FLORAND

Chapter 1

It was a dark and stormy night, and Chase had three goals. Get out of the fucking rain. Stop a terrorist. And save the world.

Goal one accomplished, he thought as he dropped soundlessly from the window into the restaurant kitchen below. Goals two and three seemed a lot less likely tonight, but at least he would have checked it out. And escaped the rain. A drop of ice water ran down his nape, and he shuddered. Jesus, it was cold out there. What the hell was wrong with this city? It was July! Somebody should have warned him all those films about Paris were bullshitting him.

City of Love. City of Light. City of snobs. City where *it rained and was forty degrees in freaking July!*

Jesus.

An LED glow dimly lit the empty industrial kitchen of the famous Au-dessus restaurant, and he shifted away from the draft from the window, scanning the space. Where to start—

The barest whisper of sound saved his life. He jerked aside just as something heavy barely missed his head and slammed into his shoulder instead. It bounced off and fell to the floor with a clatter. A pot.

Fuck.

He spun—and caught up short not at the very large, very sharp knife aimed in his direction, but at the person wielding it.

A slim blonde clad in sleek leather, her eyes cucumber cool over that lethal blade.

Oh, man. In all his career, this had *never* happened to him before. He'd been starting to think those James Bond movies he'd loved so much as a teenager had totally lured him down the wrong career path in life.

That was Violette Lenoir, right? The chef of this place? The security cameras hadn't even begun to do her justice. If they had, he'd have been fighting his entire team for the right to break into her restaurant in the cold rain.

"Hi," he tried.

Damn, that was lame. Twenty-six films, and he bet James Bond had never said "Hi" in a single one of them.

"Get the hell out of my kitchen." She reached for an open knife roll with her left hand, still aiming the butcher knife at him.

Well, he could do that. Get the hell out of her kitchen. But then (a) he wouldn't meet any of his initial goals, and (b) it might be hard to ask her out from a position of cowardly retreat. "If I could just—" He reached toward his inner jacket pocket.

A much smaller knife appeared in her left hand, balanced for throwing. "I wouldn't do that if I were you."

Damn. That smaller knife chilled the blood. He was pretty sure he could knock the butcher knife out of her hand if she came at him and not have to do anything too brutal to contain her, but if she started throwing knives left-handed, God knew how this situation would degenerate.

He wouldn't even know in what direction to dodge, the aim would be so messed up.

Damn it. People watched too much television. That was the problem. Tried to go all Scarlett Johansson on him when she should be hiding behind a counter and hoping he didn't notice her.

"I just want to show you my badge," he said.

"Really." Her voice was deadpan, and he realized they were speaking English only when her accent on the R just frissoned over his skin.

Hell. Blonde, high cheekbones, leather, French accent, aiming a knife at his throat. Maybe he was having that dream again.

"*Vraiment,*" he tried, and that damn *expression* flinched across her face. That screwed-tight, *oh God spare me* look everyone in this damn city got whenever he tried to speak their language.

After untold hours of torture by LREC classes, too.

"I'm a security consultant," he said. "For the hotel."

Her knife didn't waver. "Right. That's why you didn't have the code to enter through the door."

"I'm *testing* security," he said. "To see how easy it would be to break into this place."

She smiled and hefted her knife. "Well, as you found out—it's hard."

"Nope." He shook his head firmly. "You need better security on the windows. Which I would like to make a note of, if you would just—let—" He inched his hand toward his pocket.

The knife she held whizzed right past his ear and buried itself in the wall two inches from his head.

"Jesus H. Christ!" he yelled, jerking far too late to the right. "What the hell? You almost killed me!"

A second knife appeared in her hand. "Don't be a baby. That was three centimeters away from you. If I'd wanted to kill you, you'd be dead."

There was a God after all, and He loved him. Chase could not believe a hot blonde in leather had finally said that to him in real life.

"But who wants to go to jail?" she said. "Your president might be coming for dinner next week. If I'm not here, God knows what they'd serve him."

Interestingly, Chase had a similar worry about what they might serve the President.

The guys in Intel rated the information as only twenty percent reliable, which, in his experience, meant it was probably a figment of someone's imagination. And there never had been a successful mass ricin attack yet. But hell...if there was...

If there was, and it was in this kitchen, he was probably looking at the first casualty right now. The chef.

"I just want to show you my badge!"

"I just wanted to make sure you were clear on what could happen, if whatever you're reaching for in your pocket isn't a badge."

"It's a badge!" he said indignantly. And as he reached for it, "Are you left-handed?"

She gave him the barest of smiles, shifting her right hand just enough to let the light flicker off that giant blade. "No."

Oh, wow. "Will you marry me?"

"There are a lot of knives in this roll." She shifted the one in her left hand until her fingers just lightly gripped the tip. "Don't make me start emptying it."

"I've got a good job." He pulled out his badge. "Secure income. I'm nice to kittens and small children."

"I'm not a kitten or a child. And it looks to me as if your job involves breaking into other people's property in foreign countries and having knives thrown at your head. Your notion of security might be a little off."

"You haven't gotten a look at me in the light. That will make up for a lot." He set the badge on the counter, careful not to make sudden moves. "I'm going to slide this to you. Don't startle and kill me."

She sniffed. "I'm twenty-eight years old, a woman, and I already run a two-star kitchen. Trust me, I have nerves of steel."

"Well. You never know." He flicked his fingers, and the badge spun the three yards to her. "You could be one of those chefs who lives on her emotions. Throws pots at people's heads. Sometimes knives."

A very, very small smile. Hey, she was starting to like him.

She used the tip of the butcher knife to flip open his badge. "Chase Smith. Is that your real name?"

Ha, ha, ha. No. "You can call me Chase." It wasn't a name on any legal records, but it was, in fact, the nickname he went by, for survival purposes. His parents had had the worst taste in names in Texas history.

"How much did you spend on this fake badge, two euros?"

Probably more like two thousand, the way they inflated prices in the military. At least the one benefit to spending most of his career downrange was that it didn't come out of *his* taxes. He tended to put in more...sweat equity, for his country.

"It's a real badge!" he lied.

She fixed him with eyes so level he was pretty sure they made a little red laser point glow in the middle of his forehead. She was maybe just a *tad* trigger happy to make a good sniper, but she had the gaze down pat.

"I'm tall," he said. "I can reach things on high shelves. Very convenient in a husband."

She definitely had to suppress a smile there. "I organize my kitchen. I can reach whatever I want."

He sighed heavily. "I suppose you don't need me to open jars for you either."

Hey, she had a dimple. Damn. He was definitely going to marry her.

"Why H?" she said.

Hunh?

"*Jesus H. Christ*," she repeated, with an accented precision that was so erotic he nearly whimpered. "Why H?"

He, uh...damn. He had no idea. "I'll tell you after the birth of our first child."

5

She had *two* dimples. One on each side. And she paired them with a very haughty look up and down his body that made him just want to *beg.* "It will be interesting to see you pregnant."

He grinned. "So that's a yes?"

She caught his badge up with the tip of her knife and tossed it back to him. "You're promising to bear all the kids?"

Well... "We might have to negotiate the details. Can we have the wedding in Texas? I have a really big family."

She shook her head with a little purse of her lips that was probably illegal in his own country. All the best things were. "It won't work." She gestured at her chest with the smaller knife. "Fifty cousins. My mother made me promise to get married here."

Damn. That *was* going to be a tough one. His grandmother would kill him if he got married in France and she couldn't come. "My grandmother's eighty-six. Ailing. She can't really fly any more."

"Eighty-four," she said regretfully. "Claustrophobic and convinced America is full of people who shoot each other whenever someone cuts in front of them in traffic. Refuses to step on a plane."

Well, hell, this was looking bad. "I'll figure something out."

She shook her head mournfully, her lips pressed down but those two dimples peeking out. "It will never work."

"French people are such damn pessimists," he said, aggravated. He slipped his badge back into his pocket.

"We're not two years old going on thirteen like some countries I could mention," she said crushingly. "It's called realism."

He shook his head, deeply disappointed by such a defeatist attitude. "It's the weather, isn't it? It's got you down. Forty degrees in July and raining, hell, that would destroy anyone's spirits. Let me help cheer you up."

6

She eyed him as if she was considering it, and his spirits perked *right* up. "It *is* kind of fun throwing knives at you and seeing the expression on your face."

Hey.

"I've got a really hot body, too," he offered. "I mean, there are other sources of entertainment here." He gestured to himself.

She raised an eyebrow and ran a long, trailing look up his body that made a man glad to be alive. In more ways than one, where she and her knife-throwing ability were concerned.

"I mean hot in terms of body temperature," he said innocently. "I could warm you up." He tried to channel puppies as he looked at her with limpid eyes.

A grin flashed across that haughty, high cheekboned face of hers and was quickly bitten back.

Yes. He managed not to pump his fist in victory. He'd gotten her. A full grin.

"I'm afraid it won't do," she said mournfully. "I like a man who can focus."

"Oh, I can focus," he promised her, his voice dropping deep. *Oh, yeah, I promise I can focus on you all night lo—*

"You broke in here to ask me to marry you? And here I was thinking you'd gotten easily distracted."

Now that was a low blow. Showing up with that leather clinging to her sleek body and waving knives at him and then blaming him for getting distracted. "A man has to have his priorities straight."

"What was your other priority?" she asked dryly. "The one that brought you into my kitchen."

Oh, well...he coughed awkwardly. "Saving the world."

She stared at him with both eyebrows raised.

"One small restaurant at a time," he said gamely.

"Oh, for God's sake."

"But don't worry," he assured her hastily. "If you're about to say yes, the world can wait."

Chapter 2

If there was one thing a young female chef in charge of a major establishment learned how to deal with fast, it was cocky, physical males who thought they could push the female around.

Vi had been hoping to get a good night's sleep before tomorrow's banquet, but it wouldn't be the first time she'd pulled an all-nighter because an arrogant idiot had screwed up her plans. In her world, you handled things or you packed up your knives and slunk off to find some other career.

"I lied," her burglar admitted.

It was so redundant when the male of the species said that. What else was he going to admit to? Being arrogant? Thinking she was a cute, feisty little thing?

"Damn it." She set down the smaller knife and began to sharpen her butcher knife. "Your grandmother isn't really ailing, is she? You just said that to try to get the wedding where you wanted it. I'm going to sic my mother on you."

"No, that part was true!" he said indignantly. The dim LED lights that glowed in the kitchen all night made it hard to tell his hair or eye color. But she could see the size of him, the strong, stubborn chin, the outrageously delighted grin, and the insane cockiness. She'd nearly knocked him out, she'd planted a knife three centimeters from his ear, and she was holding a butcher knife and knew how to use it, and he was having the time of his life.

The idiot was flirting with her. That was what was so annoying about men.

Well, one of the many things.

Like how hard did she have to beat them with a pot over the head before they respected her abilities?

"Then you're not actually going to have the kids." She made her voice severely disappointed. "I knew it." She gave her mouth a bitter twist as she angled her face away. Not enough to let him escape her peripheral vision, of course. She didn't trust him for a second.

"You're twisting my words." He sighed. "I never promised that."

"Then you don't really want to marry me?" She pointed her butcher knife at him. "I hate it when men lie about that."

He gave her that wicked, hungry grin. "Honey, I'd marry you tonight, if you'd put down that knife and come over here."

"Ha." She stabbed her butcher knife in his direction. "Got you. How are we going to get to Texas and get all your family together in one night? You probably don't even have a grandmother who wants to see your wedding."

He grinned at her. "I'd get *engaged* to you tonight. And your mom and my mom can fight the wedding details out."

"Right." She went back to sharpening her knife. She did like a sharp blade. "You know, I'm a twenty-eight-year-old female who heads a two-star establishment of nearly all male chefs. Trust me, the last thing I need in my life is another cocky, arrogant man who thinks he is the shit."

"But I really *am* the shit," he protested, grinning.

She sighed. At herself, because it made attraction kick hot and hungry through her when he said that. It would make her life so much easier if she didn't find cocky men who thought they were the shit a major turn on.

"Also, I don't mean to be greedy, but could you say *shit* again in that accent? Or if you want to broaden your English vocabulary, there's this fantastic swear word you might try." He pressed a fist to his heart and stared at her like a starving puppy, as if he could just will the word right out of her. "*Fuck.*"

She narrowed her eyes at him. "Were you, like, Navy SEAL before you took up 'security consulting' or something?"

He angled his head just a little. The dim lights showed a strong jaw and a gleam in his eyes, but she still couldn't tell their color. His hair must be brown, though—not light enough for blond, and if it was black, it would be all shadow now. "You say that like it's a bad thing."

Wait, what? She'd been being sarcastic, trying to come up with the cockiest archetype of American manhood she could think of. What nail had she hit?

"I mentioned my arrogant male fatigue," Vi said.

He grinned again. "In the right circumstances, I bet you could make me beg."

This guy was so full of himself. It was disconcerting how much he made her insides tickle with that grin of his. It must be the adrenaline getting to her. Things had been so calm around here lately. It had been at least two days since she'd had to throw a pot at anyone's head.

"But that's what I lied about." He looked woeful. "I'm not really here testing your window security."

She sighed and set down her butcher knife to pick up the good-for-throwing knife in her right hand. "And I'm not left-handed." She took an easy grip of the point in her right hand, holding his eyes. "But oh, right. I told you the truth about that."

"I'm head of a security agency that has taken on as a client one of the billionaires coming to your restaurant tomorrow, and we were tasked with making sure that all of his meals would really be gluten-free."

She choked. She made a mighty effort to keep her haughty, disdainful look, but she couldn't hold the laugh back, and she had to set one of her knives down as she covered her mouth to try to suppress it. Damn it. *Never let the cocky male make you laugh.* You lost all kinds of authority that way.

"What?" he asked innocently. "He has an intolerance! It makes him bloated!"

She bit down on her lip as hard as she could, but the whole laugh escaped out into the open air. She dropped both knives and pressed her hands against the counter, trying for breath.

Her burglar grinned like a cat that had rolled in way too much catnip. "I hope you won't take this the wrong way, but you are really hot."

"Is there a good way to take that?" she challenged dryly.

"Well...as a compliment? I mean, if you told *me* that, that's the way *I* would take it."

She sighed, wishing his cockiness and physical strength and visible attraction to her didn't get to her the way they did. The *last* thing a female chef needed was to be vulnerable to that particular male combination. She'd never hold her own. "Did Quentin send you to sabotage tomorrow's dinner?"

A little of the grin faded off his face. He straightened away from the wall. In the light, his hair was a kind of blue-brown, his skin faintly ghostly. "Who's Quentin?"

"He *was* my second."

Her burglar's eyes narrowed just a little. It changed the whole look of his face, from cocky and dangerous to her equilibrium to just...dangerous. To everybody else. "Was?"

She shrugged, as if this kind of thing didn't hurt every time. Why the hell did men have to make it so hard to do her job? As if everything in life was all about them and their wants, all the time? "Well, since I'm a woman, obviously *he* thought he was the real star in the kitchen and that I was just some figurehead who was sleeping with the hotel owner."

Her burglar held up one finger. "Just a little point of interest, and not to distract your story, but *are* you sleeping with the hotel owner?"

She gave him a withering look.

He smiled. "Good."

Oh, for God's sake. As *if* that was his business. She tried to wither his cockiness again, but like most of the men she encountered in her career, his cockiness just thrived regardless.

"I mean, because I wouldn't want to have to kill your boss," her burglar said innocently.

Damn it, he'd almost made her laugh again. She rolled her eyes to cover it.

"So you had to get rid of Quentin," her burglar said.

"After he cornered me in the walk-in after everyone else had gone home and tried to prove his masculine supremacy over me, I did." She shrugged. "It was either that or cut off his balls, and can you imagine the media if I did that? My career would be finished. No one would *ever* eat at the restaurant of the female chef who cut off men's balls."

He gazed at her a moment, with a dazed look in his eyes. He gave his head a hard shake. "Hell, you're hot."

She raised an eyebrow at him. "The idea of getting your balls cut off attracts you?"

"I'll wear protection. So this Quentin...what's his last name? Where does he live?"

"I took care of him," she said dryly. That was the point, right? She took care of *all* problems cocky males presented her with. That was how she could stay chef.

Yeah, it would be nice if it was all about the food, the way she'd imagined as a kid, but she'd learned long before she finished her first apprenticeship that it was mostly about surviving in a world of sexist assholes.

"Stabbed him?" her burglar asked hopefully.

"I brought one of the pallets of milk down on his head when he pushed me back against the shelves. Mild concussion."

He weighed that a moment. "Much of a struggle before you managed to bring the milk down on his head?"

Maybe. She lifted her chin at him and braced her feet. *Even if there was a struggle, I still won.*

"Yeah, you know what? I think I'll still pay him a little visit. Don't worry, I can find his address on my own."

"I don't need a hero," she said dryly.

He raised his eyebrows. "How do you know? It sounds like you've never had one."

Chapter 3

"Okay," Chase said, getting down to business. "Let's get this done so I can take you out for drinks and get you out of those leather pants."

"I'm still holding a knife," Violette Lenoir pointed out dryly.

"Because they look uncomfortable! Come on. Admit you would rather be in pajamas right now."

"Not for a motorcycle ride through rainy streets at midnight."

"Good God." Chase had to put a hand to his heart to calm it down. "You have a motorcycle, too? Is it by any chance a Harley?"

"A Ducati."

He considered. There was no help for it. He was going to have to make a sacrifice. "I'll do all the ironing."

She raised her eyebrows.

Fine. *Fine.* "And the dishes five days a week."

"Am I supposed to be coming home from my eighteen-hour days as a top chef to make my man a steak in this scenario?" she asked ironically.

He snorted. "I'll make the steaks, thank you. I've seen what you people do to meat."

Her jaw dropped. Pure outrage blazed so high in her eyes it pretty much grabbed his dick and tried to yank him right over to her by it. Damn, that was a hot look on her. "You think *I don't know how to make a steak?*"

"You probably cut it into tiny spirals and make some commentary on Plato with it. Serve it on this much potatoes"—he held up thumb and forefinger in a stingy circle—"that you mix with, God knows, celery root or something. Beets. Who the hell knows?"

She was so mad he was going to have to kiss her in half a second or totally lose his mind. She ran that knife up and down that sharpener, the sound singing dangerously through the air.

"I'll make the steaks," he said firmly.

She slammed the knife down on the nearest cutting board. Ouch. She could take a man's arm off with that kind of cleaving action. "You like to live dangerously," she said.

"I know," he said woefully. He patted his heart with his hand. "I'm sorry," he told it bravely. "I'll try not to let her break you." He gave the Blonde in Leather his puppy look, this time channeling wistful courage. "Be gentle with it," he whispered. "It's not as tough as I look."

She rolled her eyes.

He grinned. "Grandma is going to love you."

"I'm going to call the cops now," she said firmly.

There was so much to be said for a woman who thought about stabbing him, hitting him on the head, and dismembering him before she remembered she could depend on someone else to handle her problems. "Now, Ms. Lenoir, why break your record by calling for help now?"

She winced. "It's *Lenoir*." Something different and a hell of a lot sexier happened to the R and the vowels when she said it.

Those damn French classes. "How about I call you Vi? Your last name is going to change anyway."

"I put a lot of effort into my name. So no, I'm not giving it up to some cocky idiot who thinks his own identity is inherently more important than mine, just because he's a man."

A beautiful idea hit him. "*I* could be Lenoir. That's much more exciting than Smith. I think my grandma would be okay with it. She didn't really have much choice about the name change back in her day, but she always thought Smith was boring." Well, she definitely would have, if Smith was her real last name.

16

Violette Lenoir sighed heavily. "Are you some kind of manifestation of my worst nightmare?"

"Hey." That hurt. "You're straight out of *my* dreams."

"You know I crush a hundred men just like you on a daily basis?"

Okay, not that he wanted to destroy her self-confidence or anything, but...seriously? "I'm pretty sure you don't, honey. Just because they pretend to be me in video games doesn't mean they're actually like me."

Just for a second, a flicker of genuine caution showed in her eyes, and her left hand scooped up another throwing knife. Aww, and they'd been getting along so well. He backpedaled. "But don't worry, sweetheart. I may not be crushable, but you're safe with me."

"You're not. Safe with me."

He sighed with delight. "I know."

"Are you sure your heart is as fragile as you pretend?" she asked dryly. "It looks as if bullets bounce off it from here."

"Kevlar." He thumped his chest with his knuckles, where he was, in fact, wearing a vest. "But underneath it's pure mush."

"So aim for your throat?" She hefted the left-hand knife.

He beamed at her and opened his hand over his heart in civilian pledge position. "I'd unzip my body armor for you, honey."

She sighed heavily. But her lips twitched.

Yes. He pulled a victory fist. "Now about those drinks. I don't want to keep you all night, sweetheart—" He paused. Grinned. "At least, not all night here. So—"

"No?" she interrupted, disappointed. "Because I've always had a fantasy about this counter."

Oh, hell, yeah. He sprang to attention. Coming away from the wall, a part of him rising up eagerly, and—

She held up that butcher knife, point straight toward him so he'd ram himself on it if he kept coming.

He sagged and scowled. "Was that necessary? That was cruel and unusual."

She gave a very smug, mean smile, like Catwoman licking her lips.

He regrouped. "Now *I* have a fantasy about that counter." He gave her a smile back. "I'm even down on my knees in it."

She checked. Her eyes widened just a tad, and then flickered to the counter. And back to him. She pressed her lips firmly together, but her throat moved as she swallowed.

Yeah. *Now* they were getting somewhere. He took a step toward her.

"You are like some Jack-in-the-box on steroids," she said, exasperated. "You just bounce up again, and again, and again."

"Yep," he agreed. "All night long."

She thunked her own forehead with the haft of her knife. "Look, just tell me what you want."

"Oh, honey, you don't want me to get started on everything I want from you right here. You want to be lying down for some of that."

She gave him an utterly exasperated evil look, and he laughed. "It's your own fault, you know," he said.

"That you're an idiot?" She raised an ironic eyebrow.

"The—sproing." He shielded his crotch with his hand and then made that hand spring up at attention. "You seem to have that effect on me."

"Oh, yeah, sure, it's *always* the woman's fault. Tell me what you want before I kill you."

"To inspect you from top to bottom."

She gave him a fulminating glance.

"I mean your kitchen. Did I say you? Slip of the tongue." He grinned. "Don't worry, it's not always this clumsy."

A knife buried itself in the wall behind his head, but at least she left a generous foot of distance this time. He must be growing on her.

"I don't really need to inspect you for my job, to be honest," he said. "Our files on you are so thorough, I could probably tell you what kind of underwear you're wearing." He closed his eyes a second. "Black lace," he said firmly, cupping his hands at his chest. "Push up. And then...definitely a black thong."

She gazed at him a long moment, with that narrowed look to her eyes that just excited the hell out of his entire body. "So the peekaboo pink lace would be a real disappointment to you."

He took a hard breath, as that one got in past his body armor and hit him right in the belly.

"With the little slit down the middle...?"

"Okay." He held up both hands in surrender. "I'll be good. I promise. And I'll do the dishes all seven days a week, okay? That's on top of always taking out the trash and changing the oil. Just don't tell me more about your underwear right now, okay?"

Because he had a *really* creative brain, and right now it had just paired that nice ass in peekaboo pink lace arched just so on the back of a motorcycle, and...yeah, he might explode before her eyes.

"I'd better focus on work for a minute," he said.

"No, really? You can do that?"

It was too good to pass up. He gave her a slow smile. "Honey, I can focus like you wouldn't believe."

***

The good thing about leather, Vi thought, was that it really gave *no* clue as to how much a woman was letting a certain full-of-himself idiot get to her. Panty-dampening get to her. If anybody found out, it would totally ruin her cred.

He sure as hell didn't need to know. He was too cocky already.

All the other men she had crushed were just fantasizing about being him in video games? Ha.

Unless...he really was an ex-SEAL or something, in which case...nah. He was just another braggart, right? The number of men in bars who had tried to pretend to some mysterious SEAL affiliation the year she worked in New York was probably greater than the number of SEALs in existence.

"Now, about this saving the world issue," her intruder said. "I'll admit it's niggling at me. Honey, if you would just let me get that out of the way, after that I'm all yours."

"Ri-ight." She sighed. "Because you have to do that in my kitchen. Of course you're not just a thief sneaking into the hotel from here."

He shook his head at her with grave disappointment. "Sweetheart, you're going to have to trust me more if we're going to make this relationship work."

She just looked at him.

"Have I mentioned that I save kittens out of trees? Well, one. There was this little girl crying because he was stuck and—"

"What kind of kitten?" Vi said dryly.

"An ungrateful one. That's where I got this scar." He drew a finger down an apparently imaginary line on his cheek.

"Well. As wonderful a character reference as I'm sure the kitten could give you, I'm afraid it's not here to meow on your behalf."

He gave a broken-hearted sigh. "The embassy gave you a number to call, in case, right?"

"Yes," Vi said warily.

"Call it and verify if they have a Chase Smith pre-vetting security at one of the President's potential restaurant visits in advance of his arrival."

"Potential?" She knew how this game worked—her own president had had to cancel twice before he finally made it—but *damn* she would love to land the American president. To be the one restaurant he and his wife chose to dine at in Paris. Sure, fine, some of the bloggers and other critics would make jokes about American taste to put her down, but she was a woman chef in a profoundly sexist field. She was used to dealing with crap.

"My company has men checking out some of his other top choices tonight, too, so that we can give a preliminary security assessment." For a moment, Chase Smith was inscrutable. Unyielding. Serious.

Suggesting that she'd better cooperate, if she wanted to have her moment of glory next week.

She called the number. A male voice with an awkward French accent on the other end confirmed.

Oh.

"Why didn't you just say that in the first place?" she demanded, exasperated.

"I was having too much fun, to be honest."

Fun at her expense.

"You're really *very* hot," he confessed.

She glared at him. "If I don't get to kill you, you don't get to sexually harass me."

He considered. "But the reverse is fine? I can keep sexually harassing you if you can keep trying to kill me? I can take that deal."

She kind of liked it, too, to be honest. She had to put her fists on her hips to keep from thumping herself in the head.

"But it will take me a while to finish my inspections of the place," he said. "You're welcome to go home."

Okay, maybe he wasn't a burglar, but he was still crazy. Her eyebrows went up incredulously. "Nobody gets to wander around my kitchens unsupervised. Not even for a president. There are all kinds of things you could mess up."

Chase hesitated, his eyes narrowing just the tiniest fraction.

"I'm sticking to you like glue," she said firmly.

The narrowing of his eyes vanished. Chase gave a great, dramatic sigh of relief and clasped his hands to his heart in gratitude. "Honey," he said ecstatically. "I knew I'd start to grow on you."

Chapter 4

"You're touching my ass."

Vi jerked back a step, caught herself, and glared. No, she had *not* been.

And it had taken a lot of self-discipline, too.

Chase gave her a smile over his shoulder that invited true confessions. "It's a great ass, isn't it?" He was going through the kitchen at a brisk, thorough pace, opening everything—lowboys, drawers, cabinets—scanning everything, with the efficiency of an entire security team. "I tried to get it insured, but the premiums were too high." He sighed woefully.

"All the women wanting to smack it?" Wait, that sounded a lot more erotic and a lot less like a cool putdown than she had meant it to.

It was just...it would be such a great ass to smack.

"Also." He stopped in front of wire shelves filled with martini glasses, each with a small amount of liquid caramel in the bottom, all prepped for tomorrow when the last-minute components would be added. He was a really big guy. Vi herself was pretty tall, and her boots had six-centimeter heels on top of that, but this man just filled the space. Not only was he big, but his *presence* was big, as if he had an invisible extension of himself that just stretched out to every corner of the room and took charge of it.

His ass, on the other hand, was a tight, *fine* ass. Not big at all. But it still managed to keep dominating her attention as she followed close on his heels to make sure he didn't mess with anything in her kitchens.

"Put that glass down! You're getting fingerprints on it!"

"You won't even let me have a little taste?" he asked wistfully. "That caramel looks good. *I'd* let you taste anything you want." He pursed his lips near the edge of the glass in a very...*tastable* position.

She grabbed the glass and replaced it on the shelves. "Don't touch anything! Don't breathe on anything! If you sneeze, I'm killing you."

"I'd better take care of the kids when they get sick," he decided and moved to the walk-in. "Poor little tykes. You're going to scare them into pneumonia with that attitude."

"Yeah, that's what everyone always told me. Twenty-eight, just stepping into my first starred kitchen, would be a *perfect* time to get pregnant and start a family."

He eyed her a moment and then nodded decisively. "You're right. We'd better wait on the kids. I'll warn my grandma so she doesn't harass you."

She sighed very heavily.

"She's not, like, *obsessed* or anything," he hastened to reassure her. "She's got plenty of great-grandchildren. It's more my mother you have to worry about."

"Did any of your commanding officers ever try to beat you over the head with a sledgehammer?"

He smiled and opened the walk-in. "Brr. I don't suppose you'd consider coming closer to keep me warm?"

"I thought your hot body temperature was supposed to be one of your few attributes."

"I think it's like having a fever. I'm so hot that the slightest chill in the air makes me shiver."

"The sledgehammer probably bounced off," she decided grimly. She braced herself at the walk-in door and folded her arms. "I don't care how obnoxious you are, you are not getting me to stalk off and leave you a chance to do something in my kitchens I can't see."

"Obnoxious," Chase said in a very sad, small voice. He gazed woefully at the crates of cream as if about to ask them for sympathy, and then his gaze changed, and for a second that narrow, dangerous look was back on his face. "This where he cornered you?"

That bastard Quentin. Vi smiled. "He regretted it."

"I'll just double-check to make sure he got enough bruises," Chase said in a soothing, reassuring tone. "Sometimes it's good to have a second opinion on these things. Is that gluten?" He pointed randomly.

"You're probably more likely to find gluten where we keep the flours. As opposed to where we keep the fruits, vegetables, butters, and creams."

"Is that safe?" He pointed at some slabs of butter.

"What do you mean, 'safe'?" Vi asked warily. "It tastes good. Please, dear God, don't tell me that your president is on some weird diet plan where he can't eat butter."

"He's vegetarian." Chase sighed and shook his head. "Hard to believe people voted for that guy."

"*Vegetarian?*" Vi recoiled, grabbing the edge of the door for support. Then her eyes narrowed. "No, he damn well isn't. The embassy would have said something when they called!"

Chase grinned at her.

"Okay, you know what? You can get out of my kitchens now."

"Nobody could get sick from it, right?" he said. "The butter?"

Vi stared at him. "What, you mean like *food poisoning*?" she finally realized, outraged. "No one is going to get *food poisoning* from my kitchens!"

Chase held up a hand. "Just doing my job, honey. Just doing my job."

She glowered at him and tapped her foot. His gaze drifted down her body all the way to her tapping toe, and he closed his eyes tight and gave himself a hard shake.

Then he bit back a tiny, wicked smile and bent from the waist. "What about here?"

Vi stared as his black pants pulled tight, tight, tight as he slowly bent, and then snapped her gaze away. "Of course not!"

"Anything up here?" He straightened to lift one of the heavy crates completely off an overhead shelf, holding it above his head at an angle that showed off biceps so sculpted and so perfect that they looked hot even through his shirt.

"Did you ever do any modeling?" she asked him dryly. "Or do you just practice that pose in front of the mirror?"

"It was for charity. They harassed me into it. And can I just say that I am entirely ready for this male calendar charity craze to be over? What's up with that? Why can't you women pose naked if you think it's such a good idea for charity?"

Violette's lips parted. "Like...are you *nude* in a calendar?" Her eyes tracked over that big body, most of it hidden far too thoroughly by clothing and body armor. But he had those biceps. And those buns of steel. Kind of suggested that once the vest was taken away, there wasn't going to be much of a bulge to his belly.

"My private parts are discreetly covered in it," he said loftily. And then winked. "With dog tags."

"That's all it took?"

He stopped still. "*Plus my hands*," he said outraged. "And the angle of my thigh! That—I—" For once words failed him in his indignation.

Vi gave him a sweet smile. "Just checking." Because it was much better to have in her head an image of a man whose private parts could be covered by dog tags rather than an image of one whose private parts *couldn't*, where the dog tags and chain artfully draped and entirely failed to hide the...she coughed.

He narrowed his eyes at her. Then he slowly set the very heavy crate back on its high shelf, biceps flexing, and reached even farther so that his shirt and vest drew up from his waist, showing a line of tan skin. He gave her a second with that view before he wobbled, toppled, and grabbed her shoulder for support.

"Sorry," he murmured, as he pulled her in snug for just one second and then let go. "I lost my balance."

"Yeah, I know all about that. It's amazing how many guys lose their balance around me when we're by ourselves in the walk-in."

He blinked. "Oh." He let go of her and stepped back. "I never actually thought of it that way," he said after a moment.

"I know. Maybe it's some kind of testosterone thing. The men who fall on a woman in a walk-in are always convinced they're special."

He frowned, then shifted to make sure there was a good meter of distance between him and her. Violette followed immediately of course. She wasn't going to let him get away with a thing.

"What happened to the rest of the photos from the shoot?"

"Destroyed," Chase said firmly. "Are you sure your fingers didn't brush my ass? Because I could have sworn..."

"*Destroyed?*" She didn't mean to let her voice squeak, but darn...that seemed like a sinful waste.

"Except for one copy, of course." Chase slid her a glance and then diligently examined the shelves—linking his fingers through the wire shelving above his head so that he was very clearly not touching her...and then lifting himself just slightly so that his butt tightened and his shoulder muscles flexed. "Which I have. It would be incredibly hard to convince me to share it. I'm not sure what someone would have to do."

Oh, boy, did Vi have some ideas. She could handcuff those strong wrists of his back against her bed and probably get him to do anything she wanted. Oh, yes. She had *ideas.*

He'd strain against the ties at his wrists, all those muscles in his arms bulging, his back arching as she...

"—Ms. Lenoir."

"Hmm?" She blinked up at the face bent toward hers.

His hair was streaked brown and gold, his eyes blue. Lines at the corners of them suggested that he had squinted into a lot of sun and wind and dust for his age. A broad forehead and strong cheekbones and straight dark brown eyebrows. A relaxed, amused mouth that, just occasionally, briefly, firmed until it seemed to belong to someone else entirely.

Only it didn't. Both those looks belonged to him.

And if she got him tied up to her bed, she'd not only get those photos out of him but she'd crack through that teasing manner, just shred it off him, until he was...

"Ma'am? Ms. Lenoir? Honey?"

She blinked slowly at him. He inclined that handsome chin toward the right.

Toward her hand curled over his biceps. Which he was quite politely keeping taut and bulging just for her. With a tiny smug smile on his mouth that he was trying valiantly to suppress.

She jerked back so fast she teetered. Nearly ran into the shelves behind her, jerked away before she could ruin anything for tomorrow, and—he caught her by both elbows before she could fall straight against him.

Just this firm, easy, confident catch, strong and sure. He righted her and released her, stepping back with his hands spread wide to prove their innocence.

"You really do have a scar," she said, startled. A hair thin, barely visible line that ran from just below his eye down to his jaw. If he hadn't mentioned it and his face hadn't been so close, and if she herself wasn't used to paying attention to hair-fine details in her quest for a third star, she never would have noticed it.

"Disfigured for life," he said dejectedly. "My chances are ruined. Only a woman with a good heart would look past me now to the man I am inside." He gave her the kind of piteous look the kitten had probably given him from that tree as he reached to save it.

She snorted with laughter before she could stop herself.

"Which you clearly don't have," he said severely. "Mocking my pain."

"Sorry." She tried to control herself. She *really* should not let someone as impossibly cocksure get to her. "It's just—your chances are—" Laughter exploded and she clutched her stomach. "What do you have to do to pick up women when you walk into a bar, snap your fingers at the door and then sort through the masses that throw themselves at you until you pick the one you want?"

He looked thrilled with himself. "Damn. You think I'm hot."

Merde, she needed to be more careful. He was *definitely* the type of guy who would jump on the slightest encouragement like a duck on a breadcrumb. "Are you sure that scratch wasn't from a woman trying to gouge your eyes out?"

"You don't think I'd save a kitten?" He looked offended.

"Oh, probably." Flexing muscles the whole way. She sighed.

"I get no end of crap about it." Sad look. "All the other guys, *they* get scars from knife fights and bullet wounds. Mine—a kitten."

"You do know that this scar can barely be detected without a microscope?"

"You want to look closer?" He proffered his cheek.

Maybe she should invest in some kind of foam pot. It seemed like it might come in handy with him. Something she could use to beat him over the head regularly, without actually ending up in jail for battery.

Wait. Now why would she need to make *any* long-term investments into ways to handle him?

"Or I could help you with the knife scar problem?" she offered dryly.

"I don't mean to suggest the guys are sexist or anything, sugar—"

Yeah, right. If she ever met a guy who wasn't sexist, now *that* would be something.

"—but I'm pretty sure they would give me even more crap if I got beat up by a woman."

"It's better to lose to a *kitten* than a *woman*?" Vi demanded, so furious he was *seriously* lucky she didn't have a pot to hand.

"I didn't say *I* thought so. I'd definitely rather lose to you." He looked hopeful. "Want to see if you can floor me?"

She growled.

"Physically, I mean. You've already floored me in all the figurative ways." He gave her a bewitchingly cute smile.

"You do realize that the only thing keeping you alive right now is how badly it would ruin my chances of having your president visit if I was in jail for homicide?"

"Well...there might be *one* other little thing keeping me alive," he mentioned, with this lurking amusement. As far as she could tell, amusement pretty much always lurked somewhere in him. That man had not taken her seriously once.

She gave him a blank look.

"I might be able to defend myself a teeny bit?" he suggested meekly, hunching his shoulders to try to look small and vulnerable. He completely failed to manage to shrink that tough, big body with that gesture.

She frowned at him.

"Except against pink peekaboo panties. I'd definitely lose to those."

Yeah, see. She'd had *exactly* the same thought about how fast she could get him on his knees with the right panties. *Damn it.* Why was he doing this to her?

Fine.

Fine.

She knew exactly why.

He was hot. He was cocky, in that way she utterly loved, as if his confidence was very well-founded. He kept making her laugh. And if she didn't manage to control that utterly enticing cocksureness of his—

"Oh, thank you, Jesus, I had a thought," he said with stunned relief.

She blinked. "Ah...I take it that's rare for you?"

"Well, I was beginning to think you had *permanently* fried my brain." He put his fingers to his head and gave it a slight, adjusting shake. "Look at that," he said with delight. "There are two entire brain cells there that managed to survive. Maybe there's hope."

"Why don't I share your optimism?"

He grinned at her. "Because you're French. And it rains and it's forty degrees in your country in freaking July. You're going to like Texas so much better, honey. In July, *we* hit 114! Plus, there are stars."

"Not Michelin ones, there aren't." Might as well go open a restaurant in the Antarctic, as far as Michelin was concerned. "That thought you had?"

"Oh, you're going to like this one, honey. I thought it on your behalf, in case your brain was fried, too." A hopeful look.

She rolled her eyes.

31

He grinned. "Listen to this brilliance: failing to control me doesn't mean you've failed to control your kitchens, lost hard-earned respect, exposed yourself to sexual gossip from your staff, and ruined your career. Isn't that beautiful?" Just like that she was against a wall, and he had his hands braced on either side of her head, laughing but with a heat in his eyes that curled all through her. "Like right now. If you fail to get a handle on me, your entire career doesn't suffer for it." He smiled down at her. *Down*, even though she was a tall woman and wearing heels. "Pretty fun, right?"

Well...yeah. It was almost irresistible fun. Because if she could get him out of her actual kitchens, it was *true*. She could tangle with his cockiness all she wanted, flex her strength against his and maybe, for once, *not win*, and the next day, she could stride into her kitchen and still be in charge of it. Nobody would be gossiping about her. Nobody would be thinking that since she let him roll her under him in a bed, she was under him now in her kitchens, too. She could have just, like, *fun*.

With that hot body, and that irrepressible cockiness, and that sense of humor. That refusal to take her seriously, that ability to turn every single damn thing she said into a joke, could have devastating effects on her authority in the kitchens. She'd dealt with enough men who tried not to take her seriously, thank you.

But here...she could just let him drive her crazy and *enjoy* it. Drive him crazy, too.

Hein. For only two functioning brain cells, he'd managed to come up with a halfway decent thought there.

It almost suggested that a man who could manage to turn every single thing she said back on her, and nearly get a laugh out of her every time, might be far smarter than he was currently playing.

A wisp of caution ghosted through her.

Those blue eyes laughed and challenged. Those big biceps were just a few centimeters from her head. "I'm all done here," he murmured. "I guess you pass muster."

"I...*what?*"

He made a little moue and held up a cautious hand. "You run a fairly tight ship."

"I run a—*fairly*—" She should never have put down her knives.

"I guess my client will be okay in your hands," he said. "Your food probably won't kill him."

She gasped. Rage turned her brain red.

"It must be fun being a woman sometimes," Chase said.

"I—what?"

"Well, *I* have an almost irresistible, maddening urge to just grab you up and kiss you. And I have to control that. But if you gave in to your irresistible, maddening urge to hit me, I'd probably just enjoy it."

He probably would, too. It made her *sizzle* with fury. Like nothing she could do could get through the arrogance of certain males.

"Don't be so sure," she said. "I fight dirty."

He bit into his lower lip to control his grin, but it smirked out at the corners. "Me, too," he allowed, in a deep voice that made the thought of fighting *dirty* just run over her whole body and heat it up.

"You're *so* lucky I haven't killed you yet," she said, staring up into those blue eyes and that laughter and arrogance.

He fought to control the twitch of his lips. "If my luck fails, I'll try to defend myself."

Annoying jerk. He could probably control her just by shifting his body five centimeters and grabbing her hands. She could feel it all through him, the power, the size, the training, all held off her by his own arms. "I take it you don't think that would be too hard?"

"Nope." And just as she started to glare, he said with naïve pride: "I took karate when I was a kid."

She blinked. He pushed himself off her, giving her space. "I got to blue belt," he bragged.

33

She choked. And then just thumped her head back against the wall as she started to laugh.

"Damn, it's hard not to kiss you," he said. "*Jesus*, you are driving me crazy."

And he strode out of the walk-in and to the end of one of the lines, as if she actually *was*. And he considered it his full responsibility to control any urges she created in him, too.

She stared at that broad back. He looked over his shoulder. "So are you in any hurry to get to bed?"

Blue eyes, tan body, that grin and that cockiness, all in her white sheets...

"Or do chefs keep late hours?"

"It, ah, can sometimes take us a little while to come down off the adrenaline," she said cautiously, not sure she wanted to follow where he was going with this. And not sure she wanted to shut it down, either. She really did usually have a lot of adrenaline to release, and right this second, she was quite sure she wouldn't calm down for *hours*. Possibly weeks.

"Because I'm a poor, lonesome tourist in this country." He looked pitiful.

"Oh, for God's sake."

"And you're the nicest, most welcoming Frenchman—woman—I've met all day."

She tried to stuff the laugh back inside, she really did, but he was just *impossible*. "What did the others throw at you? Bombs?"

"They did that—*thing*—whenever I spoke." He pinched at his lips with his fingers. "And then they answered me in English. Every time." He frowned and shook himself, as if shaking off a horrible nightmare. "It was brutal."

"Poor baby."

He gave her a disgruntled look. "You know, being a beautiful blonde Frenchwoman who wears leather and stiletto heels has given you a *real* lack of empathy for victims of snobbism."

She snorted. "There are plenty of people who try to snob me in Paris."

An eyebrow went up. He looked her up and down. "And how does that work out for them?"

She smiled.

He smiled back. His eyes were laughing, and heated with interest, but they were also so...warm. As if he really did like her, and not just think she was fuckable. "What do you say, honey? I assume it's still forty degrees, but the rain has stopped. Would you save your country's reputation? Be an ambassador for peace? Show a poor, lost tourist the sights? Hopefully on the back of your motorcycle? Maybe even let him drive it once?"

She held up a hand. "You are not driving my motorcycle."

A heavy, put-upon sigh. "Fine. I'll ride behind you."

It was only after he'd settled on the bike behind her that she realized how often he pushed for something really outrageous—the chance to drive her motorcycle, a marriage in Texas, babies—to get the thing he really wanted, which the technique made seem much more normal in contrast.

"I've got a knife on me," she said, as those hot, strong thighs framed hers and his pelvis nestled up against her butt, his arousal very evident.

"If you need to stab me, do you mind aiming above the waist? I'd way rather lose my spleen than my balls."

Chapter 5

His team was going to make him pay for this for the rest of his natural life, but what else was he supposed to do? Drug her? Yeah, *that* would be subtle. No way she would wake up from being drugged and not run straight to the police and create an international scandal.

Conversely, now what could she say? *A guy broke into my kitchen in the middle of the night. I bought his story, took him off on a motorcycle with me, and...and...then he turned out to be a lying bastard and...*

Wait. Stop that negative thinking right there. There was *no* reason for her to find out that he was a lying bastard. Also, covert operations and being a lying bastard were *not* the same thing. They'd even had a class on trying to tell the difference.

Just because a man was covert didn't mean he couldn't meet a hot girl. Other men met women in the line of their work. It wasn't like he would be able to tell any other hot French woman what he really did for a living either, and he was deployed here for the next six months.

He, Jake, Ian, and Mark hadn't been able to believe their luck when they'd gotten their assignment. *Holy crap, Europe? Where there were women and, and...Eiffel Towers, and...women.*

The weather in July had been a bit of a shock, but the woman part was working out just fine.

Oh, yeah, he was hooked on covert ops. He was so hooked he was freaking effervescent. In fact, his dick was starting to feel like a corked champagne bottle, getting too shaken up.

This whole operation restored his faith in God and Hollywood, that was what it did. It was too bad he wasn't Catholic, or he'd go light a candle in one of these cathedrals that dominated the city. "Are you going to insist the babies be baptized?" he asked at a light.

She gunned the motor and accelerated so fast from the light he had to grab her tight. He grinned and valiantly managed not to kiss the nape of her neck or squeeze any inappropriate parts of her and mess up her driving.

"It would be okay," he said soothingly at the next light. "Grandma would be really happy, actually. She's from one of the old Spanish families there. Tried like anything to get my mom to baptize us."

"Do you actually know how to be quiet and focus, ever?" she said.

Well. If she put it like a *challenge.* He'd gotten her out of the kitchens, without having to drug her or kidnap her or do anything else to the restaurant's top chef that might tip Al-Mofti off to how close they were on his trail. So maybe now he could quit trying to keep her distracted and just shut up and enjoy the view.

And the feel.

Her between his thighs, her in control while he just wallowed in pleasure. That sleek leather-clad body. Her grace and strength, the way his weight on the bike challenged her at first, and how quickly she adjusted to it, back in perfect, sexy control of her machine within a couple of blocks. He was so freaking aroused he was embarrassed at himself, pressed up tight behind her on the bike like that. Hell, he hoped he didn't *really* embarrass himself. That might be possible, with the vibration of this bike, the erotic over-stimulus of having her right there in control of him and yet at his mercy, and the fact that she was so freaking hot.

He tried to focus on the city, all the lights shining off its wet pavement and buildings. Aww, she was—that was kind of sweet, actually. She was taking him on the Seine. Cutting left toward all these gloriously glowing buildings, a fountain leaping in front of a magnificent old palace— "L'Hôtel de Ville," she said, and it looked and felt so different when she was saying it than when he was studying the layout of the city as part of a mission briefing.

He started to...not relax into it, exactly. When pretty much every atom in his body was focused on crawling into her pants, *relaxed* wasn't quite the right word. But to enjoy this part, too—the view. The ride.

Maybe he'd been a little harsh on this city. In certain lights, in certain conditions, it was a hell of a view.

Bridges arching over dark water, building after majestic old building glowing magically against the dark. She crossed one of the bridges and slowed for a light, Notre-Dame in their sights, the ancient view oddly...moving. *Hell, Grandma, you should get on a plane just to see this, you'd love it.*

Vi pulled her form-fitting leather sleeve back to check her watch. "Oh, only fifteen minutes before it goes out," she said, and shot them left across a bridge and left again and then just bent into the handlebars and gunned it.

In the scarce traffic of the after-midnight weekday streets, she raced so fast he ducked into her and held on, all the already overstimulated cells in his body revved even higher and hotter by the speed. *God*, she had control of that Ducati. Cutting slick and sleek through what traffic there was, blazing past the long, stately Louvre, the streets sparkling up at her headlight as they sped toward the Eiffel Tower.

They reached the esplanade across the river from the Tower just as it went out. But—"Made it!" Vi exclaimed, jumping off the bike and heading toward the parapet, taking her helmet off as she strode.

Boots on stone. Long, ground-eating stride. Leather. The Eiffel Tower snubbing him by going out just before he got to it, in forty-degree weather in July.

Life was *good.*

Also, if he got more aroused, he might honestly start trying to talk her into public sex. So there were dozens of tourists around and they'd end up on YouTube. So his career would be shot. Was that the end of the world?

And just then the black Tower started sparkling like someone had laced champagne with gold leaf flecks and shaken up the bottle.

He rested his hands against the wet parapet beside her, giving himself something solid to hold on to. The sparkles just danced and danced against the shadow of the Tower. Hell, that Tower made him think of...himself, actually. The sparkles would be his sense of humor, and the shadow would be...

He looked away from that shadow down at his own personal, honest-to-goodness Bond girl. Who was pressing her black-gloved hands against the parapet and gazing at the gold-dancing Eiffel with a pride and pleasure that made her look like a teenager. "Damn," he said. "I should have proposed *here.* Can I do it over again?"

She rolled her eyes and didn't even bother to glance up at him. So he had to nudge his body into hers, of course, to get back all her attention.

She slanted a glance up at him, adding ten more degrees to his already overheated blood. Her eyes still sparkled from the Tower, and yet they held this speculative wickedness.

Hell, she was thinking about it.

He'd already gotten lucky tonight, just by her throwing knives at him, but she had a look like he might get Super Duper A-Meteor-Must-Be-About-To-Hit-Me *Lucky.*

He nudged her some more, using his bigger body to bump her gently around until he could close her in against that parapet. Jesus, he was going to go out of his mind. Even that much contact just sizzled through his brain and entire body and made him want to see if he could rip leather with his bare hands. "I give you full permission to tie me up," he said.

She blinked. Then she got this smile on her lips that flooded him with red heat and made him want to kneel at her feet and *beg*.

"If you need to slow me down," he said.

"Now why would I want to do that?" she purred.

Oh, holy hell. Oh, yeah. *Yeah.*

"I'm kind of, maybe"—he took deep breaths—"rushing you."

"That's the only way to do a one-night stand, isn't it? Rush into it and enjoy every second?"

A one-night—? His lips parted, and then his dick just roared up in dragon-rage at his brain. *Shut the hell up. Just go with it. Don't argue with a damn thing.*

"*Definitely* enjoy every second," he breathed, letting his hips settle against hers. Finally. And *hell* but that was not enough.

She stood on tiptoe, which dragged her body against his as she brought her mouth to his ear. The dancing Eiffel lights behind her turned starry red. Or was that his brain? "You're very sure of yourself," she murmured, with that brushed pure-sex accent of hers. He was pretty sure the Rs just reached down and physically started stroking his dick. "Are you that...*cocky* in bed?"

"I—I can—" *Speak. Think. Complete a full sentence. Breathe.* "Take direction, too."

She brushed her lips down the side of his throat. Oh, hell. She really might need to tie him up. It was so hard not to just grab her butt and grind himself against her, the muscles of his arms might snap in the fight against himself. "I'm fully convinced of your ability to come in two seconds as soon as you see my panties," she murmured.

Hey.

But, hell, that might be true.

"But what I want to know is, do you have any...stamina?" she breathed as her lips brushed back up his throat to the underside of his chin.

Ooh. The nice, loud mental slap of a gauntlet thrown down. He did love that sound.

"Honey, I can promise you one thing." He curved his hands around that gorgeous leather-clad butt and pulled her up into him so he could bring his mouth to her ear. "If I get you in a bed, you're for damn sure not getting any sleep tonight."

"But I have that billionaire's banquet tomorrow," she protested. Or it was kind of a protest. She might be just teasing him.

But he didn't want to risk it. "Fine. I'll set an alarm and stop at three."

She pulled back enough to raise her eyebrows at him, biting her lip. Amused, but sexy amused. Like she, too, found laughter erotic. "You'll set an alarm?"

"A loud one." He showed her his watch. He was surprised that watch didn't include a miniature missile launcher for all the damn things it could do. "Otherwise I'll never notice." He gave her a slow smile. "I told you I could focus."

"Yeah, but you brag quite a lot," she said.

Hey. What? When had he bragged? He'd been staying so humble all evening. He'd barely even flexed a few times.

She rocked her hips ever so gently against his. "So I guess I need...proof."

There had to be a meteor headed for the Earth. Or an alien invasion or something. Those alien invasions always did attack the Eiffel Tower first.

He was exactly the guy Hollywood would expect to leap into the breach and fight them off if aliens did show up about right now.

But for once in his life, if the bomb dropped, he would *love* to be the last to know.

"Oh, yeah, honey." He bent and captured her mouth. "Let me prove myself to you."

Chapter 6

"I can't figure out how to do this," Chase said, and Vi stopped with her key in the lock and looked over her shoulder.

"It's your first time?" she said blankly. That was...extremely unexpected. But...kind of...wow, that would be kind of...

Chase gave her an incredulous look. "No."

Oh. Yeah. Probably just as well that was a very short-lived fantasy.

"But it's my first time with *you*," Chase said. "And you've got me—so—" He made a gesture as if his head was exploding. "If you tie me up, how am I going to be able to touch you to make sure *you* have fun? And if you don't, how the hell am I supposed to not rip your clothes off?"

"They're leather," Vi said and opened the door.

"Gnaw them off with my teeth then," Chase said and, that fast, turned her back against her own door and pushed it closed. He looked like a hunter who had just sprung a trap on an unwary young wolf. Amused and delighted with himself and very, very predatory. He dropped down to a knee, his hands bracing to either side of her hips, still pinning her to the door. "Maybe I'll start the gnawing—right—here." He leaned in and pressed his mouth straight to her leather-covered crotch.

Vi made a startled sound and jumped, clutching at the door frame behind her.

"Shh," Chase murmured, his lips moving against the leather. "It will take me a while to gnaw through this. Just relax."

"Oh, my God." So much hot arousal fogged through her she couldn't see through the red and gold clouds. Oh, God. She pressed her head back hard against the door.

Chase closed strong hands around her thighs and pushed them wider, bracing her. And bit her, right between her legs. A gnawing leather-veiled pressure against the lips of her sex, and she dissolved, slickening her panties.

"Leather and you, wet," he said and pressed his face straight between her thighs and *nuzzled* there. "Christ, they should make a perfume." He nibbled again.

Vi whimpered, trying to crawl backwards up the door.

He tightened his grip on her thighs. "Hold still, honey. You challenged me, now take your throw." Those teeth, against her leather. "There are worse ways to lose, don't you think?"

Oh, God. She clutched his head, then grabbed the frame again, bucking as she twisted toward and away from what he was doing all at once. Her brain was lost somewhere. Wasn't *he* the one who was supposed to be in her power up here? She was supposed to be smiling wickedly right about now, reaching ever so slowly for the zip on her jacket, lowering it a centimeter at a time as he finally, finally, lost control of that glib tongue of his and just stared.

"It might take me a while to work my way through all this leather this way," Chase said as he took a long, slow bite of it—and of her with it. "Maybe you could tell me more about what panties you're wearing under it? Give me some motivation?"

He had not even been conceivable as a person who existed when she put on her panties that morning. She couldn't even remember. "Black lace," she said randomly, writhing against the door. That seemed like something that would keep him motivated. "At least—in front. In back there's not much at all. "

"Yeah?" He loosed one of her thighs to run his one finger down the seam of her pants and up, up the cleft of her butt, where a thong would go, under that leather. She writhed, pressing herself against that finger. "Now that's a nice goal, right there. The thought of you on your hands and knees on your bed, with nothing but a thong on and me standing right behind you. How we doing on this leather, baby? Am I getting through?"

"No," she said. "Yes. No. *Not enough.*"

"Well." He sat back on his heels and cocked his head up at her. "*You* have your hands free. You could help."

She stared down at him—that wicked humor in his eyes, but all that hunger, too. More and more hunger. It made him look...dangerous. Like a man with well over twice her strength, who knew exactly how to use that strength against far bigger and more lethal enemies than a knife-throwing chef.

"I should have known you couldn't handle me on your own," she said.

His face just lit in this wicked, wanton way, like a hellion who'd finally broken out of a monastery. "Oh, honey, you like to live dangerously, don't you?"

"Yes," she admitted, on the giddy rush of that danger as he slid his grip of her thighs up to the uppermost possible point, his thumbs sliding deep between her legs to pinch folds of leather and her up to his mouth. His elbows came into play, forcing her legs to stay spread.

"I think I'm handling you...just...fine," he purred, as his thumbs and teeth worked her.

She had an intense level of self-confidence, and she thrived on adrenaline, but she liked to be in control, too. Well, normally, she *had* to be in control. Even a male top chef had to maintain control at all times in his kitchens, but because she was a woman, running that starred kitchen full of arrogant and physically intense men did not allow her to falter in her control ever. Not for a millisecond.

I can falter here. I can give it all up and love *it.*

45

No consequences tomorrow, just the sex-filled adrenaline charge of playing with this hot and cocky guy who could...handle her just fine.

The arousal of what was happening to her kept pushing up her body in huge hot waves, flooding out all thought, leaving nothing but burning, frantic pressure in her breasts, in her brain, between her legs. This itchy longing heat that spread at the nape of her neck, at the base of her throat and down over her chest, at the insides of her elbows, behind her knees...everywhere.

"Well, let's try this," he said and worked his mouth around to the discreet black zip that ran over her hip. When she'd bought these pants, she'd originally thought that near-invisible side zip, with no button since the pants had no obvious waistband, was part of their sexy appeal. Now, as his tongue teased the zipper's pull tab up so that his teeth could close around it, she arched her body back against the door and cursed the day she hadn't bought pants with a normal center closure.

He laughed low in his throat as he worked the zipper down in his teeth, pressing her thighs back more firmly against the door when she writhed too hard. "Oh, honey, I'm kind of glad you threw that challenge at me, because I am having so much fun." He nuzzled his face between the spread panels and bit her hipbone, a teasing little nip. Then he caught the bikini strap of her underwear between his teeth and pulled it a couple of centimeters from her body before releasing it so that it snapped against her skin, a playful sting. "Honey, this looks like black cotton to me. Were you lying to me about your underwear?"

"You actually thought I would wear pink peekaboo panties to work all day in a hot kitchen?" she managed.

"Sweetheart, I could probably imagine you in pink peekaboo panties in any situation whatsoever. Be a sweetie and pack some for our honeymoon, okay?"

Him and his wedding jokes. She tried to roll her eyes, but he just smiled and lifted her thighs onto his shoulders, pushing her back up against the door so that her feet no longer touched the ground. Oh, God. She sank her hands into his hair. He rolled down the waist of her pants, folding it over rather than pulling it down, so that it revealed just a couple more centimeters of her pelvis.

"I'm going to die," she panted incredulously. Where had this man *come* from? Her entire experience of men had just been exploded out to the edges of the known universe. Maybe he was some kind of superhero come to Earth from the planet Sexton.

"Oh, yes, you are, honey," he purred in that crazy drawl of his. "*Le petit mort,* right?"

She winced, even through that much adrenaline and arousal. "It's *la. La petite mort.*"

He pulled his head back and frowned at her. "Did you just correct my French? At a time like this?"

"Never mind," she said. "You can...keep going here."

"Do you know how frustrating it is to have people dissing on my French all the time in this damn city?" He drew a finger very slowly down the center of her black panties, to where the folded band of leather stopped him. That damn leather. "Because I could maybe give you some idea. Of the frustration. Of what it's like to work a long...long...long   time   on   something   and not...get...anywhere." His finger twisted along the edge of that band.

"Oh, no," she said, trying to climb the door again, clutching him too hard with her thighs. His shoulders and neck seemed perfectly able to withstand the pressure, though. "No, no, no, no, no. No lessons in frustration."

He grinned, slow and wicked. "But it hurts my feelings," he said woefully. His finger wormed its way down under that folded band, stroking in far too short and limited a motion. "And this makes them feel all better."

"Oh, my God." She fisted his hair, trying to drag his head closer.

He didn't let her, for just long enough to let her know she couldn't make him if he didn't choose it, and then yielded, dipping his head in close to nuzzle his face against her panties and that damn band of leather. "God, I love this smell," he said.

She'd met some pretty physical men in her life, men who liked to live with their senses wide open, but she'd never ever met anyone as unadulteratedly *physical* as he was. He just wallowed in the pleasure of everything about his body, and hers.

It drove her absolutely out of her mind. Her brain shut down for it and let her become purely physical, too.

"It's not lace, but I think I'm enjoying these textures, too," he said wickedly, stroking his finger down between the tight leather and her very wet panties, rubbing them against her.

"The texture could maybe stand to be a little...firmer," she said, bucking.

"I know." He sent her that wicked grin. "But making you ask for it is a hell of a lot more fun."

"If you ever fall asleep around me, I'm going to tie you up and make you *beg*," she swore, clutching his head.

"Hell, you'd kill me," he realized, on a note between awe, hunger, and genuine alarm. "And here I've been revealing all my weaknesses for lace and knife-throwing leather, too. Now *that* is a deadly warning." He opened his mouth over her panties for a deep hot breath against her.

Violette might actually have whimpered. The heat in her body had reached such a point she was surprised she didn't burn her way through the door.

"You're so hot," he said. "If you'll unzip your jacket for me, I might be willing to give you a little more pressure down here." A teasing rub of his mouth over her panties.

Vi fumbled with her jacket zip as she tried to get it off. He did *not* help—teasing her, breathing on her, blowing gently against her. She finally got the damn jacket off and just threw it somewhere.

He looked up at her and tilted his head consideringly. "Okay, that's not going to do it. You're wearing a T-shirt!"

"You promised," she said between her teeth.

"I promised a *little* more pressure." He pressed his thumb against the leather, where it shielded her from the pressure she really wanted. He did press, but with that leather in the way...she gripped him, arching, fighting for what was so maddeningly elusive.

"If you want a *lot* more pressure, like in a...rhythm"—he blew her a kiss, his eyes so laughing and so aroused—"I think I'm going to have to insist you strip at least down to your bra."

"When I tie you up," she swore, "it's going to involve...silk...and pink peekaboo panties...and maybe, if you're really good at this, my mouth." His thumb jerked a little against her. Ah, yes, *almost* what she needed. She twisted to try to get more of it, but he pulled it away. She swore. "And you're going to cry."

"You first," he said, and rubbed his finger leisurely deeper through her weeping folds.

"Oh, hell, yeah," she said and yanked her T-shirt off, throwing it across the room.

"Now *that's* a view a man can get inspired by," Chase said reverently, gazing up her torso to the black, lace-edged bra that cupped her breasts.

Yeah, she could get inspired by her view, too, down at that cocky, handsome man on his knees before her with his rogue's humor as he used that beggar's position to take all the power over her he wanted.

"How bad do you want it, baby?" he murmured, in a deep, deep voice that seemed to vibrate against her skin as he pressed his mouth to her panties. "Bad enough to come right here? With me watching?"

She whimpered again, her nails digging into his skull, her thighs trying to lock around his head like a vice. He forced them back open with an ease that shot even more heat through her. Her legs were *strong*. They should be strong enough to give his hands some resistance. And yet he pressed her inexorably wide again.

"Bad enough to come like this?" he coaxed in that deep, rich drawl, angling an arm so that he could still brace her thigh with it and press the leather against her sex.

She bit her lip, closing her eyes, breathing fast, chasing it.

He deepened the pressure, the leather riding against her in just the right spot. And began to work it. Her body relaxed in relief at the deliberate rhythm. Now he *meant* it. Now he was going to let her—

"I like this," he breathed along the upper edge of her panties, then followed it with a stroke of his lips, as his thumb kept up that steady rhythm.

"Oh, *merde*," she said, and came suddenly and dramatically, this wave crashing through her body that jerked her hard against the wood. Her elbow hit the doorknob and she grabbed onto it, rocking and rocking against him, utterly helpless before the massive rush of pleasure, this great flash flood of it, filled with adrenaline and surprise and delight, that just crashed through her and obliterated her.

"Hell, you are fine," Chase said, hauling her into his arms as he came to his feet, hand still riding between her thighs as he found her bedroom and tossed her onto the bed, stretching the orgasm out, making it last.

It was too hard to last that long, though, and she pressed her hands over her face, shuddering and shuddering.

"Baby, baby, baby," he muttered, pulling at her leather pants. He peeled them down her legs and came over her, his hand sliding back now under her panties to freely touch her slickness. She jerked a little, so vulnerable there now, almost too vulnerable for open touching. And yet she liked it soo...ooh...she moaned, shifting.

"Yeah, yeah, yeah, yeah, yeah," he muttered, hand delving along the length of her in long strokes up and down. "Yes, go. Keep going. Oh, yeah."

The waves came back at her, taking her again, this flood-tossed, I-can-barely-breathe-now second orgasm like being borne exhausted back to some shore.

"Oh, God." She bit into the side of her arm as the waves slowly lapped down and let her rest. "Oh, God."

"You and me both, baby." Chase was stripping off clothes and his vest, shoving them off his body with the speed of a firefighter in reverse. "God, you are so damn fine." He kicked his underwear off his ankles and stood there completely naked.

Oh, wow. Wow. Wow. And he said *she* was fine. She had never seen a body so ripped and hard in her life. If-I-wrestled-a-T-Rex-I-would-win hard. Tough and big and utterly cut.

"*Bordel.*" She brought her hands to her lips. "*Tu es...*"

"Oh, God, yes, tell me dirty things in French," he muttered, coming down over her. "And then translate. Translate every. Single. Word." He kissed her, hot and deep, taking her mouth like he was fucking it, this devouring pleasure.

Having given her two orgasms and won his challenge, he was quite obviously focused on his own pleasure now, and she loved it. She loved that kissing was part of his pleasure, this glorious, deep kissing, over and over and over, as his hands gripped her head and dragged down her body, as he found the catch of her bra and got it off her, as he slid both his hands to grip her butt too hard and then got her panties out of the way.

"Did I win that challenge, honey?" he managed, his voice rough as he scraped his jaw down her throat and suckled against her collarbone.

"What if I said you didn't?" she couldn't resist asking as she wrapped her thighs around him.

"Then you sure as hell better not complain and beg me to stop five or six orgasms from now." He cupped her breasts. "Oh, fuck, these are so pretty. Are you daring me?" He paused with his thumbs held just above her nipples.

She hesitated.

His eyes narrowed just a little, and that blue gleamed dark with the love of challenge.

"No," she decided quickly. "No, uh, not...this time."

He grinned in pure triumph.

"Well, I'm daring you to *do it*," she said, and wrapped her thighs tight around him, sliding her hands under her legs to grip his butt as hard as she could.

He loved that, his butt muscles clenching as he thrust toward her. "Fuck, half a second," he remembered suddenly and rolled away, scrambling for his clothes. He sheathed himself so fast she actually wrapped a hand around him to double-check he had done it right.

He grinned, thrusting into her hand in luxurious pleasure. So she squeezed.

"I must have a guardian devil," he breathed. "And he's finally beaten that damn guardian angel off my other shoulder. *Thank you.*"

That *thank you* seemed to be directed more toward the guardian devil than to her, but she smiled, feeling about as smug as a woman could who had just had two orgasms and was no longer in a rush herself but ready to thoroughly enjoy driving a man out of his mind. She squeezed and drew her hand up the length of him and then back down.

He flipped her over, lifting her hips. She smiled as she braced on her forearms and arched her back.

He breathed a series of awed curses. She lowered her cheek to her pillow and rubbed it there, just for the pleasure of the texture as she savored his delight.

His hands caressed her butt almost worshipfully, as if she was fragile, those calluses shivering up through her body everywhere. Then he bent and bit her butt, just hard enough, with just enough tickle from his jaw, to make her yelp a little and laugh.

He rubbed his hand between her legs from behind until he could slip a finger into her sex in a slow, luxurious exploration and a verification that she was ready. She squeezed all her inner muscles against his finger.

He gave a low, burring sound of pleasure, thrusting again and then again, working her, making sure. She stretched her arms awkwardly behind her, taking her own weight on her face and shoulders, as she grabbed for his butt and managed to reach his thighs, pulling against those great muscles.

He arched her a little farther to make his access easy and then with a sighing *fuck* of delight thrust into her.

Mmmm. She pulled on him harder, bringing him deeper. "Don't stop."

"Please tell me that's not a challenge," he said as he thrust deep, deep, deep enough that she gave a little gasp and had to relax her muscles again. "Don't you dare ask me to keep this up for a damn hour."

She smiled into the pillow. "All right, then, hurry up." She tugged on his thighs as hard as she could from that angle.

He bent over her back, his voice that deep, luxurious drawl. "How about I take my own sweet time?" He drew a callused hand down her spine.

She shivered with pleasure. After an intense day on her feet, controlling everything, there was perhaps nowhere on her body hungrier for touch than her back.

"Like that, sweetheart?" he murmured, broadening his strokes of her back to her shoulders, then tightening his hands on her shoulders as he thrust deep into her again. And deep again.

God, he felt good. She bit into her lip with the pleasure of it, shaking her head a little against her pillow as every texture, cotton sheets, skin, pressure inside and out, became delicious. He stroked down her arms, found her hands, and threaded his fingers with hers, locking her hands to the mattress. "And that?"

She nodded against the pillow.

"I have died and gone to heaven." He thrust harder, his fingers tightening on hers. "Well...maybe not heaven, but somewhere a lot dirtier and more fun."

"Don't stop," she whispered into the pillow.

"I tell you what, honey. I can't promise not to stop. But I sure as hell promise you I'll do it again."

And, by God, he did.

The second time was in the shower, in this long, slow, mercilessly sensual stroking of water and helplessness, too much sensation everywhere, while he laughed low in his throat and lifted her and kissed her and manipulated her body every way he wanted to, until he finally pressed her wet against that wall, with the warm water pouring over both of them, took her mouth with his, and fucked her senseless.

Almost literally. She was limp and somnolent from exhausted pleasure as he carried her and a bundle of towels to the bed and stretched her out on it, patting her dry with a kind of possessive smugness. And it was 2:50 a.m. when she fell asleep.

***

In the dark room, Chase propped on his elbow a while, smiling as he watched her sleep. She'd turned away from him, and her blond hair spilled over the sheets and her back, her arm flung out to the edge, her knee drawn up. She wanted to take *all* the bed, didn't she? It was *hers.*

He rolled onto his back, with one hand behind his head, and checked his watch. Three o'clock. The smile slowly faded. If Vi had been awake, she would have seen his face go faintly grim, inscrutable, a blank, lethal contemplation. In the dark, where no one could see, he looked like a hardened killer anticipating battle.

But, of course, if she had been awake, he wouldn't have let her see that face.

Time to go.

He rolled out of bed smoothly and silently, dressing without a sound. Vi didn't even move in her sleep. He pulled open the drawer of her nightstand. No paper. But there was a journal lying on top of the stand. He opened it, flipping past what seemed mostly menu ideas to a blank page. It was one of those expensive journals he hated to rip up, so he hesitated a moment over it, pen in hand, then smiled a little as he wrote quickly. He set her alarm clock on top of it to hold the journal open to the page, so that she would spot it when she turned that alarm off.

Then he strode out without looking back.

Chapter 7

"So how did your fishing expedition go?" Mark asked with a crisp edge to his words, as if they'd spent too long on a temperamental grill. Being team leader of a group of men like them who had been sitting still for far longer than their temperaments could handle was not for the faint of heart.

Chase leaned back in his chair, locked his hands behind his head, opened his mouth, closed it...and a great, beatific grin spread across his face.

"I'm going to kill him," Jake informed Mark. "God damn it. I spent the whole fucking night on a roof in forty degree rain. Isn't it *July*?" Half Irish and half God knew what—mountain lion, probably—Jake had golden red hair and skin that should currently be deeply relieved to find itself in a rainy climate. The dense layering of dust-toned freckles on his skin had pretty much left no non-freckled space, after the Middle East.

"I had to keep her distracted!" Chase said. "Her brain scrambled. You know." He grinned, feeling so big he was going to explode any moment. Hell, she was fine. "Who wants to be the best man?"

From the doorway, Ian snorted. "No woman is dumb enough to marry you. She was just using you for sex." There was a grain of truth to that which snuck under Chase's skin. Special ops always did have more trouble getting a woman to marry them and stick with them through deployments than finding someone to have sex with.

"It's true love," Chase said loftily, instead of admitting that. "You're just jealous."

Possibly true. The gods had showered multiple ethnic blessings on Ian, as if each race in his ancestry had assigned him his own personal fairy godmother at the christening to try to form the ideal twenty-first century man, and, in consequence, he found it even easier than the rest of them to pick up women. He had possibly gotten a little bit spoiled, therefore.

Near him, their French RAID liaison, Elias, gave Chase a jaundiced look. The tall, black-haired, and bronze-skinned member of France's elite counterterrorism unit had been born of an Algerian father and a French mother in one of the poorer *banlieues* outside Paris, and he had reacted to the 2015 attacks kind of like someone might react to discovering his brother had turned into a raging zombie cannibal and was eating out the brains of their parents.

In which case, Elias had chosen the role of Rick Grimes.

"Did you come here to help protect the civilian population or inseminate them?" Elias asked coolly.

Chase grinned at him. "Worried about protecting your womenfolk?"

Elias just raised one eyebrow. How did French men manage that damn eyebrow thing? Chase tried it, involuntarily—he *always* had to try physical challenges as soon as he thought of them—struggling to wiggle one eyebrow over the other, and sneezed.

"I know you don't know much about restaurants in America, but trust me, a twenty-eight-year-old two-star chef can protect herself," Elias said dryly.

Chase's grin widened. Damn, she'd been hot wielding those knives. "She sure as hell can."

"So I'm just going to assume she has lousy taste in men."

Hey. "Maybe she's desperate." Chase yawned and stretched and rubbed his knuckles against his chest. "Real men, you know. She probably never met one before, growing up here." He shot Elias a bird.

"Well, she'd have to be desperate if she thought you were one," Ian said from the doorway. He folded muscled arms across his chest and gave Chase a competitive look. "Or exhausted."

"Ego depletion," Jake said judiciously. "Eighteen hours handling a top kitchen. Decision fatigue, man. Give her a chance to sleep and she'll wonder what the hell she was thinking."

Chase scowled, slouching a little in his chair. It was not that he thought they were right, *obviously*, but still...

Damn it. They were probably right. Part right. They *all* knew the research on decision fatigue, kind of essential to anyone in special ops. Shit.

"I'll go introduce myself to her, and *then* she'll wonder what she was thinking," Ian said and grinned. "But that's okay. I don't mind giving her a second chance to find the right man."

"Okay, you know what—?" Chase started to stand.

"If we could focus on the main subject," Mark said with that too-long-on-the-grill note to his voice. Long, lean, dark-haired Mark had a quiet manner and a bony angularity to him that always managed to convey the impression that he was a nerd, which was kind of hilarious considering his physical abilities. The iron man geek. Who had the nerves to deal with men like Chase, Jake, and Ian.

Chase subsided, Ian relaxed back against the wall, Jake gave them both a sardonic glance, Elias gazed heavenward, and they all paid attention.

"Chase. Other than chasing tail, anything?"

And Chase settled down. Way down. Into that cold place, where his heartrate dropped, where his focus was perfect. He didn't think he was a psychopath, like people always liked to claim about special ops, because his emotion switch was usually full on. But he knew how to turn it off. That empty, calm clarity that took over his brain and body when he did.

"Nothing," he said. "But..." And he dropped his head back, staring at the ceiling. "Is there any more on that ricin rumor?"

SOCEUR, United States Special Operations Command, Europe, was coordinating special ops with the French for one primary reason. Obviously, SOCEUR, too, would do anything and everything in their power to help prevent additional attacks on French soil, and they'd been instructed by the President himself to assist in any and all ways they could to track, punish, prevent.

But Al-Mofti was their highest value target now, and the reason SOCEUR had more or less crowbarred their way into operations here. Al-Mofti had been the mastermind behind the attack that took down a Paris-New York flight over the holidays, full of hundreds of French and Americans going to visit families, usually with their little French-American children with them on their way to see grandma. There had been a symbolism in the attack, to hit both France and the U.S. at the same time, a strike right at the heart of where the two were most vulnerable and most united.

And every person in the room and all the way up their chain of command to two presidents would kill that motherfucker if it was the last thing they did.

Mark shook his head grimly. "They've gone entirely dark."

Chills prickled up Chase's arms. He hated it when terrorists went dark. Especially when several of them in Paris and Brussels went dark together. Especially after the word *ricin* had been picked up by the CIA. Especially when one of the men they were tracing on his return from Syria was the cousin of Violette Lenoir's pastry chef and had been seen on the street of the restaurant, using a phone for a purpose they hadn't been able to trace. Damn encrypted chat apps.

Fuck, that kitchen was a nightmare. Jesus, they had shelves and shelves of half-prepped desserts sitting there overnight. Someone with a code, which probably covered all the upper levels of staff, could come in early and...

...and the first they'd know about it was when people started to get sick. And there was no cure for ricin.

They had *nothing* on the head pastry chef, nothing at all except the relationship with that very problematic cousin.

But what if...

That was what a counterterrorist unit had to deal with. That huge, horrible what if.

Who would be on the front line if the crazy bastards did manage to use ricin?

Violette Lenoir and all her staff. Handling all the food. Tasting it before it went out.

"We need to shut it down," he said abruptly. "Find some excuse that gets the kitchen closed until after the President's visit or we nail the bastards. Something that doesn't tip them off. A plumbing problem or something. Rats?" No, shit. Vi would be *pissed* about rats. He'd seen the way those critics reacted in *Ratatouille*. Watched it during one fucking cold winter in Kandahar, where even a rat's vision of Paris had made for an enticing contrast. "An electrical issue. Small fire."

"That's your call?" Mark assessed him steadily.

There had never been a successful mass ricin attack. But Chase had seen far more than his share of aftermaths of attacks with bombs and AK-47s, and they crowded up in his brain suddenly, sent ripples of horror down his skin. "Yes," he said flatly. "It's too big a risk."

"The chef can't know what happened," Elias said. "She's got to be left as much in the dark as anyone. We can't risk tipping them off."

Chase's jaw tightened grimly. Yeah. He knew. "Fuck, she's going to be pissed. She was really excited about the President's possible visit."

Elias was watching him. That sardonic look had faded beneath a certain tough sympathy. "Don't worry. She's a Michelin two-star chef at the age of twenty-eight. Trust me. She can handle anything."

Chapter 8

"Salmonella?" Vi stared at the health inspectors blocking her access to her own kitchens with no regard for life or limb. Health inspectors were getting more and more suicidal these days. "In *my* restaurant? No, there damn well was not!"

"We're sorry, Mademoiselle Lenoir," the lead inspector said woodenly. "We have reports from a dozen people whose one point in common seems to be having eaten here last night."

"That's not even possible!" Vi said, outraged. "My team's hygiene is *impeccable.* I know the source of everything we serve." Even as she said it, she was running things through her mind: eggs from her brother's farm, honey from the rooftop rosemary gardens and beehives of their own quarter in Paris, no oysters last night it wasn't the season... "Let me see this—" She started to push by him.

He stepped to the side to block her, and something flickered through her. That was a very *adamant* block. A police officer kind of block. Or a military man's block.

"*Pardon, mademoiselle.* It's a public health emergency. Until we track down the source, we need to close the restaurant and run tests."

She narrowed her eyes up at the health inspector, who certainly seemed to work out a lot in his down time. The set of his shoulders reminded her quite a lot of... "Is this something to do with Chase Smith?"

"Who?" the inspector said blankly.

She folded her arms to keep herself from stabbing someone. A health inspector, for example. "That's not his real name, is it?"

"I have no idea who you're talking about, *mademoiselle*," the military-mannered inspector said formally.

"*Bordel de—*" Vi stabbed her finger at him. "These are *my* kitchens. *You tell me what is going on.*"

"We're investigating a salmonella outbreak," he repeated woodenly. "That seems to have started here."

"So it's true then?" a voice said from behind Vi to her right. "You've been forcibly shut down for salmonella?"

Vi pivoted to see—with a shock of horror—a television camera pointed her way. Oh, *fuck.*

"Mademoiselle Lenoir, would you care to comment?" a perfectly coiffed brown-haired man asked, posing beside her before the camera and extending his microphone.

"How could I care to comment? I just found out about it! How do *you* know about it already?" She tried to see which news station they were from.

"Twitter," the journalist said.

Bordel de merde. "It's on Twitter already?" Vi said, her stomach sinking as if she'd swallowed a bucket of rock.

The journalist nodded with an appearance of sympathy. "As I'm sure you're aware, taking you on as chef here created some controversy, and your changes to the menu have been...splashy. Do you think a salmonella outbreak at Au-dessus supports those who have always claimed you were too young and too...flamboyant...to handle the job?"

Fuck, fuck, fuck. Oh, shit, any minute they were going to bring out the "woman chef" thing. And she might have to hit somebody. "I think you'll find there's some other source to this salmonella outbreak." She looked at the health inspector grimly. "Let's see those tests."

"I'm afraid we'll have to ask you and your staff to remain off the premises while we conduct the investigation," the military-like inspector said stiffly.

"Oh, no, you damn well will not." Vi forgot all about the television camera. "Mess around in my kitchens without me there? Over my dead body."

***

"*Salmonella*?" Chase demanded between his teeth. "Out of all the possible excuses for shutting that restaurant down, they went with the only one that would do someone actual harm?"

Mark propped his butt against the table behind him and folded his arms. "They said it was the perfect cover. It stirs up doubt. Al-Mofti might have to make calls to find out what was going on, and maybe we can get a location. *Was* there a ricin attack attempt? Did one of his men carry it out? Did they get caught and this is our cover up? He'll want to know. And the more of his men he tries to communicate with, the more chance we have of tracking him down."

"I said a kitchen fire! Plumbing!"

"You've got to admit it's better," Mark said.

Maybe. If Chase turned off all thought of individual consequences and went into his cold place. Kind of a lousy, crappy place to go when it came to a gorgeous, vivid, life-filled blonde in leather.

"Better only if you consider destroying a chef's career a minor side effect," Elias said, his voice very even and cold. "*Putain*, but you people have no idea of culture. Maybe later you can build a McDonald's where her restaurant stood."

Ice entered Chase's soul. "I thought you said she can handle anything."

"I suspect she can," Elias said. "But that doesn't mean her *restaurant* can. Or her current *career* can. Food poisoning. At a restaurant already at the center of every critic's eye this year, as they love her or hate her or swear she'll never make it. *Merde*, it's a top chef's worst nightmare."

63

"At least she's alive," Mark said. "Which she wouldn't be, if she were exposed to ricin. She probably has friends who aren't alive, from the last Paris attacks."

A grim look settled over Elias's face. He didn't have to tell them that he also had friends who were no longer alive. They all had friends who were no longer alive, these days. "Who the hell made this call? Were my people involved or was it the damn CIA?"

"It's a coordinated initiative," Mark said wearily. Within their team, that was working fine, but on a larger scale...it had already been a nightmare coordinating operations between the CIA and the military when they only had one country involved. "That's all I've got."

One of those visions of Violette Lenoir dying of ricin again. Not rippling under him in a glorious orgasm, shining with life, but wrenching in death, convulsions going weaker and weaker, until all of her was gone.

Sometimes he really wished he had gone into ranching or something for a living. Surfing. Skiing. Something else challenging and daredevil that didn't stuff his brain with so many visions of so many different moments of dying. His brain was so damn good at switching out the real bodies seen with those of the people he most cared about, too.

A lot of people claimed his breed were psychopaths. But Chase knew how many of them had gone into the military not because of too little empathy but too much. They'd seen those bodies jumping from the windows of incredibly high buildings rather than burn alive, and the pain and the fury on their behalf had been too much. *I'll get those bastards back for this,* the teenage boy thought. *I'll make sure it never happens again.* And he enlisted.

Maybe that teenager adopted some traits of psychopathy later. Learned how to turn off that empathy switch, because what else were you supposed to do, when your mission night after night might be to slip into someone's compound while he was asleep and kill him? But he wasn't born that way. The problem of that teenage boy who enlisted wasn't that he was born with too little heart where others were concerned...it was that he was born with too damn much, and he didn't know how to give enough of it, except with his actual blood.

"I just think they could have used some excuse besides *food poisoning*," Chase said. Damn it, and he'd been the one to say he didn't care what they came up with. "What the hell was wrong with the kitchen fire excuse?"

"This leaves Al-Mofti in greater doubt, which gives us that many more chances to finally pinpoint where that bastard is."

"Yes, but..." Chase logged into Twitter and found #audessus #vilenoir. Oh, shit. A sick feeling grew in his stomach. What the fuck? Had some asshole just called her a "dumb c***", with a "women don't belong in a real restaurant" added on? He was going to kick somebody's ass. "Can you retract it? Correct it?"

"Chase," Mark said firmly. "You have to hold it together. We'll run 'salmonella tests' for a few days, follow any leads we might get, and later we can say the salmonella cases were traced to something else and nothing to do with the restaurant. I hope I don't need to remind you that stopping Al-Mofti is our top priority."

A vision of Flight 997's family members, the screaming agony of the mother of the little girl who'd flown by herself for the very first time to see her grandparents and now would never be coming home. "No," Chase said, feeling sick. "No."

"And *do not tell her*," Mark said. "We still don't know what, if any, connection her pastry chef might have with any of this. We need *doubt*. We don't want anything certain to slip out."

Fuck.

Chapter 9

By four that afternoon, Vi had one thing on her mind: Chase Smith.

If she ever found that slimy bastard again, she was going to kick him so hard in the nuts he wouldn't even be able to *look* at a woman he wanted to screw for months without wincing.

Not that she knew what the hell was going on, but she knew how a man's eyes flickered when she caught him out. Like, *You're married, aren't you?* Or *Navy SEAL.* She knew what normal health inspectors looked like, and she knew they didn't bar her from her own restaurant. And she knew what it was like to be screwed by a man who didn't see her body as anything more than an enjoyable byproduct of his running his tank right over her life.

You're lucky you snuck out without leaving your number, you bastard. She rolled her right shoulder and touched her right cheek, where both had been bruised when the police had to forcibly remove her—pushing her against the wall by the restaurant back door and cuffing her. More good fodder for the cameras.

Putain, she might have broken Twitter.

Fortunately, her arrest had been a catch and release deal. The police had just wanted her to calm down and *give up her own restaurant into the hands of imposter health inspectors.* One of them had even told her a pretty woman like her shouldn't get so upset, she should show more class. And she hadn't even been able to deck him, because all the power was in his hands, and he would just have arrested her again, and this time kept her locked up.

She glared back at the Commissariat, the main one on the Île de la Cité, where she was pretty sure she'd been taken just to put more distance between her and her restaurant in the Tenth.

Then she checked her phone. Yeah, that "c***s don't belong in the kitchen" Tweet had been reTweeted 2753 times. With her tagged each time. She didn't even want to check the hashtags. Her publicist would have to handle that one.

Merde, now Twitter was claiming she'd food poisoned the President of the United States? That had been a *prospective* visit *a week from now.*

She threw her phone in a long arc from the point of the Île de la Cité into the Seine, and stood there, her hands on her hips, watching that phone sink down into brown water and the mud below like her life.

Fuck.

How had this just happened to her? She had been at the heights and still climbing, a rising star, glowing bright and determined to keep climbing. Controversial, yes. Flamboyant, yes. "It's pretty but is it art?", yes. But any woman worth her salt in this field had to face that crap.

The same way she had to face the way so many onlookers cheered her fall now and threw rotten eggs and tomatoes at her while she was down in the dirt.

She shoved her hand through her hair and stared at a passing barge, tempted to swim out to it and beg the captain to take her away from this city. Maybe she could change her name, change her hair, change countries, and start over.

A movement to her left, a man coming in too close to her personal space, and she pivoted so fast she nearly drilled a hole through the cobblestone with her heel. Some jerk wanted to harass her right now? Bring it.

But it was Chase. Big, tan, easy-moving, gold-streaked brown hair, with those blue eyes and the lines around them from squinting into who knew what. Bullets?

As cocky as ever. Checking her out, with that quick *I-own-that-now* flick up and down her body. Larger than life, hard-bodied, absolutely sure of himself. Except for that guilty smile on his mouth.

A wave of memories washed over her—his hands all over her body, inside her body, his face as he looked down at her butt, his mouth on her...all while he knew he was going to bring her life down around her ears. Her fingers curled into her palms.

"Hi, honey," he said, just cautiously enough that she *knew*. She'd been his roadkill, hadn't she? And now he had a guilty conscience.

"You." Her fist clenched.

He held up placating hands, like a cheater calming down his little woman after she caught him with another girl. "Now, honey," he started.

She hit him.

***

Chase had a split-second to control his instinct to duck, and he managed it. Took it on the chin.

Vi's hand connected with a force that shouldn't have surprised him, and he shoved off with his feet for good measure, so that the punch sent him flying back into the river. He grabbed a deep breath as he flew, hit the water with a loud splash, and sank out of sight.

Okay, let's just hang out down here for a while, give her a chance to calm down. Given all the free-diving he'd done, he was tempted to give it a full five minutes just to panic her—best way to break through anger, right?—but he didn't want her actually diving in after him. Well, he kind of didn't. Ruin that leather of hers. So he came up after three, expecting to find her hovering on the edge of the stone quay, getting anxious.

69

She wasn't even looking at him!

She was—oh, fuck, she was huddled over her hand, her face twisted in agony.

He leapt out of the river, water flinging off him. "Honey—" He reached for her wrist.

Her hands flew up, and he barely saved his eyes. One of her nails raked up his cheek, as she went for them.

He grabbed both her arms, taking firm control of her. She kicked him in the groin.

Ow. Damn it. He should have kept that vow to wear protection around her. Hunching over himself, he glared at her. "Was that the fuck necessary? *Ow.*"

"Fuck you." She clutched her wrist, her face a mask of pain.

"Honey." Damn it, had she *broken* her hand on his jaw? And he'd been so damn cocky about letting her hit him. It had never occurred to him that *she'd* get hurt. "Let me look at it. Please?"

He was vaguely aware of the audience they were gathering, all the other couples or groups who had been hanging out on this stone island in the middle of the Seine now focused on them with varying degrees of fascination, wariness, and willingness to intervene to help Vi. He kept the awareness of the crowd and its potential for trouble in his peripheral, but mostly he focused on Vi.

Who had all her rage focused on him, green eyes like two of her own knives. "You ruined my life. Go to hell."

"I didn't! It wasn't—" He bit his teeth together over the words.

I didn't come up with the food poisoning thing.

But he *was* the one who had said the restaurant needed to be shut down.

"You didn't ruin my life?" she said very precisely. "I've been climbing my way up through macho kitchens since I was *fifteen*. I run a *two-star restaurant*. I worked eighteen-, twenty-hour days for the past thirteen years. And now this will be the only thing the world remembers about me. What the hell do you think you haven't ruined?"

He shoved his hand over his face. "Can't you still do all that? I mean—those people who give stars don't even *like* the American president, right? They'll probably give you an extra one for poisoning him."

And she hit him again.

Or she tried. This time, he did duck, shifting with her attack so that her body flew half past him, guiding her wrist, bringing her back up so that he locked her against his body, back to him. "Honey—"

She stomped on his foot. With that stiletto heel. *Fuck, that hurt.*

He hefted her up so that she couldn't reach it.

She kicked him in the shins.

Ow. "Will you *stop*?" He let her go, putting some space between them. At least she wasn't as likely to break her foot on him as her hand.

Phones were out in the crowd around him. Yeah, this was definitely ending up on film, and some people were bound to be calling the police. Wonderful. If he got arrested, there were some people higher up his chain of command who were going to skin him alive.

If she got arrested a second time in one day, they might actually keep her in jail.

"Honey, we need to get your hand looked at, and—"

"If you call me honey one more time, I will kill you."

He hesitated. "Hon—bab—sweetheart, listen."

"And not sweetheart either!"

He frowned at her. "Mademoiselle Gorgeous, then, fuck."

"Mad-moi-selle!" she shouted.

71

"What?"

"You pronounce it *mad'moiselle!*"

Wasn't that what he had just said? This damn language. "You're getting hysterical." And thank God she didn't have her knives on her. "Will you just—"

"Hysterical?" Her fist clenched.

Oh, hell. He took the coward's way out and just went ahead and threw himself back in the water before her fist could actually make impact.

He came up starting to get just a little mad himself and gripped the edge of the quay, glaring up at her. "Are we done yet?"

Her eyes narrowed to slits, and she gave a look at his hands that made him jerk them back from the edge, just in case she decided to stomp on them with those stilettos. He gripped a ring halfway down the stone wall of the quay instead, out of stomping reach. Some people in the crowd were starting to laugh and applaud her. "You can swim, right?"

She took a very wise step back from the edge. Which she probably thought put her out of easy grabbing reach. Sometimes it was a *real* temptation to show her what he was made of, but he should resist the urge to toss her into the river herself to cool her off.

Really.

Resist.

Hard.

Although the expression on her face when she came up would be—

Resist!!

"Oh, we're done." Vi spun on her heel, striding away.

He leapt out of the water and caught up with her, also resisting the urge to grab all the phones he passed and throw them into the water. It would only escalate the situation. If he got in a fight with a mob of civilians at four p.m. in the middle of Paris, he was going to ruin his own career.

And he'd put far too much blood and sweat and effort into his own career to—

The thought faltered. He looked down at Violette's head, his eyebrows drawing together. Remembering the burn scars he'd seen on her arms and hands, when they made love. The calluses from handling knives.

He'd joined the military when he was eighteen. She'd been doing this since she was fifteen. Fifteen. He was pretty sure his voice was still cracking on him at embarrassing moments when he was fifteen.

Within his team, reputation was everything. You were a badass, and you kept your shit wired tight, or you got forced onto another team, and your career was over.

Reputation.

He looked down at her proud face, the way she fought to keep from showing her pain.

"Hon—swee—Vi. I'm sorry."

That long stride of hers faltered on a rough paving stone. She flicked a glance up at him.

"I would never," he said quietly, "in a million years have caused you harm." *Except that I did. And it was at least half my choice. And even right now, I could lessen the harm if I broke security and told you the truth. But I won't. Because it's my job to save the world.*

And you...you're strong enough to handle this.

I bet you're strong enough to handle anything.

It was an amazing thought. He'd never met a woman as strong as he was. Hard to wrap his mind around when she kept looking so much smaller.

"I didn't know—" He stopped and pressed his lips tightly together and shook his head. He grabbed a deep breath, as if going underwater for another long dive. "Vi. Will you *please* let me look at your hand?"

She scowled and looked away from him, cradling her wrist.

LAURA FLORAND

Okay, now she was just being stubborn. But he knew all about stubborn. Stubborn wasn't even an adequate word for the sheer bullheaded, don't-yield-to-anything-ever determination of the men he worked with. It made it confusing to go out among ordinary people, actually. He kept expecting to run up against granite wills, and instead he just walked through everyone, their wills so flimsy they were almost immaterial. Most of the time, it took conscious effort to even *notice* that the average person actually did have a will of his own.

A wisp-of-fog will, easily ridden over or through by a man in a hurry.

And yet those same men who would ride over the wills of average people and never even notice would also throw themselves toward a suicide bomber for average people and put their own glorious wills entirely out, forever...and never think twice about that either.

He'd done so much damage to her. And yet it really had been for her own good. To save the world. Her.

"Please," he said again. "Just to make me feel better."

"I don't want you to feel better," Vi said. "You should feel like shit. I hope you feel like shit for the rest of your life."

Well, all right then.

"Just to make you feel better then," he said. "Damn it, Vi, I think it's broken." It was starting to swell alarmingly.

"If you try to lay one finger on me ever again, I will stab you," she said.

Well, a guy knew where he stood with Vi, didn't he? No game-playing. In fact, a man used to running right through everyone else like wisps of fog hit her like a brick wall.

He liked it—liked the nice, resounding smack of his will meeting hers. But it made getting a woman to do something just a little more complicated when she refused to let him take charge of her situation.

74

"Are you just going to *ignore* it?" he demanded, starting to get desperate. She was clearly in agony and too proud to show it.

"I'll get it taken care of myself." She strode on.

He sighed. "Fine. I'll just walk along with you in case, at any point during the process, you need to hit me again. Don't aim for the jaw next time, okay?"

***

Vi managed to get him kicked out of the hospital room, by the simple process of telling the staff that she didn't want him in the room with her. So he had to sit in the waiting room, thumb-fighting himself, feeling big and stupid and useless, for what seemed like hours.

See, this was why a lot of the married guys preferred to be downrange. On the job, they were used to being the baddest shits on the planet, taking names and kicking ass, the best of the best of the best...and then they got home, and they turned into these big, useless lugs. None of their skills fit, and their wives were giving them sad, woeful looks because they'd forgotten the anniversary of the day they first kissed or something.

On the thought, Chase pulled out his phone and put the previous day's date in his calendar to pop up as an annual reminder. Yeah, that was one mistake he wasn't going to make.

He searched "Violette Lenoir" on his phone and winced at the titles that now filled the first five pages. He paged forward, finding older articles and blog posts about her as the chef of Au-dessus. Some critics hated her, but others loved her, and one thing her food did was make people talk. The energy in it, the sense of passion, the way it evoked the city and the life of her quarter.

The web showed images of dishes where the artistic dots and squiggles and lines of sauces on a plate he associated with fancy restaurants had been taken to a whole new level. Instead of fine lines so elegant that it seemed as if looking at the food would make it faint, she had plates where color splashed across them with the drama of a young, rebel artist flinging paint. She had plates that spoke of graffiti and rebel theater and the artists' workshops that filled her corner of Paris. A plate called "Belleville", which evoked, apparently—he checked the blog post explanation—the funky glass studios in that area, with blown sugar for the glass. Oh, that one had come from Lina Farah, her pastry chef. The one with the suspicious cousin.

He found a three-minute video of the kitchen in full swing and watched it with some fascination. The reflexes and precision, the way those knives moved across a cutting board or sliced through a fish, the constant intense physical action. Interesting the careers people chose. A lot of these guys would probably have made good soldiers, maybe even elite ones like him if they tried, but they'd focused on feeding people instead. That worked, he guessed. They were both important jobs for keeping people alive.

And damn but Vi was hot, running that kitchen. The way she moved, the way she cared about every single thing that happened, the way she took control, with confidence and authority and no hesitation to make demands. That three-minute video clip was way too short.

More photos. There were dishes that used honey from the rooftop beehives and rosemary gardens Vi and a couple of other chefs had set up in a cooperative above their street. Dishes that honored a director friend's ambitious, indie theater project with its dramatic, slashing style. Dishes that made him think of leather and studded boots and maybe a piercing in an unexpected place, of tattoos, of laughter and impractical ambitions and funky art.

In her hands, food wasn't elegant and refined and as fragile as fine china. It was glorious, the source of life, abundant, rebellious. It was in love with her part of the city, with the people in it, and it was something you could *sink your teeth into*. Exactly the opposite of what every other three-star restaurant was doing.

And people loved it, or hated it, and said she should lose the stars she had, or said they hoped she would get her third star, that the culinary establishment had gone down the wrong path with their elegant wisps of food a long time ago, and it was time for a new generation, time for Vi Lenoir.

Or that was what they had been saying.

Now, of course...he arrowed back to the first pages of the search results. Now all they could talk about was catastrophe. "Is this the end for Vi Lenoir?" "Can Audessus survive?" And those were the formally written pieces. Unfortunately, Twitter was one of the first search results, and it was full of sniping, constant 140-character chatter, of ugliness and misogyny but also of people who were furious about that misogyny: "It could come from the spinach leaves! Why are you blaming the chef? #becausesheisawoman".

He bent his head and rubbed his shoulder. Fuck.

After a wait that shouldn't have seemed long to a guy who had been through sniper training but which somehow lasted ages, Vi finally came out with a black splint that immobilized all but the thumb and index finger of her right hand. Chase leapt up, coming to her.

"Broken, then?" He tried to reach for her forearm, so he could lift her hand up for a better look, but she jerked away and cold-shouldered him.

He cursed. "I should have ducked."

She spun on him. "You know what you should have done? You should have not played the cocky shit who can have anyone and anything he wants, when all that time, you were planning something that would ruin my career. You're no better than Quentin."

He stopped stock still. Quentin…the guy who had tried to *rape* her? The guy who had assaulted her in her own walk-in, so that she had to bring a case of milk bottles down on his head? Kicking his ass so bad he never even looked at another woman again without flinching in fear had been next on Chase's to-do list.

"I was *not* planning anything that would ruin your career," he said between his teeth. "You were secondary."

She swung on him, and he dropped into a squat just in time for her splint to fly over his head.

"Will you stop?" he yelled. "You're going to hurt yourself again if you keep this up!"

"I need my knives." She stalked off.

He followed. "Secondary wasn't the right word."

"Fuck you."

"I mean, it all—it had nothing to do with you, okay! I just…happened to run into you and didn't want you to call the police."

"I will kill you," she said, in a monotonous scary voice, like a relentless robot, striding out the hospital doors.

"Vi! Damn it." She hailed a taxi. "I *can't* talk about this. Just—can you trust me that I had nothing to do with the food poisoning thing?" Well, maybe *nothing* wasn't quite the right word, but…but… "I never meant you to get hurt!"

A taxi pulled up.

Damn it. Ten taxis in a row would drive by him in this city, and she got one within five seconds? How could a man do a proper grovel in these conditions? Rain started to spit at his head again, and it was all he could do not to shoot a bird at the sky.

She yanked the door open and then grabbed the edge of it, locking her eyes with his. "You had *nothing* to do with it?"

Well...he shoved his hand through his hair. It still felt absurdly short to him since his shift to Europe. In Afghanistan, he'd had a beard and shaggy hair. "More or less nothing," he said. "I mean—it wasn't my *fault*."

"You're pathetic," she said, and climbed into the taxi and slammed the door.

He stared after her as the heavens opened up and started pouring icy rain down on him again.

Pathetic?

The next time he saw one of those movies about romantic, magical Paris, he was throwing popcorn at the damn screen.

Chapter 10

Anyone would think a woman who had frequently had to shower off with sliced fingers or second-degree burns on her hands could handle having a hand in a splint. Vi even had a variety of vinyl gloves and plastic bags around to keep a wounded hand dry, although the doctor had said that wasn't necessary with this splint.

But somehow, standing under the water with her arm thrust out past the shower curtain and the pain from the fracture trying to eat its way through her brain, her head suddenly thumped against the dripping wall.

At least with the water pouring over her face, she couldn't tell if she'd lost the battle against the stinging in her eyes. At least she'd broken down in private, not like some nineteen-year-old in a chef's reality show, when everything went wrong and the top chef judges tore her work to pieces in front of everyone, and the video of her flushed cheeks and wobbling voice was on YouTube forever for the whole world to see.

Fucking YouTube. She'd drowned the clip with as many TV appearances and "how to make Vi Lenoir's famous so-and-so" video clips as she could, but that old reality show clip still rose to the top.

This one would, too. Everything from today—her face when she learned her restaurant was being closed for salmonella, her getting arrested, probably her hitting Chase. It would take over the Wikipedia page on her. It would drown out all her accomplishments, everything she'd done.

Her eyes stung harder, and she stared up into the water to make sure that sting was coming from the shower and not inside her.

Idiot. She kept her face turned up into the shower, until the water was cold, until it was icy, and finally she had to drag herself out from under it, shivering uncontrollably as she bundled herself in pajamas and bathrobe and fuzzy slippers. Normally she just blazed right through the chilly weather, barely noticing it, but this afternoon, the cold summer had seeped into her bones. She felt like ashes, trying to remember the glory of when she had been flame.

The knocking on the door made her brace. The code on the building door had so far kept out the media who had been lying in wait, but eventually some journalist would be enterprising enough to duck in after a legitimate resident, pretending to be someone's friend.

And she couldn't even call the police. Maybe she shouldn't have thrown her phone away without having a landline.

She checked the peephole. Chase.

She hesitated. But then she did open it, mostly because it was hard to hit someone through a door, and braced it, ready to slam.

"I brought you something," he said hopefully, drawing his hand out from behind his back. A pair of red boxing gloves dangled by a string from his finger.

Vi almost laughed. A little start of a laugh that got choked by pain and exhaustion and anger.

"That way, if you want to hit anything..." He held them out.

She closed the door immediately, before he could get to her again. Hadn't she already let him ruin her life once?

She stood for a moment on the other side of the closed door, expecting another knock, expecting him to argue or plead or state his case.

But there was silence. She peeked through the peephole again.

He'd *gone*? Just like that? Not even *arguing* with her about it? The guy who could argue his way out of Château d'If, probably via hot sex with the prison warden's wife?

She scowled and flung herself on the couch and stupidly started crying again.

Damn it. She scrubbed her hands over her eyes and stared at the ceiling, taking deep breaths.

After about ten minutes of trying not to contemplate the ruins of her reputation, she heard another knock.

Only masses of flowers were visible through the peephole. She hesitated.

But Lina or Célie might come by. In fact, she was kind of expecting—wanting? not wanting?—to have to deal with the sympathy and fury of her friends as soon as they could get to her.

So it might be them, right? She could tell herself that, anyway, as an excuse to open the door.

Boxing gloves bounced against it, where Chase must have left them dangling on the knob the last time.

This time, he shoved his foot in the door immediately, bracing it open as he lowered his arms to proffer the masses of flowers.

"What did you do, rob a florist?" she said. *I hate you.* But the cold and the tears must have defeated her, because she couldn't get up the physical courage to break her other hand on him. And she'd be damned if she'd dull any more of her blades on him. She'd started her knife roll when she was fifteen. Buying her first precious blades, adding to it as she could, keeping everything carefully honed, *her* knives, her work, her life.

He sure as hell didn't deserve to have any more of them dulled against the wall by his head.

"They didn't have any bouquets I thought were worth you," he said, so matter-of-factly it was confusing. It should have been a dorky attempt at a compliment. But it sounded as if he was just saying what he meant. "So I went for quantity to try to make up for it." He thrust them at her.

She tried to close the door on him.

He blocked it with one big shoulder. "Hone—I mean, swee—I mean, Mademoiselle Gorgeous."

She arched her neck and stared at the ceiling, counting to a dozen. The number of roses in one bouquet. The others were more creative—gorgeous combinations of flowers that she recognized from the display in front of the florist just down the street. Maybe she could stuff them all down his throat. "You can say *ma'moiselle.*"

"What?"

"You don't have to pronounce the D if it's too hard for you." Although the careful four chunky consonants and drawled vowels of his attempt at *mademoiselle* were starting to grow on her somehow. If she didn't hate him, they might be charming.

He stared at her a second. "I hate your damn language." He thrust the flowers right into her chest, so that she had to either take them or drop them. "Except when you speak it. When you speak it, it's beautiful."

He let go of the flowers.

She dropped them.

"Damn it, Vi." He bent to pick them up. "Now you're just being rude."

"*You ruined my life.*"

"I *sav*—" He bit the word off abruptly, turning his head away, jaw set.

"And on top of that, you used me!"

"I...*used you?*" For the first time since she'd met him, anger flared in those blue eyes. "Last I checked you had a really good time!"

She tried to slam the door on him again. It bounced off his shoulder.

"Look, nobody made you take me home last night! I would have been happy to take you out for a while first."

She grabbed one of the bouquets from him and hit him over the head with it.

"You're gorgeous!" He pulled the bouquet away, white petals from it clinging to his hair and on one cheek. "You're so damn *fine*. Hell, you are fine. You're so fine it makes my brain shrink little bitty and then explode." He pressed his fingers into his forehead and then flared them out to indicate. "If you wanted to make me court you, you think I wouldn't have done that? You chose to go fast. I did *not* use you."

She glared at him, both insulted and stymied. Because she made all her own choices, and made them proudly. And it was true that she'd chosen him.

Knowing he was arrogant, cocky, uncrushable, stubborn, and doing *something* that was really out of line, knowing that he was challenging her and teasing her and deliberately misleading her, she had still taken him home. Because all the adrenaline in her just focused on him like he was where her energy could find its home. Because he was deliciously hot...and she was an idiot.

Plus, in her defense, she had watched way too many Hollywood films and halfway thought his behavior was normal for an American.

She made his brain shrink little bitty and then explode?

His blue gaze drifted over her, and all that hard energy slowly softened out of him. "You look like you could use a cuddle or a punching bag. I have more practice at the punching bag role, but I could definitely try the cuddle."

"I hate you," she said. "Go away." But she didn't try to close the door on him again, just turned around and trudged back into her apartment. Her slippers shuffled.

All her proud stride, with her clicking boots, reduced to a shuffle. Oh, hell, and were her eyes red? Could he tell she'd been crying?

She spun around, ready to attack him with flowers again to prove her strength.

He moved lithely past her and into the small kitchen area, setting the gloves on the bar and reaching up into her cabinets. Failing to find vases, he made do with some of the larger water glasses, making a mess of the bouquets as he tried to divide them so that they would fit.

He ended up with every single water glass she owned spread across the counter, each holding as many stems as it could, and gazed at the awkward deconstruction of the beautiful bouquets a moment, framed by red boxing gloves, then sighed.

He did look kind of...cute, over that disarray of flowers.

Damn it, Vi. She kicked a slipper against the floor in lieu of kicking herself.

"Has no one given you *flowers* before?" he asked incredulously. "Where the hell are your vases? Wait, don't tell me, let me guess. You broke them over the last guy's head when he pissed you off, and that's why he's not around any more."

She mostly didn't date. She looked like she did, she knew that. But the reality was that men hit on her, of course, and then when she actually took them up on it and went out with them, they quickly turned into wimps who found her too much to handle. She didn't give into them enough, she fought for too much space for herself when they wanted all the space and wanted it by automatic right, not by virtue of any effort.

She'd gotten kind of tired of men who thought she made a great sex object but not such a great, pliant girlfriend, and she'd mostly given up on the dating thing recently. Ever since she took over a two-star kitchen, she didn't have time for a social life anyway.

Which was probably why she'd been so deprived she'd taken up with the jerk in front of her and been willing to play *his* sex object. "Did I mention I hate you?"

He picked her knife roll off the counter and set it on top of the kitchen cabinets, where she would have to climb up on something to reach it. "It's come up a few times."

"Then why are you still here?"

"Well, I'm hoping to talk you round before the wedding. Otherwise, if you try to knife me when the minister says 'You may kiss the bride', it's going to cause a hell of a scandal in my family. Not as bad as the one at my cousin Ty's wedding, but still."

Wow, what had happened at his cousin Ty's wedding? She bit back on the question, furious with herself for being tempted to ask it just to see what other B.S. he made up. Damn it. This man was *impossible*.

He had *ruined her life*. And here he was acting like that was no big deal, because of course to him it wasn't.

"It doesn't even matter to you, does it?" she said.

"What doesn't?" he asked blankly, and she grabbed a couch pillow and threw it at him.

It knocked over half the glasses, and he flung himself to catch them, managing to make sure not a single one hit the floor.

The flowers and water, of course, spilled everywhere, and he got quite wet. "Damn it," he said plaintively, looking at the mess of flowers. "You sure do take a long time to calm down."

He tossed the pillow back to her gently and patiently started reforming his awkward bouquets in all the glasses, adding water carefully and setting the array back in a line on the counter.

"My life," she said between her teeth. "That doesn't even matter to you, does it? It was never worth anything in the first place. Compared to yours."

He stopped messing with the flowers and just looked at her for a long moment, holding two lilies. "I'd take a grenade for you without a second thought. So I guess it depends on your valuation system."

Her lips parted involuntarily. She stared at him.

"But I do that kind of thing all the time," he admitted. "Put my life on the line. That's almost like you saying you'd risk second-degree burns or cutting off a finger to make me something special to eat." He nodded to her bare right arm, where the scar from one really bad splash of oil would show all her life. "So I can see why you could say that doesn't count."

Well...it wasn't that it didn't *count*, exactly. It seemed terribly...wrong, at the minimum, to say that a man's willingness to *die* for you didn't *count*. But...but...she thrust her hand through her wet hair, frustrated. How was it that a man could die to save your life and still not respect that life? How did they *do that* in their screwed up heads?

"Honey—I mean Mademoiselle Gorgeous—I can't tell you what's going on. I was brought in to test security, that's all. The rest was just an excuse to keep flirting with you. But I will say that I'm pretty damn sure that *nobody*, not even the stupidest idiot on the planet, weighed your life against *one* other life, even the President's, and thought it wasn't worth as much. Now they might—and I'm just theorizing here—have weighed an ignorant little lie they didn't realize would affect you against a few thousand other lives and, yeah, sold you out. But I couldn't say for sure, because I'm just inventing all this off the top of my head and have no idea of anything."

"A few thousand?" she said numbly.

He shook his head, his lips pressing together until just for a second he looked like that grim, lethal man she'd glimpsed when he heard about Quentin. He stuck his lilies in the glass, saying nothing.

"Was someone going to blow the restaurant up?"

He said nothing. The firm line of his lips changed him radically. He looked trustworthy, even, and...scary. Like someone even she might not want to mess with.

Well, that would explain why they would want to clear the restaurant. It might even explain why her career had been sacrificed to do it. But...this was Paris. Why would Americans have been involved in stopping a terrorist attack here? In *warning* of one, yeah, sure, but French special police would have been the ones to take action.

"Was it some kind of sting? You caught somebody? Some kind of arms-trader or bomb-maker or financial handler for al Qaeda or ISIS or something?"

He said nothing.

He looked different, with that tough, tight expression on his face. Her fingers touched her mouth. "Have you *killed* anybody in the past twenty-four hours?"

A flat, blank glance. "I'm just in private security, honey."

Private security for whom? The CIA?

"Mademoiselle Gorgeous," Chase corrected himself.

"Did your president ever plan to come to my restaurant at all? Or was that all just part of some sting?"

Chase said nothing.

"*Putain de merde.*" She beat the pillow against the back of the couch, slamming it multiple times. "I can't believe my whole career was ruined over some fucking—stupid—*cover-up.*" She slammed the pillow again. "Americans don't have the right to intervene here. I should take this to the media."

"Take what? Sounds like a pretty wild-eyed story to me. The kind of thing a woman chef who bit off more than she could chew and then failed would come up with to try to cover for her own inability to handle a man's job."

"*Merde*, I hate you," she said viciously, her hand fisting in the pillow.

"Yeah." He sighed, and just for a second, both the cockiness and the grim lethalness slid off him, and he looked...sad? Not the puppy-eyes sad thing he did when he was playing her, but real emotion. "You've mentioned."

Vi slumped down onto the couch. It took a lot to make her slump. She'd thought she'd gotten it out of her system in the shower. But her day sank on her, the weight and the frustration of having her whole life randomly ruined just when she'd thought she was reaching the stars, so heavy and so dark a weight that sometimes even her anger couldn't fight it, and it settled on her like unending despair.

Her butt slid slowly off the couch, because she just couldn't bear to sit that high up, and she slumped on the floor against it, burying her head in her hands. Well, in one hand, and in one chunky splint.

"I hate this," he said. "I really hate it. It *does* matter to me, Vi."

Not enough to tell her the truth or anything, though. "Go to hell."

A knock sounded. Vi lifted her head and gazed wearily at the door, and after a second Chase went to it himself. He gazed through the peephole. "Do you have a friend who's Middle Eastern? A girl? Shorter than you. Pretty. She's with another woman with dyed red hair who's kind of curvy and cute and is carrying a metal box that has DR marked on it." His face had gone grim. That expression he had when he forgot to keep joking, that always raised the hairs on her arms. As if a superhero had dropped his genial secret identity and suddenly she was in the presence of lethal force.

The kind of lethal force that let her throw knives at him because he thought it was kind of funny.

Damn it. Had he found it *cute*?

"That sounds like Lina and Célie." His wariness and racial profiling reinforced her idea about some kind of terrorist sting. And pissed her off on Lina's behalf. Lina was always getting this kind of crap. Sometimes she ignored it, sometimes she made ironic comments, but there were days, Vi knew, when it wore her down, and days when it made her really mad. "You know, her family has lived in France for two generations now."

But she was still "Arab", while Vi, with her blond hair, was "French." Even though Vi was no "Frencher" than Lina, of course. Her father was of old French peasant stock—farmers for centuries—but her mother was Polish.

Chase gave a shrug of acknowledgement—not too much guilt about profiling on *his* shoulders. "What about the box?"

"Célie is chef chocolatière for Dominique Richard. It sounds as if she brought chocolates." She stared at Chase. "Do you think—wait a minute. If you think it's a bomb, why the hell are you still standing so close to the door?"

"To keep an eye on them," Chase said flatly.

"They're my friends! Are you *paranoid* or what?"

Chase glanced at her briefly. Vi had a brief, echoing sense of a vast distance between them, as if they came from two alien worlds. *Caution isn't paranoia if people genuinely are trying to kill you most of the time.*

Her lips parted, and fear wrapped a fist around her. Not for herself. For him. "They're my friends," she said very quietly. "Lina's my pastry chef. I've known them for years."

Also, if you think someone might have explosives…couldn't you come hide behind the couch or something?

Chase gave her a rueful smile, as if his excess of caution was just an amusing quirk, and that hard *I-could-kill-anyone* expression vanished so completely she could almost forget it had been there. He opened the door, a friendly smile on his face.

Célie and Lina pushed inside, frowning at him as they passed him. "Who are you?" Célie asked bluntly. She was trying to grow her winged pixie cut out, wanting to reach shoulder length, but all her attempts at styling the burgundy-red hair at the current length left her looking like a pixie who'd gone savage and been living in a thorn bush.

"A friend of Vi's," Chase said at the same time as Vi said, "A jerk."

Célie looked back and forth between them, her eyebrows going up and her lips quirking a little. "Ah." And then, the flicker of humor disappearing, "*Merde*, Vi, are you okay?"

"Super." Vi kicked her coffee table.

"The team is in an uproar," Lina said. "But you're their hero right now, getting arrested like that on behalf of the restaurant. Also, I think Mikhail and Amar might be single-handedly waging a Twitter war in defense of the restaurant. You know how those two get."

Vi smiled a little. Explosive. Emotional. Arrogant. Easily insulted. Damn, she loved her team. "I'll take everybody out tomorrow. All the drinks are on me." She gestured as she spoke, forgetting her splint.

"What happened to your hand?" Lina took three long steps toward her. Her thick black hair bounced in a ponytail of glossy curls. "Did you hit somebody or something?"

"You know me too well." Vi stared morosely at her hand. Her right hand, too. She didn't mind throwing knives left-handed, but if she tried to fillet a fish that way, she was going to end up stabbing herself.

"You didn't pick a fight at the Commissariat, did you?" Lina asked warily. "No, that can't be right, they let you out."

Chase returned to the flowers, gazed at them a moment, then tried shifting tall flowers for short ones to see if that improved the look of the makeshift array.

"Where did you get that scratch?" Lina asked Chase coldly.

"A kitten," Chase said, with an attempt at that woeful look he'd given Vi the night before.

"I'm not a fucking kitten!" Vi yelled, kicking the coffee table extra hard.

"Oh." Chase touched his cheek, discovering the scratch her nail had left when she'd tried to gouge his eyes. "That one." He felt it a moment. "I forgot about that."

Vi thumped her head back against the couch. "I hate you." Even fists, knives, scratches didn't make an impact on him. Okay, she hadn't actually tried, with the knives—she hit what she aimed at—but still. She could probably shoot him, and the bullet would bounce off. So how could she expect *herself* to make an impact?

"Who the hell is this guy?" Célie handed the box of DR chocolates to Vi and stood between her and Chase, her hands on her hips. "*Oh, purée*, Vi, did you fall for one of the police officers who arrested you? I saw that video. They looked pretty rough with you to me."

"They did?" Chase's eyes narrowed. He scanned Vi's body.

"I'm fine," Vi said. She was mostly extremely pissed that the police had been able to handle her body as if it was their right to control it. But she hadn't resisted arrest, just tried to force her way into her own restaurant. "And he's American, Célie. Clearly he's not police here."

"Well, where did you meet him? Why is he still in your apartment if you hate him and think he's a jerk? Since when do you go for military men?"

"Civilian." Chase tried to slouch his shoulders. "I swear." He didn't seem that intent on convincing them, though. He seemed more amused by the pretense than anything, except for a tiny second when his eyes flicked to Lina and there was something narrow and cool in them, assessing her reaction.

Célie looked at him a moment. Her eyes narrowed, and her head tilted. "Since when?"

"What makes you think I was ever in?" Chase said.

"I recognize macho military when I see it." Since her boyfriend had just gotten out of the Foreign Legion, she certainly should recognize it. "It's a whole different look and swagger from macho non-military." Another look Célie should recognize, given her boss, Dom Richard.

"I used to be in the military," Chase said firmly. "But now I'm a civilian."

"How long ago did you get out?" Vi asked. "Forty-eight hours ago?" Just in time for a black ops mission in an allied sovereign country that would be illegal if he was still in the U.S. military?

He gave her a bland look.

"Why don't you bring one of those glasses over here, so I can see the pretty flowers?" Vi asked tightly.

"No. Then you'd just throw it at me, I'd have to clean up glass shards, I'd miss a tiny shard, and sometime in the night when you came to get a drink, you'd forget your little slippers and you'd cut your foot. And think how guilty I would feel."

Vi took off a slipper and threw it at him.

He caught it and gazed at the cute brown bunny face on the toe for a second bemusedly.

"You see how damn *patronizing* he is?" Vi asked her friends between her teeth.

"Oh, yeah." Both other women folded their arms to gaze at him, and Vi felt an instant's relief.

93

Because Célie and Lina *got it.* They had worked their way up through macho kitchens just like she had. They'd fought for the junior international title together, three women on a team who'd had to prove they weren't some symbolic gesture to appease the media, that they hadn't been "given" the place on the team at the expense of inherently more qualified men. Lina, with a double whammy, had had to face down the belief that she was symbolic diversity and a symbolic female and in no way *a real, high-achieving person* who could kick ass.

Lina and Célie knew exactly how infuriating it was to literally *hit* a man to try to get revenge for his destruction of your life...and end up with your own hand broken while he patted you gently on the head and tried to look after you.

And pretended all of this was too much for your pretty little head and wouldn't even tell you *what the hell was going on.*

"How am I patronizing?" Chase asked incredulously.

Célie and Lina rolled their eyes and looked empathetically pissed off.

"Nothing I do can even hurt you," Vi said. "The little woman."

Chase gazed at her a moment, and then walked over to her, a white flower still in his fingers. With her on the floor and him standing straight, his size loomed over her.

"That hurts me," he said quietly, gesturing to her position on the floor and finishing with her splint. "That hurts me a lot." He crouched, slipped her bunny slipper back on her foot with a gentle, callused touch of her ankle, laid the white flower carefully over her knees, and then straightened and moved away from her again.

Vi sighed and scrubbed her forehead with her good hand. What he had just done did not change the sexism here at all—in fact, it just underlined his inherent belief in his own strength versus her fragility—but...there was a sweetness to it, too, that just kind of wormed its way inside her anger and wiggled in there, in a troubling way.

"Also, this is kind of sore," Chase said, from the counter, rubbing his jaw where her punch had landed. "How bad is the bruise?" He angled his jaw toward nearby Lina with a pitiful, anxious look.

Vi rolled her eyes, but in there with that wiggly, annoying sweetness there slipped his damn *humor* again, making her want to laugh.

And her *life* was shattered around her in utter *ruins*.

He was so annoying.

"So what's the deal?" Célie put her hands on her hips and stood, braced in a position so that Chase would have to get through her or jump over the coffee table if he wanted to touch Vi again. "Do you want me to hit him?"

"I've been doing that. He enjoys it."

"I can call Joss if you want me to," Célie said.

Lina and Vi frowned at her.

Célie held up her hands. "You're right. You're right. We can handle him ourselves."

Damn straight they could.

"Who's Joss?" Chase asked.

"My boyfriend," Célie said.

Chase nodded politely. Like a man who might be willing to let another man get in a punch in order not to make him look bad in front of his girlfriend.

Célie frowned. "Foreign Legion," she said menacingly.

Chase cocked his head. "Really? Some of those Foreign Legion guys...what regiment?"

"2e REP." Célie held his eyes. "Commando."

Chase's eyes lit. "Real-ly. Now *that* might be fun."

Vi sighed.

"Not that you aren't fun, honey," Chase said quickly. "It's just a...different kind of challenge."

"Will you *go away*?" Vi said.

"No," Chase said indignantly. "When I got here, your eyes were red and puffy. Now look at you. You're breathing fire again. I barely know your friends. How do I know they're not going to coddle you and cry over you and let you sink back into despair again?"

Célie and Lina stared at him, outraged.

Vi wanted to kill him. He'd *seen* she had been crying? And he'd had to go and *tell the whole world about it?*

He hid behind upraised arms. "Okay, don't *everyone* start throwing things at me at once. I might not be able to duck all of it."

Célie pointed a finger at him. "You need to be quiet."

"Good luck with that," Vi muttered.

"And you need to tell me all the details." Célie pointed at Vi.

"He broke into my kitchens, I threw a few knives at him to teach him the error of his ways, he got scared—"

"I *what?*"

"—and asked me to call the embassy. They swore he was just part of their advanced security check, and you know...I *really* wanted the president to come next week, so I...well, I fell for it. Like an idiot. But I did watch him like a hawk the entire time. And made sure he couldn't go back to the kitchens after I got him out of there."

"Oh, is *that* what you were doing," Chase murmured idly. "Watching me like a hawk." A little smile curved his mouth as he inspected a long lily and finally gave it a glass by itself.

Vi shot him a bird. He slipped his middle finger into his mouth and sucked the tip of it absently, studying the flower.

Grrrr. She needed more things to throw.

"And this morning I woke up to the food poisoning story."

"There are rumors on some of the Arabic language channels that American special ops are moving on extremist groups here," Lina said.

Chase gave her a quick, assessing look. "Are there."

"You know, you can read Arabic without being a terrorist," Lina told him darkly.

Chase said something Vi couldn't follow, but it sounded vaguely like the Arabic she heard in the Métro often enough and occasionally when around Lina's grandparents.

Lina looked at him blankly for a moment, then raised one eyebrow. "Your pronunciation is terrible."

Chase sighed deeply and gave the flowers a look that begged them for sympathy.

"You speak three languages?" Vi said, impressed despite herself. To master French and English seemed pretty normal to her, but Arabic was a whole other level.

"Apparently not," Chase said dryly. "Apparently I only read them."

"Are you really from Texas?" Because nothing she had ever heard about Texas indicated that its denizens did anything but wear cowboy hats and guns, ride horses, and act macho. Oh, and there was the oil thing. They definitely didn't interest themselves in other languages or in anything outside Texas, she was pretty sure of that. Unless Spanish? "Do you speak Spanish, too?"

Chase smiled at her and said nothing.

Hunh.

Vi contemplated that a moment. "Say something in Spanish," she said suspiciously.

"*I soñado toda la noche de las cosas que puedo hacer para ti con la lengua*," Chase said promptly.

Vi frowned at him. *Lengua*, the only word she could guess at in the sentence, either meant language, which would be a perfectly normal subject of conversation right then, or...tongue.

He smiled at her beatifically.

Vi slumped deeply and stared at her bunny slippers. Energy tried to defy the slump. She was starting to get the urge to leap up and start pacing around again.

"So," Chase said. "How hard is it going to be to recoup your reputation as a chef?"

And there went her spirits again, down, down, down into the depths of a dirty river. "Impossible."

He held her eyes, raising his eyebrows just a little. "How hard is it going to be if you give up?"

She stared at him. Her eyes narrowed. "Really impossible."

He grinned at her. "So 'impossible' is a pretty flexible word."

"Can I have my knife roll?" Vi asked.

His grin widened. "Only if you can get past me to get it."

She came to her feet.

He looked delighted. "Don't mess up the flowers, okay? I'm just getting them to look right."

Everyone in the room looked at his flowers. Stems of mismatched length flopped in random ways in wide-mouthed glasses.

"What?" he said defensively.

Célie and Lina bit down on their lower lips. Vi put her hands on her hips. Energy was starting to course through her, now that she was on her feet again. She kind of missed her boots. "This isn't the kind of thing a chef can come back from, Chase." Well...*she* was planning to, one way or another, but that didn't mean he should make light of how hard it would be. "Think about it like if you were to shoot the wrong guy. Maybe it's the same."

"Not quite," Chase said quietly and evenly. His eyes met hers, and for just a second she had one of those disorienting glimpses of depth and seriousness. "Because when I shoot the wrong guy, he's dead. And he never comes back from that."

Oh.

For a second, all three women were still, this little shock wave at the hint of a job they could barely begin to imagine.

"That's why I went into private security," Chase said blandly. "No actual shooting ever comes up, and the pay is much better." He smiled at them, full wattage. "You girls hungry? When's the last time you ate, hon—Ms. Lenoir?"

"Yesterday," Célie said when Vi didn't answer. "Come on, we all know that. That's why we're here."

Chase reached into the basket of brown eggs Vi had on her counter and started cracking them into a bowl.

"Being a top chef is all about reputation," Vi said, still trying to get the degree of damage done to her through his thick head. "You build your reputation on your abilities, but if people can get hold of anything to destroy that reputation—something like this—then it's gone. This would knock even a top male chef all the way back down the ladder, but as a woman, people have been looking for me to fail from the start." Since she was born, in fact.

Célie folded her arms across her belly, protecting her guts in visceral sympathy for the blow Vi had taken to hers, nodding. Lina looked grim. As pastry chef, the blame didn't stop with her the same way it did with Vi— her name didn't front the restaurant—but she still felt the responsibility, and it could even quite easily turn out to come from the pastry side of the kitchen. The eggs, the custards, the sauces.

Chase nodded, too, matter-of-factly. And held Vi's eyes. "So you're going to quit?"

Vi stared back at him. Her lips pressed. "Do you have a *death wish* or something?" *Quit!*

"Why is he still alive?" Lina asked Vi curiously. She shook her head in some wonder. "Either this whole food poisoning thing is slowing your reflexes, or you must really like him."

Hey! *Shut up, Lina.*

Chase perked up, giving Lina a hopeful look and then eyeing Vi again, like a puppy starved for affection.

"I feel sorry for him," Vi said. "He's a civilian. Easily scared by a few thrown pots."

A little crease showed in Chase's left cheek. He smoothed it out. "I should have tucked my tail between my legs and run right then." He met Vi's eyes. "But I didn't have it in me."

Vi's teeth snapped. "If you don't quit implying that *I* might have it in me if you don't give me this little pep talk, I might have to kill you."

"Seriously, you hooked up with this guy?" Lina said.

Vi flushed. She hadn't realized it was quite that obvious that she'd actually hooked up with him.

"He's worse than Joss!" Célie said. "About deciding he knows all about your life and what's good for you. How is that even possible?"

"Do you have some kind of *radar* that pings the most arrogant guy in the city for you, every time?" Lina said. "How do you even find these guys? Now you know why I like geeky, shy guys."

A tiny flicker of Chase's blue eyes toward Lina, just this hint of a narrowing of his eyes as if he was filing away information. But it was over so quickly Vi might have imagined it.

"I'm shy," he said to Vi.

Oh, for God's sake.

Chase tried to look bashful.

Vi clapped her hand to her forehead, and, once again forgetting her splint, bonked herself in her own eye. *Aïe.*

"Have you ever thought about opening a restaurant in Texas?" Chase asked hopefully.

"*Texas?*" Vi recoiled. "Nobody can catch stars in Texas."

"Okay, you know what? I'm going to take you out on my grandparents' ranch in the middle of the night, and then you try to tell me that again."

Vi rolled her eyes. She'd seen real stars once in a while. Weak things in a gray sky. They weren't that impressive. "What do they eat there, rattlesnake?"

Actually, what if she did a dish with rattlesnake and—

"We eat good beef," Chase told her, eyes narrowing. "And I don't think someone who thinks snails and frogs are food has room to cast aspersions."

"Do they eat cactus?" Vi's head tilted. "What does that taste like? You could do something kind of fun with cactus and—" She broke off.

Chase grinned, looking very pleased with himself. "And if these idiots in Paris don't know how to appreciate you, people in Texas would find it hilarious that you food poisoned the President."

"I did *not*—damn it, he hadn't even arrived yet!"

Chase continued as if she hadn't spoken. Kind of like the Internet. "Don't chefs of your standing usually start opening second and third restaurants about now? No, seriously, this is a good idea, Vi. You could spin this in your favor. In fact, if you named the restaurant something like *Potus' Last Meal*, you'd probably draw a crowd just because they'd respect your balls." He paused, and his eyes lit with fervor. "Actually, you need to open it with that name in *Washington*. Oh, hell, that would be hilarious. People would *love* you. Plus, it's a lot shorter commute to where I'm stati—where my house is, in the U.S."

Vi could almost start getting a vision there. It would be kind of fun to take her career international. Be crisscrossing the globe, building herself into...this heady glimpse of herself ten years down the road, one of the most influential female chefs in the world. Hell, drop the *female*. One of the most influential *chefs*.

"Balls," Vi said, instead of admitting his pep talk was working. "Always has to be something inherently male to show you have nerve, doesn't it?"

Chase sighed. "Are you ladies going to cut me any slack at all?"

"No," Vi said. "It doesn't matter how little rope we give you, you still manage to hang yourself. In fact, I'm starting to think that if the only rope you had was the one tying your wrists tight to something, you'd still manage to hang yourself." Oops. Had she just let it slip that she had multiple times imagined tying his wrists to something so he'd be at her mercy?

Chase grinned, as if he'd read right into the depths of her dirty mind. "Not that I've never had a fantasy about three women tying me up, I admit, but she's got a boyfriend in the Foreign Legion"—he nodded to Célie—"and I'm monogamous now."

"Since when?" Vi said very, very dryly.

Chase gaped at her. "Since last night! You never listen to a word I say, do you?" He scowled. "If I dismissed everything *you* said, I'd be taking flack about sexism again."

Vi pressed her splint and her bare hand to her face a long moment. "I think I need to go fix my hair," she finally told Célie and Lina. "I really wasn't expecting company."

"I've got some aspirin, if you need it," Lina said sympathetically.

"You know, I've got to give you credit, Vi," Célie said, as Violette headed toward her shower. "I thought your last guy set the record, but you have finally found the most impossible guy in the universe."

CHASE ME

Chase beamed and patted himself on the back.
Vi slammed the bathroom door.

Chapter 11

Chase was having a hard time holding steady. Humor had gotten him through some tough shit in the past, so he clung to it, like he always did, but Vi was messing with his ability to compartmentalize, waking up *emotions*. And not fun, happy, adrenaline-charged, she's-so-damn-hot emotions either. Those made him feel as if he'd finally fallen into one of those Hollywood action films about men like him.

No, these were the scary kind of emotions. They were *vulnerable*, and even though they seemed to reside in his middle and his head, he couldn't figure out how to fit body armor and a helmet on them no matter what he did.

The swelling sense of failure—*I didn't protect her, a civilian hit by my own unit's friendly fire*—the powerful desire to fix it, this morass of other emotions that he didn't even have names for but that swelled up at the sight of her in a bathrobe and fuzzy slippers, like someone who wasn't a Bond girl right that minute but who needed a man who could sweep her up close and warm and hold her tight until all the bad went away.

He'd mentioned it, that he could try the cuddle. But she clearly realized that wasn't in his normal skill set. She'd gone for the option he was good at—taking flack. It was such cute flack, too—slippers and pillows and a bouquet of flowers. Adorable, when compared to AK-47s.

After he'd fielded her friends' probing questions for a while, she came back out, her straight blond hair silky dry, as if she was about to head out somewhere glamorous for the evening. She'd abandoned that fluffy bathrobe and slippers, but she hadn't really gotten dressed, just put a bra on under her black camisole top, still wearing black pajama bottoms, barefoot.

The combination of that silky, pretty hair and the quieter intimacy of her attire hit him like a punch in the gut.

It troubled his stomach, this tumble of a fantasy a man like him never got to actually have. Women loved to date men like him, loved hot sex, loved, yes, the *idea* of marrying guys like him, but they never really lasted through the actual him. The man who was too tough, too impervious, too able to ride roughshod over almost everyone without even realizing it, and, of course, who was gone most of the year.

The knit camisole clung to a slim, athletic body that moved now not so much like a whip cracking, as it did when she was taking on the world, but like a dancer winding down from a long performance—the energy subdued, but all that grace and strength still obvious in the lines of her body and in every casual move.

To his surprise, she didn't go back to sending verbal jabs his way, or throwing things at him, both things he could handle. Okay, that he *enjoyed* handling, except when he was too stupid and cocky a shit and his damn showing off made her end up with a boxer's fracture.

She seemed...quieter now. Thinking. She took the bar seat across from him, pushing a couple of his makeshift vases to the side to rest her chin on her good hand.

He sliced a pat of butter, feeling weirdly self-conscious. He hadn't felt self-conscious since he was a teenager. What the hell?

"Heat the pan first," she said.

"What?"

She grabbed his wrist across the counter, and the pat of butter he'd been about to add fell to the stove. "Heat the pan first. It expands the metal and gets rid of any invisible porousness, so the eggs are less likely to stick."

He smiled at her fingers circling his wrist. Hell, he was easy. But he liked having her grab his body and manipulate it however she wanted. He wished she'd do that to a lot more than his wrist. "I thought I was adding the butter so the eggs wouldn't stick."

"You're adding the butter for flavor." She let go of his wrist.

It was all terrifyingly enticing—her sitting across a counter from him while he cooked a simple omelet. Of its own volition, his hand rose to draw a strand of her hair through his fingers. Soft and silky, still a tiny bit damp.

He expected her to bite his hand or something, but she just let that proud chin of hers rest on her fist, letting him play with her hair the same way he'd let her control his wrist and gazing at him as if she couldn't figure out what to make out of him.

You can't make much, he almost wanted to warn her. *I am already what I made myself.*

That was another thing that blocked him from those quiet moments of intimacy. Women, whether they admitted it or not, usually wanted to change a man, mold him to who they were. But he, like most of the men he knew, was just too hardened by the life, too stubborn, too confident. He had that will before which everyone else's dissipated like ghosts.

And so he kept being him, and...well, here he was. Not divorced yet, which was something of an accomplishment in his field. Surrounded by a band of brothers. But...alone.

He hadn't felt lonely the other night, when he met her. He'd felt cocky and sure of himself, quite willing to take her dares and ask her to marry him.

But seeing her vulnerable this evening made him vulnerable, too.

He didn't know what to do with vulnerable. Pull on body armor? Crack a joke? Bring up his weapon?

He gazed down at the pan.

"You know what would be good with an omelet?" Vi said. "Truffles."

Chase's contact with truffles was confined to the chocolate ones his mom made for Christmas and which had always turned splotchy brown and grainy by the time they reached him in Afghanistan. He'd hide with them inside his hooch anyway, eating them slowly and closing his eyes as tight as he could to try to pretend he was home for Christmas.

Célie's and Lina's eyes lit up when Vi pulled an open plastic zip bag out from her refrigerator and unwrapped a dark, dirty looking lump. A pungent, earthy smell filled the room immediately. "A real one?" Célie said. "It's July!"

"From Australia," Vi said smugly. "Top grade, too."

"Australians grow truffles?" Lina said doubtfully, as if Vi was suggesting something sacrilegious. "Real ones?"

"Taste it." Vi started to slice off a sliver and cursed as her splint made that awkward. Instead of letting that stop her, though, she pulled out a cutting board and braced the mushroom on it, clumsy but managing. "I'm not sure we could ever use them in Au-dessus, because critics would have hysterics, but maybe Texans wouldn't care." She cut Chase a sardonic glance, but then focused on cutting three very fine slivers and gave one to each of them.

Her face had changed. Her eyes were glowing with pleasure to offer this.

Chase's sliver was rich and earthy and unlike anything he had ever tasted before. But he knew to say, "Mmm," and to use about the same tone he would have if Vi had just wrapped her hand around his dick.

Besides, it tasted rich, full, amazing—and it made Violette's eyes glow.

"Wow," he said, for good measure.

"Wait until you taste it in an omelet." She began slicing fine slivers, hands still amazingly deft even with one partially immobilized.

107

"Want me to slice it?" Chase touched her wrist.

Vi yielded the knife to him with the ease of someone used to delegating to sous-chefs. "Slice it fine. Very fine." She bent to pull out two more skillets and set butter to melting in one, white wine to reducing in another, while Chase sliced. He eyed her sidelong. She was smiling a little as she worked, relaxed.

Well, hell. He'd finally figured out how to calm Vi down. Give her food to work with and hungry people to feed. That was what made her happy.

And she hadn't been able to do it today, in her moment of crisis. Because he'd had her restaurant shut down. So he'd been party to not only the worst thing that could happen to her, career-wise, but to eliminating the way she *dealt* with bad things that happened to her. Her cooking.

She added flour to the butter, a rich, nutty scent rising off it, then whisked in the reduced wine and something that looked like sour cream but that she called *crème fraîche*. She dipped a spoon in it and put it to his lips, to make him taste the difference.

He smiled, loving the fact that she wanted to put flavors straight into his mouth.

She took the bulk of the truffles he had sliced, grabbed the knife and minced them even finer, then dumped them into the sauce, putting the skillet on the back burner to warm gently. "Now for the omelet."

So he melted the butter with a sizzle and started to pour the eggs in.

"You'd better let me do it," Vi said.

Seriously? He couldn't even make an omelet right? "You should see me work a grill."

Vi actually grinned. "For an omelet?"

"Everything is better with a grill," he said loftily.

She *laughed*. And slipped between him and his pan, so that he got to stand with his chest brushing her back and one hand against the lower counter by the stove, framing her like they were...*together* or something, her body shifting against his as she rapidly twirled the pan with the egg in it rather than pushed the egg around with the spatula. Her hair smelled really nice, so fresh from the shower, and the warm, hungry scents of butter rose from the pan and mixed with white wine and truffles.

She was messing up his ability to compartmentalize. She was accessing all the emotions he set aside in a box for when he was back home.

And some new emotions he had no idea what to do with, since he and the men he spent his life around dealt with their deepest emotions by pretending they didn't exist.

Might as well take the appearance of unicorns in stride as handle the emotions that rose up when a slim, proud woman stood with her hair brushing his chin as she worked in the circle of his body, holding a spatula with the thumb and finger she could still move with that splint on, where she had broken it on his jaw. Broken it because, to her, he had destroyed her life as if she was nothing.

She would never understand that he'd been protecting her life, as if it was everything.

What did you do with those emotions? When you'd spent ten years trying to box them up in a little carton labeled "impossible things" and pack them out of the way?

He knew what he *wanted* to do. He wanted to let his head slowly tip forward until it rested on her head and sigh some of his size and strength out so that he was small enough to fit in this space and just stay there a moment, with his eyes closed, breathing her in.

Just as well that she'd probably elbow him in the ribs or something if he did. Kept a man on his toes.

In what was so deceptively close to the shelter of his body—he *felt* like he was sheltering her, but she probably didn't feel that way at all—Vi dribbled the truffle sauce down the center of the omelet, folded it, sprinkled it with a pinch of some special sea salt, and slid it on a plate for Célie and Lina. Then she set about making another one.

"Let me try." Chase brought his other arm around before she could shift away, taking the pan and the spatula and holding them around her, so that she was captured by his body while he worked.

Mmm, yeah. *Nice.* A man could really enjoy learning how to cook this way.

And she still didn't elbow him in the ribs or anything.

"Like this?" Rather than move the spatula around the pan to spread the eggs, she had held the spatula pretty still in the middle of the pan and twirled the pan rapidly to get the eggs to spread. So he tried that, just clumsy enough that she made a little sound of protest and placed her hand over his bigger one to guide him.

He grinned down at the back of her head in triumph and caught sight of her friends eyeing them with a great deal of thoughtfulness. *Go away*, he thought to them. *You're...whatever that French word is. De trop. I want this time. Me, mine. You're messing it up.*

Plus, Jesus, the last thing a man feeling this vulnerable and this full of *emotions* needed was an audience.

But he didn't say that.

In fact, after they ate the most delicious omelet he had ever had in his entire life—it took *omelet* to some phenomenal level, and she'd managed that in only a few minutes' work—he ended up washing the dishes in the background and then settling himself on the floor on the margins as the women drank wine and he frowned over the French label on Violette's pain medication and tried to figure out how dangerous mixing the two was. Probably less dangerous than running off on a motorcycle with a strange man who had just broken into your kitchens, but still...at least *that* risk had had a very high reward potential, right?

She ignored him, so it took him a while to realize she hadn't even opened the damn bottle of painkillers yet. Too tough, hmm? Well, he'd seen some friends go down a bad road that started with painkillers, so maybe just as well.

She did drink a couple of glasses of wine, and he just watched the gathering and kept his mouth shut, except when the sympathy from her friends seemed to be starting to prey on her courage. Then he would say something randomly provocative to make her spine stiffen again.

He smiled, sipping his own wine in his corner. He did like that straight spine of hers.

Mostly he kept out of it and didn't try to grab that intimacy for himself because...well, he remembered.

All the times he had gone over to a married buddy's house after one of their own was killed, all the times they'd hung out on a deck drinking beer and reminiscing about the stupidest, funniest, craziest things that friend had ever done, while the wife put the kids to bed and brought out a couple more beers and maybe squeezed her husband's shoulder and gave Chase a sympathetic I-hurt-for-you-too look but let them have that time.

He wondered if Vi would ever do that for him.

He wondered if talking her into marrying him meant more than hot sex and fun challenges and finally having his own kids to play with but was...deeper. Quieter. More...there.

Her eyes lifted suddenly and met his. Their gazes held for an odd moment. He was the one who looked down.

He looked back up almost immediately, feeling almost—and this was surreal—*shy*. But she had already turned her head. A moment later, when he was watching vibrant Célie as she spoke, he thought Vi looked at him again, but couldn't catch her at it.

That was okay. The less she looked at him, the more he could watch her. That fine, proud chin of hers, the beautiful cheekbones, the way her hair slid over her shoulder when she turned her head, making his own skin itch to know what that felt like sliding over his.

Watching her made him feel naked.

He frowned into his nearly full wine glass and then set it aside, resting his head against the arm of the couch behind him, trying to turn his brain off. Just be in the moment.

He was good at being in the moment, but this one scared him. He kept wanting to escape out of it to long-term planning or worrying about the past and future, because the moment itself felt too wide open and full of wishing.

It was after midnight before Vi's friends finally went home. Chase sank his butt more firmly into the floor as they kept giving him insistent glances while they were getting their things. Célie jerked her chin at him and said something low-voiced to Vi.

"It's okay," Vi said. "I want to talk to him."

Damn talking. But that sounded like a reprieve, where kicking him out was concerned, so he stood to shake hands good-bye with the women.

They looked at his handshake bemusedly. But neither of them offered to do that kissing thing instead that they'd taught him about in his LREC training.

By the time Vi had closed the door on her friends, he had managed to get back to one of the two couches and stretch out on it, making his body as heavy and supine as possible. A two-hundred-pound man who was sitting up—well, you could almost expect him to be able to get to his feet and get going. But supine...good luck moving *that.*

Vi stood with her hands on her hips looking down at him a moment.

"I'm listening," he said.

"Yeah, but you're not giving answers, are you?"

It would be so nice to get it off his chest. Just tell her. *I did make the call. I couldn't risk it, honey. Have you ever seen what ricin can do? I had to save you. Your team. The world. In case.*

But instead of losing all plausible deniability for his country and this operation, he could only shake his head with a little sigh. "I'm just in private security, honey."

She gave him an annoyed look, but he really must have worn out her annoyed-look muscles, because this one lacked punch. Slinging herself down on the other couch, she crossed her long legs at the ankle and rested her head on the opposite arm.

"Mademoiselle Gorgeous," he corrected himself.

"Oh, shut up." She closed her eyes. He smiled at her. He couldn't help it. She was so pretty, and every time she told him to *shut up* or threw something at him, he got such a charge out of it. Besides, he would way rather she fight him than go down without any fight at all just because she had no visible opponent.

She opened her eyes again and caught him smiling. Oops. Green eyes gazed at him a long moment. "I've known Lina for years," she said suddenly. "She's a fantastic pastry chef, and if you guys are suspecting her of something just because her grandparents came from Syria and Algeria, you're racist idiots."

Not suspecting, no. But she did have that cousin. Of course, Chase had cousins himself, and if he had to take the blame for everything a couple of them did, he'd be in jail right along with them.

Still, no harm in stirring the pot. See if Lina mentioned to anyone the suspicious American military guy hanging around Vi, see if that tenuous is-anything-wrong information spread in certain directions, if Chase's ambiguous appearance in Vi's life and the salmonella story stirred up enough doubt to pick up chatter and phone calls they could trace. Or see if there was no reaction at all and no need to worry so damn much.

About Vi's beloved city getting bloodied again, about her tasting one of those caramels or something, happy and alive...and then the ricin setting in. About watching her die. No antidote, no cure.

"I could take a shot at the cuddle." He tried not to sound too desperately hopeful for one. Especially since the idea of a cuddle made him feel a bit like his first HALO jump. Looking out from a plane at twenty thousand feet and realizing that, after all, he *did* have a fear of heights. At least when he was that high and had to jump.

Her eyebrows crinkled, and she gave him a look as if he was the most baffling man ever invented. He was pretty sure that was just due to a peculiarly limited experience with men, because, hell...he'd been about as open and straightforward as it was possible for a man doing such highly classified work to be.

You're hot. Can I come home with you? Oh, I can. Hot damn. Will you marry me? Not sure yet? I'll keep asking.

"I'll just...try it, okay?" He shifted off his couch. Vi wouldn't like being the one trapped between the couch back and him, so he eased his body down between the back of her couch and her. After all, she was smaller, and if he wanted to break free, he could just move her. If he locked her in, she couldn't get free unless he let her, and she would *hate* that.

She didn't hit him or anything when he lined his body up with hers. Either he was growing on her, or she was just exhausted. He was kind of tired himself. He hadn't slept in over thirty-six hours.

He laid his arm over her waist, shifting them gently until her back was nestled against his chest, her butt against his groin—*nice*—and he could smell her hair without being suffocated in it.

He checked her expression. Ironic.

Ha. She expected him to try to turn this into sex, didn't she?

Well, he would just show her.

He caught a firm grip on his will. That didn't stop him getting aroused, because even his will had limits.

But he didn't *do* anything about it. He held her. Quietly.

And it really was kind of like a HALO jump. After you got yourself out of the plane and started free-falling, it was both adrenaline-filled and peaceful.

Maybe it was even more like a HAHO jump. You got your chute open early, right after you left the plane, and then just floated through beauty for forty miles, until you had to land and go kill somebody.

No. It's not like anything that involves blood or guns at all. He adjusted his compartments in his brain sternly. Sometimes it would help if he had a greater variety of references. For all that he had done pretty nearly any impossible physical challenge known to man, since the age of eighteen *all* of his own training in those physical exploits involved guns or explosives at some point, or possibly knives.

He wondered if most of her experiences involved at some point getting burned.

His finger touched the splattering of dots of paler skin on her forearm. Grease, probably. He reached the black splint and traced over it gently. "I'm sorry about this."

"Sorry that I hit you?" Vi asked incredulously.

He nodded. It made his nose brush her sweet-smelling hair. Made him damn grateful he still had his sense of smell. A lot of guys had lost theirs. IEDs or even minor things...turned out that sometimes even small impacts on the head could mess up the sense of smell. One of the many things that, once lost, you never got back. "I was being an ass. You never could have landed that punch if I hadn't let you."

Vi stiffened indignantly. "*Let* me?"

"You telegraph, hon—gorgeous. And that whole thing about staying under on purpose to make you worry about me, when your whole life had just fallen down around your ears? Yeah. An ass."

"Staying under?" Vi said blankly.

Hey. "You did notice I went into the river, didn't you?"

"My hand hurt."

"I was under three minutes!"

"You showered off since then, right? Because that thing is filthy."

"I've been dragged through worse," Chase said wryly.

To his surprise, Vi touched *his* hand. With her good hand, she traced over one of his knuckles, all the way down to the tip of his index finger. She touched a scar and then another small scar, the kind a man picked up from all kinds of things when it got so hot he didn't want to wear his gloves—the gravel flying up in rotor wash, a slide down a rough slope. She took his hand and turned it over, studying the calluses from handling weapons and weights and climbs. "Yeah. I'll bet," she said so quietly it was almost as if she was talking to herself.

Her words gave him the oddest feeling. As if she could almost understand things about him. A woman who'd been challenging herself in tough conditions since she was fifteen. As if they might come from opposite worlds and yet somehow...like spoke to like.

She had her own calluses—the pads at the base of her fingers and the smooth, tough skin where a knife handle fit between her thumb and index finger that was not too different from the ones he had from handling guns. He traced them. "You've got great hands."

She gave a startled twist of her head, trying to catch his expression.

"Strong." He closed his hand over her unbroken one in a solid claim of it. "Pretty."

She forced her head around farther, finally far enough to stare at him. Jesus, first she had no vases for flowers, and now a compliment on her hands surprised her? "Do you have really lousy taste in men or something? Who the hell have you been dating before me?"

Her lips parted in astonishment.

He bit down hard on the urge to lean forward and kiss them. He was *not* going to turn this into sex. Her expectations of him were way too low already.

That would teach him to have sex on the first date. *It was hard to sell a woman a cow when...*

"Well...not you," she said finally, a little wryly, as if *him* summed up something pretty...unique.

A warm glow tried to swell under his breastbone, like a bubble he was a little afraid might pop and do something unpleasant to him. He'd never had to fight dolphins to the actual death, but he'd been on deep water training exercises against dolphins defending harbors, when every time a dolphin punched the hell out of you with a tagging device, it meant that in a real attempt to infiltrate an enemy harbor you would have been given a dolphin-delivered embolism, instantly lethal. She was like a dolphin—fast and sleek, and she'd hit him out of nowhere.

Okay, and it would be *so* helpful right now if he had any metaphors that didn't involve somebody getting killed.

"I'm just going to go ahead and reset your bar for men a little higher." He snugged his arm around her more firmly. This whole cuddle thing felt fantastic. He was glad he'd gotten himself to jump out of that safe plane into it.

"For the next man?" Vi said, constrained. She relaxed her head back onto the arm of the couch so she wasn't looking at him any more.

He frowned down at the top of her cowardly head. If *he* was braving this, damn it... "My grandmother would kick my ass if I ever got a divorce. So no. Not for the next man."

Tough it up, Vi, hell. I'm trying to let down my *guard.*

"Oh, for God's sake," she muttered. But she didn't try to elbow her way free of him or anything.

He smiled, dipping his head into her hair to hide it and just to enjoy her scent at the same time. Damn. This cuddle stuff was *really* addictive. He might should go easy on it.

But he didn't pull away, shifting their hands so that he half held hers and she half held his, running his thumb over the soft spots and the callused ones, the inside of her knuckles, the lines of her palm.

"You've got pretty nice hands yourself," she said suddenly. The warm bubble inside him spread, not like a lethal embolism, but dissipating through him in this fuzzy, golden glow. Hell, she'd paid him a compliment. A direct, sincere one. "Strong. Capable."

"I'm late for my manicure, though," he said sadly, turning his hand over to stretch out his fingers and display the lousy state of his cuticles.

She gave a little choke of laughter, and his arm squeezed her in involuntary pleasure. *Ha.* He'd gotten her to laugh again.

He closed his hand around hers again, holding onto it. He wondered if one of those French guys she was used to dating could get away with kissing her hand. Because, well...he kind of wanted to.

His cheeks heated, and he bent his head into her hair again to hide them, even though there was no one else to see.

"Hey. Vi," he said, low.

She didn't say anything, but she gave what might be interpreted as an inquiring squeeze of her hand.

"I'm not so good at the poor, pitiful you stuff. Where I come from, a man's life isn't over unless he's actually dead. And you don't seem pitiful to me. You seem brave and beautiful."

A little breath moved through her body, and her hand tightened on his.

"So I guess what I'm trying to say here is...if you need someone to kiss your skinned knee, I'm actually pretty lousy at that. But"—he gave her a little squeeze, pressing her more snugly against his chest—"I've got your back."

He braced for her to say something satirical like "and a knife ready for it?"

But she didn't.

She must really, *really* be tired, was all he could figure.

Her fingers linked with his, securely, as if *she* was claiming *him*. A little sigh ran through her body. He waited a while, running through all the other things she probably wanted to talk about and trying to think what he could say besides "just in private security, honey."

And then finally realized that she had fallen asleep.

Hunh.

He stared down at her blond head. Now he felt all backed up with things *he* wanted to talk about, but...

For Christ's sake, what was wrong with him? Couldn't he just appreciate that he'd been saved by a snore?

But still, just...*sleeping* like that. Letting herself go completely vulnerable.

With him there.

He couldn't quite adjust to the impact of trust. He kept staggering under it.

Either she was incredibly naïve about human nature in general and men specifically—which didn't seem *quite* Vi's modus operandi—or...it was him. She could go to sleep around *him*.

He lay there forever trying to wrap his mind around that.

Chapter 12

"Do you always get up this early?" Chase covered his eyes with his hand and stumbled to the blinds to peer outside, then flinched back. "Good Christ, the sun's still in the east."

"It's already seven!"

"Jesus." He pressed his hand down. "The first time the sun comes out in this damn country, trust it to do it at an hour like that."

"What is wrong with this country?" Vi asked, instantly indignant.

"Oh, don't even get me started."

Vi put her hands on her hips and glared at him.

He peeled his hand back a little to eye her. "Look," he said appeasingly. "It's better to work this out before the wedding. That alarm, honey. Please dear God that's got to go."

She winced guiltily and searched his face. She needed the siren alarm clock to jerk her out of bed, adrenaline rushing to her sleep-deprived rescue. She'd learned that as an apprentice. But this morning, when the siren went off, he'd rolled out of bed, grabbing her as he went and slamming her to the floor between the wall and the bed, his body crushing hers as he looked around, keeping her covered and keeping low as he tried to figure out what was going on. Her good hand had gotten trapped against his heart, and she'd felt it pounding madly. It had taken her a few tries to get through to him that it was just her alarm and everything was fine.

Now, of course, he was playing the clown.

"All I'm asking is that you tiptoe out of the room and keep the blinds drawn, okay? Unless you're wearing pink peekaboo panties, in which case it's okay if you wake me up."

"What are you even doing in my apartment at all?" And in her bed? The last she remembered was the couch, and she couldn't quite wrap her mind around the fact that she'd apparently fallen asleep so deeply with him there that he'd been able to lift her body and carry it into another room and she'd never even noticed.

"I couldn't just leave!" He acted as if she had impugned his honor. "You needed your sleep. And I had no way to lock the deadbolt behind me."

"That didn't stop you last time." Not that she was bitter about him sneaking out of her apartment while she was asleep last time *at all*. She'd knocked her alarm clock and journal to the floor in her scramble to turn it off that morning, before it ruined *his* morning, and then she'd realized...oh.

Oh.

He wasn't even there.

And that had *not* been a letdown. Not at all. It had been exactly what she'd expected. This morning, now. This morning was *weird*.

"You had a much lower chance of having drawn the attention of crazy people last time! I thought the knob lock would be enough to hold off the hordes of attackers for three hours."

"Yeah, well, thanks for not overstaying your welcome." But her mouth turned down despite herself.

For no good reason. She'd been entirely relieved that morning, of course. Nobody wanted to face the consequences of a wild hook-up the next morning.

Nobody. Definitely not Vi.

Chase rubbed his eyes with one big hand and then slowly lowered it and studied her a second. "Hey. I had to get to work."

"Yeah, security has really crazy hours," she said dryly.

"Says the top chef."

She found herself biting back a smile. *Damn it.* If only she wasn't so susceptible to his complete inability to be crushed or defeated by anything.

The man would be *hell* to live with. He would *never* be willing to lose an argument.

Not that she was *in any way thinking about living with him.* She knew he was just bullshitting her about the marriage thing, and anyway, who wanted to live in Texas? They had rattlesnakes there.

"Past tense top chef," she said. "Thanks to you."

"Honey, *nobody* can make you a past tense but yourself. And you know it damn well. That's part of what makes you so beautiful." He blew her a kiss.

"I need to buy more soft objects." That kiss made her want to throw something at him, but somehow...she wanted the something to be soft and cuddly. A cute, fuzzy stuffed animal, maybe.

Mentally she kicked herself.

"Or a black lace thong," he said out of the blue. "Possibly you could wake me up if you were wearing a black lace thong." He examined her hips with a gimlet eye.

"*Oh, purée,*" Vi muttered.

"Or those black cotton things you were wearing the other night. Or maybe even plain white cotton. That would probably be okay."

She definitely needed to buy more soft objects to throw.

"Or whatever you're wearing now. Let me see it to make sure."

Vi struggled not to laugh or, even worse, drop her hands to play with her zipper. *Stop it, Vi.* "I've got to get to work."

Maybe she could climb in through that window before the inspection teams came back.

Do something adventurous to claim her life back.

Because after that she had to face the hotel owners. The two people who had hired her, who had supported her as she took the restaurant in a completely new direction, who had ignored all controversy in their firm belief she could do it. A flamboyant female chef in a field so dominated by males its sexism was its own legend, she could take Au-dessus all the way to the top. Three stars. Nothing to hold her down.

"I could be quick," Chase said plaintively.

Vi snickered. "I've never had any doubt of *that.*"

His eyes gleamed. Oops, she had challenged him. Scruffy and tousled, he straightened from the wall.

"No," Vi said.

He scowled. "Damn it, hot sex was one of my primary motivations for getting involved with you, you know."

Vi started to laugh. It just bubbled out of her, far too much of it for his ridiculous sense of humor, but once it started, it felt too good to stop.

"Later, I fell in love with you for your mind," Chase said soulfully, trying to gaze deeply into her eyes.

Vi doubled over.

"Also your spirit," Chase murmured. "So fine."

Vi waved his nonsense away with her splinted hand. "I've got to get to work."

"Half a sec." Chase rubbed his hand over his hair to half-straighten it, yawned, and then, in that one blink of an eye, no longer looked sleepy at all. "I'll drive you."

Vi stiffened. "I drive myself."

"Sorry, honey." Chase crossed the room in a couple of strides and took her splinted hand. Lifting it, he kissed the visible tip of her constrained fingers. "Not for another three weeks you don't."

Vi froze. She'd thought about all the challenges she'd have cooking. She'd actually cried—not that anyone better ever find that out—in the shower as she tried to wash her hair. But still, somehow, in her vision of herself, she was cutting through Paris on the back of a powerful motorbike, in charge of herself and her destination.

She stomped her foot hard and began to curse. A long, colorful string.

"Wow," Chase said admiringly. "You're better than some of those Legionnaires I've worked with. Do you want me to teach you some Spanish words to mix in?"

"I want my life back!" Vi yelled.

"You know, you might want to consider another place for hitting a man than his chin, if a little boxer's fracture is going to throw you off your stride so much. I know the chin always attracts amateurs, but it's a great way to break your pinky if you haven't had training in how to properly throw a punch."

Vi made a sound like a growling dog and stomped off, grabbing her leather coat.

She couldn't pull it on over her splint, because the sleeves were too tight.

She threw it on the floor and cursed some more.

Chase smiled at her as if she was some vision from heaven. "You are just all energy, all the time, aren't you? Here." He held out his own leather jacket.

"What are you going to wear?"

He shrugged. "You?"

She narrowed her eyes at him.

"Well, you will wrap your arms around me and hold on tight to protect me, won't you?" he asked, big-eyed and anxious.

"You idiot. You know perfectly well that won't help if we get in an accident. Your skin will get ripped right off if you're not wearing leather."

"So will yours," Chase said calmly, pushing the jacket at her.

Vi folded her arms. "No."

He gazed at her a moment. His own eyes narrowed. Unstoppable force met immovable object.

Chase picked her jacket up off the floor, produced a lethal folded knife out of nowhere and sprang the blade, then sliced up half the sleeve. Vi gasped. "Here." He handed it to her. "Now your hand fits. Satisfied?"

Vi grabbed the jacket to her like a wounded child. She loved that jacket. She loved it so damn much. It made her feel sexy and strong, able to handle anything. When she had it on and the handlebars of her bike under her hands, she felt as if she could go anywhere, be anyone, do anything—a limitless potential that made it clear that she was doing and being exactly what she had always dreamed of doing.

Tears welled up in her eyes before she even knew they were coming. "You—damn—*bastard!*" she yelled to cover them.

Chase looked at the way she was clutching her jacket, looked at his knife, looked at her face—and suddenly was absolutely horrified. "Honey, I'm sorry. I'm sorry."

"Just to get your way!" she yelled. "Just to win against me. You *ruined* it!" She needed that jacket to face this day. She *needed* it.

This horrible, fucking day, where everyone would be talking about her, everyone bashing her, journalists hovering around her, inspectors blocking her out of her kitchens. She *needed* it.

"I didn't realize it meant so much to you," Chase said hurriedly. "It's your special gear, isn't it? That you made sure was just perfect for you? Honey, I'm *sorry.*"

"You would have known if you *asked!*" Vi yelled. "Before you did it! If you'd *asked* if it was okay if you *destroyed something of mine!*"

He looked down at his knife, shamefaced.

"I could have worn my damn denim jacket for a few days! I could probably have taken off the splint long enough to get my hand through! I could have bought another jacket to use for a while! I could have done all kinds of things that it was *my choice to do or not do*, but you're the damn man, so obviously you got to ride right over *me*!"

Like he'd ridden over her *life*, damn him. And wouldn't even admit he'd done it.

"Damn it." All that stubborn will had folded into remorse. "I'll buy you another one."

Oh, yeah, like she could just open up another restaurant in Texas or Washington? Since he'd smeared Au-dessus for some freaking operation he wouldn't admit to?

"What, do you think just any leather jacket will do? That you could find in a store in *July*? Do you think the problem is that I can't afford to buy my own damn clothes?"

"No," Chase said, big shoulders sagging. "I'm sorry."

"I hate you," Vi said. "And you're not driving my motorcycle, and you can get the hell out of my apartment. I don't ever want to see you again."

***

Riding the Métro to the hotel was miserable. All of her strength and belief in herself got crushed down there, until she was reduced to one of the masses that crowded into the cars, no better or more special than any of the other eleven million people in the city. Some guy sang songs behind her about her butt, and she couldn't even hit him, because she needed to have at least one functioning hand for the rest of the day.

It was horrible to face her meeting with the owners feeling so small. A knot swelled in her throat like it was absorbing too much water, all those tears she couldn't possibly let herself shed again. Not here. Not now.

She fought down the sting in her nose and at the backs of her eyes. She swallowed down the knot.

She took a hard breath.

And then she lifted her head and just faked it—overdoing the aggression, overdoing the performance of confidence, overdoing everything. But at least doing it, as she made herself stride in.

And down the street, hiding in a doorway, Chase's heart squeezed tight and he kicked the wall because he couldn't actually figure out how to kick himself.

Chapter 13

"Yeah, you screwed up." Jake flexed his shoulders, balancing upright on a narrow chimney, gazing at the rooftops of Paris. The sun was angling down in the afternoon, and it was actually a pretty nice day. Maybe Paris in July wasn't always rainy and cold?

"Fuck, yeah." Ian hauled himself through the skylight and found a balancing point on the narrow point of the roof, also pausing to take in the view. Elias was out ahead of them, moving like a black panther across the rooftops. A little light urban jungle training, since they still had no word to move on Al-Mofti.

"I know," Chase said. "I *know.* I can't believe I fucking did that. What the hell?"

"I would have kicked your ass so bad." Jake shook his head, vicariously pissed off already. "If you'd ruined my gear like that."

"I *know.*" Chase winced into himself. "*Fuck.*"

"I mean, seriously." Jake grabbed the clay chimney tops, vaulted over them, and ran along the ridge of the roof to leap without pause across a narrow gap to the next one. He glanced back. "Seriously kicked it."

"I *know*!!" Chase leaped after him, slid down the zinc slope of the roof, landed on a flat rooftop below, rolled and came to his feet. A couple of pigeons scattered. Ian dropped beside him. In the distance, they could see the Eiffel Tower and Notre-Dame. Behind them the Sacré-Coeur. The sounds of the city echoed up from the street, the noise of cars amplified by the particular acoustics of the straight buildings.

"And right when she needed it," Chase said, low. "When she was facing the worst day of her life. I wish we didn't have to delay the 'test results' for the salmonella so long." Yeah, if they could just catch that bastard Al-Mofti, all kinds of things about the world would be better.

"That's the worst day of her life?" Jake's freckled nose crinkled. "Having to deal with getting blamed for some bad eggs or something?"

"She's a civilian," Chase reminded him. "Their lives are different."

"Yeah," Ian muttered, heartfelt.

"Plus, it's her rep," Chase said. "It's like she lost a weapon or...I don't know, was a *coward* or something. It's bad. It'll follow her for all her career. It could even *end* her career." A pit opened in his stomach even saying it. Because she clearly loved her career.

What if he had fallen that time he was hanging upside down and slipping in BUD/S and broken his arm? He would have been out, his whole life derailed, and he would never have become who he was.

Knowing what was at stake, he'd been able to draw on one last desperate burst of strength to make it over the top.

Making that moment the wrong analogy. Succeeding had, in the end, been under his control.

So it was more like his old swim buddy from BUD/S, Kev, whose chutes had gotten tangled in a HAHO jump and who had gone into a spin, probably lost consciousness—God, Chase hoped so—and plunged twenty thousand feet to his death.

Oh, fuck.

Sometimes, it would be really, really nice if some of his personal analogies for a ruined life didn't involve an actual *ruined life*.

"I kind of like it," he said low. "That this is the worst thing that could happen in her life. I'd like to keep it that way, you know? Makes me feel as if we're fighting for a reason."

"Yeah." Jake kicked the flat rooftop and slanted him a curious, envious glance, the kind of glance Chase sometimes slanted at married buddies when he saw them hugging their wives and playing with their kids.

"Makes me feel strong," Chase admitted, very, very low. "Like I screwed up about her jacket, but at least I got something else right."

Jake contemplated the street below, his shoulders hunching a little, his mouth rather grim.

Christ, had Chase started talking about *emotions*? Jesus, even when she wasn't around, this woman made Chase talk too much.

He flung himself across the next gap, just catching the edge of the roof with his toes and throwing his hands up to grasp the ridge of the roof before he could slide off, hauling himself up and running along the narrow ridge. Ian and Jake caught up with him a couple of rooftops over.

"Not a bad idea," Ian said to Jake. "I'm not saying my idea, that we go see the Mona Lisa, was a bad one either, but I can see why this was on your short list."

"A lot less crowded up here," said Jake, the mountain lion. "Mark's gonna kill us for going when he was busy arguing with those CIA idiots at the embassy. We'll have to come back out."

"Changes the whole dynamic when you don't have to go shoot somebody," Chase said. "And no gear." Well, they probably all had guns on them somewhere, but no *obvious* gear that would get them arrested. "Kind of peaceful."

They considered that peace for a moment, and then, almost in unison, all focused on the largest nearby gap between roofs—over two meters and with a six-floor drop. Nobody even had to talk about it. They were *all* going crazy, spun up for this mission and stalled while the head shed dithered over information. Chase wasn't the only one capable of breaking into restaurants just to add a little interest to his life in these circumstances.

Elias dropped back beside them, with a rough sound of gravel, astonishingly light on his feet. "Having trouble keeping up?" he asked, green eyes glinting.

Yes, there might be just a tiny bit of rivalry between the French elite counterterrorist units and the U.S. black ops with whom they were currently in wary cooperation.

Ian took off immediately at the challenge, flying over the gap with efficient grace. Chase and Jake followed, and the four of them ran, jumped, rolled, slid, swung for a while, until the next flat rooftop invited a pause for breath. Damn, Paris looked beautiful up here. It looked exactly like all those movies, which was kind of amazing. Mostly by the time they got to go to beautiful places, those place were half-destroyed, often by their own side's bombs.

Paris looked...well, Paris looked like *Paris*.

And we're going to keep it that way, too. Fuck those bastards who want to destroy it.

"You started doing this when you were a teenager?" he asked Elias. "Playing on the rooftops like this?" Parkour.

Elias shrugged. "We didn't have much money. It was kind of my way of owning the city."

It was a pretty nice city to own.

We'll always have Paris, some guy had once said. Chase was pretty sure it was a good thing for the world to always have.

"We'll get them," he said, firmly. Conviction meant everything. There was no room for doubt. They got their targets, period.

He believed it, the same way he had to believe in his ability to take that two-meter jump over a thirty-meter drop. No hesitation, no doubt, just do it.

Elias said nothing for a long moment, gazing at the streets below. Then, without any of that sardonic edge, just low and firm: "Thanks." He met Chase's eyes. "It's nice to have you guys on our side."

"Don't mention it," Chase said, meaning it. "Hey, I'll catch up with you guys, okay?"

"Why?"

"I had a little visit I wanted to pay to that apartment over there." Chase smiled and took a running leap to catch against a balcony.

***

Vi's team was the best. The life of them, raucous and heated on the terrace, relaxed Vi, and she grinned at them as she ordered them another round of drinks.

That was right. Who the hell *did* care if their reviews on Yelp and Trip Advisor were now down to an average of two stars out of five, thanks to all the trolls who had found it hilarious to go online and laugh at the "food poisons the president" thing? (Even though the American president was *still sitting in Washington, DC,* and hadn't even boarded his stupid Air Force One for Paris yet.) Who cared what idiots thought?

She took another sip of beer, just to help her not care what idiots thought.

Her *second*, Adrien, a dynamic twenty-two year old with a passion for food and theater and art that blended well with hers, and a young man whose sense of command wasn't predicated on sexism like Quentin's had been, leaned forward, gesturing, his black hair flopping over a high forehead as he articulated every way the idiot trolls could go choke on their fast food burgers and die.

Amar, chef de partie, scraggly beard and hair caught in a small ponytail but nevertheless escaping in frizz in all directions, gesticulated, forgetting his beer glass and then sipping the beer that spilled off the back of his hand while everybody laughed.

Lina slouched back in her chair, amused at something Mikhail had said, but not quite as easily laughing. The pressure might not be as acutely on Lina's name as it was on Vi's, but nobody knew where the damn salmonella had come from yet—*if* it even existed, which Vi still refused to believe—and if it came from the pastry kitchen, the guilt would feel horrible.

If there *was* salmonella, Vi would really rather it came from her part of the kitchens. Nobody else to blame. *The buck stops here.*

She squared her shoulders. Because these shoulders could take it.

Beyond Lina, Vi could glimpse the great statue of Marianne in the center of the Place de la République, where very, very recently she and everyone here had left flowers in memorial, weeping. Dozens of huge protests for all kinds of issues had filled République since then, of course, a sign of how the city pulsed with life no one could put out. Right now, a group in roller skates was dancing to a boom box from which, occasionally, a particularly loud sock hop refrain reached them.

Lights played with the dark everywhere—the red lights of cars braking, the warm lights spilling out of cafés, bouncing off red awnings to pick up additional tones, gleaming in shades of warm and dark off paving stones, and glowing from street lamps against the great white marble base of Marianne and over the skaters, the people watching the skaters, the groups passing and crossing, heading toward home or stopping at the cafés and bars.

Vi loved this quarter. The kind of place where students and young people just starting their careers could still afford to go out, where the theaters were full of music and comedians and small, quirky plays.

Screw the critics. She had her faithful. They'd come back.

She didn't cook for the critics of the world anyway. Nor for the president of the United States and his First Lady, however nice that would have been. She cooked for the people of this quarter. The workers and the children of immigrants and the artists and the actors, the young people with good jobs starting to move in as the quarter got more and more expensive, the people who came here to hang out because the other side of Paris was too pale, too fake, too BCBG and bourgeois for them. They wanted to keep it real.

"Thanks, guys," she told her team. "It's nice to have you on my side."

Up on the rooftops, she caught a glimpse of four silhouettes running and leaping and smiled a little. *Des traceurs de parkour.* It was always fun to catch a glimpse of them. Like a glimpse of luck. Of energy. Movement without rules. She should do some kind of dish that evoked parkour. Height and vertigo and no limit to the lines of movement.

No limit. And if you had a bad fall, you picked yourself back up.

And avoided the kind of man who pushed you down mid-leap.

She nodded to herself firmly. *Avoid him.*

And let that be a lesson to you: the next time you catch a burglar red-handed, don't sleep with him. As ways of meeting men go, the fact that he's breaking into your kitchens is never a good sign.

Chapter 14

"What part of *go away* do you not understand?" Vi demanded, keeping the chain on the door.

"I brought something." Chase held up a small backpack.

"Did you do something to Quentin?"

"Quentin?" Chase looked vague. "Small guy, kind of scrawny?"

"He always seemed big to me," Vi said dryly.

"It's funny how many different perspectives there are on size and power, isn't it?" Chase smiled at her happily.

"He called me, screaming about me siccing criminals on him."

"Must have a guilty conscience if he's that paranoid."

"Chase!"

Chase shrugged. "I may have provided him a quick demonstration of what it's like to be struggling in the hands of someone bigger and more powerful who can do whatever the hell he wants to him." Just for a second, that cool, grim, lethal look showed under his easy charm.

All the hairs on Vi's nape rose in response to that look. Then Chase winked at her, the look entirely disappearing.

"Did you *hurt* him?" It wasn't her fault that a greedy *I hope so* clenched in her at the question.

"Well...hurt." Chase shrugged and spread his hands. "People have such a wide range of pain tolerance. I didn't cut his balls off, at least. Not this time."

Vi was probably supposed to be relieved about that.

"I wanted him to have something to look forward to," Chase explained. "In case he ever thought about trying to mess with you again."

"Chase! Damn it. Starred chefs move in a small world, you know. I have a reputation."

"For being someone a man shouldn't mess with unless he wants his ass kicked?"

"For kicking those asses myself! For *not* needing some man to handle my problems for me!"

Chase considered that. "That's a really good point, honey. To explain my own point, I thought you did handle that problem yourself. I hadn't even met you when you gave him a concussion and fired him. I just wanted to reinforce your point. We don't know who else he might have assaulted in his life. He probably didn't start out with the entitlement to take on someone like you. Probably went smaller and more vulnerable until he built up his sense of impunity." He frowned as he thought about it. "Actually...maybe I should go ahead and cut his balls off." He half-turned back toward the stairs.

Vi had never really thought about possible previous attacks in Quentin's past either, and now that she did...it was an ugly, ugly thought. Vi had been a pretty, female, teenage apprentice in a kitchen full of men on power trips herself. That was when she'd taken to making sure she had a knife on her.

She caught Chase's sleeve. "Maiming a civilian sounds like a career ending move to me. At least it would be one in our military, I'm pretty sure."

He hesitated. Frowned. Subsided. Then remembered: "Not that I have to worry about that any more now that I'm a civilian."

Vi fought the urge to wrap two hands around his throat and just strangle him. "Look, other than driving me crazy, was there something you wanted? If you say sex, I'm going to shove you down the stairs."

He smiled. "Honey, if you want to say no to sex to me, no shoving is necessary. I'd be sad, and my heart would be broken, and my life would be ruined, but still...*you'd* be okay."

Damn it, how did he manage to be so funny and so annoying and so damn *solid and reassuring* all at once? "Chase. Why are you here?"

"I told you." He held up his backpack. "I brought something."

"I don't care."

"Also some food." He held up take-out that clearly smelled of the Chinese restaurant down the street. "In case you haven't eaten again today."

"It's one in the morning." So the night was still young.

"Yeah, but this is the first time your light has been on when I've swung by. And certain people are far too fussy about crossing ethical lines when asked to ping the location of your phone." He scowled.

"My phone is in the river. What people?"

Chase coughed. "Oh, you know...hacker buddies." He changed the subject quickly. "Honey, also, please don't take this the wrong way, but if you don't want to let a man into your apartment, you shouldn't open the door at all. I could break that chain with one shove."

"But then I'd knife you." Vi smiled sweetly.

Chase rested his head against the jamb and smiled a little. "I'm so crazy about you."

"Yeah, well, I know this is going to be a hard one for you to absorb, but just because *you* want me doesn't mean *I* have to give you what you want. That's because I'm not a *thing.*"

"I'm sorry," he said. "I'm *really* sorry about the jacket. I shouldn't have done it. I was a stupid, arrogant ass."

Okay, well, they agreed on *that*. She gazed at him a long moment and sighed. "Fine, you can come in." But only because she still had absolute faith in her ability to handle him. Also because that big, hot body, those blue eyes, and the way he looked at her, like she was his personal gift from heaven, just got down into her middle and heated her all up from the inside out. "But don't touch anything."

"I'll try not to sneeze, too," he said solemnly.

"What?"

"You already forgot?" He clutched his heart. "Our first meeting?"

"When you broke into my restaurant, planted salmonella or something, and ruined my career?"

He ignored that. "It was so romantic. 'Don't touch anything! Don't breathe on anything! If you sneeze, I'm killing you.'"

"I had good instincts when I first met you. The sad thing is how fast you turned me into an idiot."

Chase licked his finger and made a sizzling noise as he touched it to his shoulder.

"Oh, *purée*." Vi strode back into the apartment, leaving the door open. Although it was really true about that sizzle. He fried her brain, that was the damn problem.

Chase strolled in behind her, his size and his presence immediately taking over the whole apartment. "Can I touch your jacket?"

"You've done it enough damage. I threw it away." When she'd come home, she'd stuffed it into her trashcan so she could go ahead and get that wound over with and never think about it again.

Chase got the jacket out of the trashcan, and when she frowned at him, he pretended to stifle heavy sneezes, casting terrorized glances at her with each one.

"*Quel imbécile*," Vi said. But already she was trying not to laugh.

139

Chase smiled and sat down on the floor in front of her coffee table with the jacket. Digging into his backpack, he began to pull out tools of some sort—things that looked like they could punch holes, and things that looked like they could pound and clamp and...were those sewing needles?

Lining them up, he pulled out an iPad and searched something. She peered, unable to contain her curiosity. Instructions for sewing leather.

Her jaw dropped.

He turned the slashed jacket sleeve inside out and began to run some kind of grooving device over a cut edge.

Vi stared.

"Might as well take your shower," Chase said. "I'm not sure how long this is going to take, and you're making me self-conscious."

"You can get self-conscious?"

He shrugged.

She *did* want to wash off the scents of the bar. She went into the bathroom, keeping her shower quick, very aware of how safe she felt doing that with him in her apartment. She didn't even feel as if she needed to lock the door.

Slipping into her yoga pajama bottoms and cami, she came back out to sit at the kitchen counter and watch him.

Like the night before, just having him here started to work on her. His presence slipped in, twining its way with the comfortable feeling of her pajama bottoms and the relaxation of her shower, as if not only could he feed her need for adrenaline rushes but he could be the way she eased off that adrenaline, too.

As if he was making himself part of her quiet. That time when she wasn't ready to face the world, when she wasn't ready to take on all comers. When she let her guard down, replacing a chef's coat and knives or leather and boots with pajama pants and bare feet.

140

She couldn't figure that out. This guy was hot sex on a stick and trouble all over, and he was *obviously* excellent material for a hook-up—if he didn't ruin a woman's life the next day, exactly what she should have expected from an arrogant male. But a woman clearly would be an idiot to let down her guard around him.

The last man on earth you'd want to have see you battered and tired and defeated. She ran her fingers through her hair, to try to make sure it didn't look battered and tired and defeated.

He didn't pay any attention to her, stubbornly setting up the two sliced edges of that sleeve in a clamp and now trying to thread a needle with his big fingers. It took her a while to realize that there was the faintest tinge of color on his cheeks.

"Do you want help?" she asked finally.

He shook his head.

"Do you want to eat?"

"It's one o'clock, honey. I ate a while ago."

She voice-activated a little music, her wind-down playlist. He tilted his head a second and then smiled a little. "Pink?"

Vi found herself grinning. "I'm still a rock star."

"Yep." He said it simply, giving her one flick of a glance that was like being licked with a flame. The heat of respect, admiration, attraction. "How did it go today?"

Not awesome.

"Fine."

His smile faded. He looked at her a long moment, waiting.

"I mean...you know...great."

His lips twisted. He waited.

"It was great to get out with my team. They needed it, and I needed it. But..." She shoved her toe against the counter. "I just can't *do* anything. The restaurant is closed until the inspections are over. So I just have to *sit* there and *take* it. I can't cook anything. I can't make flavors come alive and send them out to all those would-be critics to tell them *now* say something else. I can't focus on my work and my world, on doing what I love, and just forget all those damn yappy dogs out there exist. So I just get...torn down and torn down, while all I can think about is how my life is getting sucked down the drain. I hate it. God, I hate it."

He gave a grimace of empathy.

"I talked to the owners, and...they're not blaming me or anything. They're trying to be supportive. But they took a huge risk on me, because they were excited about me, and..." She shrugged, no words to convey how much she hated to repay them with this.

Chase grimaced again. As if he understood. "Why don't you own your own restaurant? You know you're the kind of person who would really rather the buck stop completely with you."

"The cost, in Paris. I'm twenty-eight, I've been climbing fast already. Owning my own place is my next step. I might not even have any choice about it. This might knock me right down the staircase, so I have to start back up from the bottom and open my own place even to get a chance to cook again."

Chase said nothing for a moment, his face grim as he worked. But then he said: "You know what I like about you, Vi? One of the things. You take it for granted that you will start climbing back up. You're not going to stay down there defeated."

She shrugged, not understanding the compliment. Of course she was going to start climbing back up. How could anyone be willing to stay at the bottom of anything? "If only I could just *cook* again. Act. Then I'd barely even care, you know?"

Chase nodded and focused on his stitching for a couple of careful double stitches. "Once," he said suddenly, and his voice choked oddly and he stopped. He took a breath and rolled his shoulders, doing a stretching thing with his neck as if to loosen up his throat. When he resumed, his voice was steady again, although lower than usual. "Once a team of ours went down in the Hindu Kush. They were overrun and...I was one of the two men on the QRF. The quick reactionary force—that's the back-up, if a mission goes wrong. We got on that helicopter so damn fast, ready to go. To save them or go down trying. I know that sounds...sacrificial or something, but that's not really what it feels like. It's just the way we're made, you know? You'd be the same. You'd find it way easier to be taking bullets and at least giving out some of your own than sitting on the sidelines helpless."

Her body tightened all through her at the shock of what he was saying. He was talking about real bullets. Not movie bullets. *Real* bullets, aimed at his *body*. That strong, warm, human body and that skull that might seem thick enough to stop a bullet, but...wouldn't. Her breath froze in her chest. She stared at him.

"The same way if you were on a team that was losing badly, you'd way rather be out there with your teammates giving your all to turn it around than sitting on the bench," he tried.

It's not exactly like a sports team, Chase. If you're fielding bullets instead of soccer balls. If you might die. If your teammates do die. God, her heart hurt all of a sudden. As if someone was stretching it in two big hands and it was starting to tear.

"And the fucking assholes in command kept the helicopter grounded," he said low and viciously. "They wouldn't let us fly out. They said they didn't want to risk losing another chopper and even more men and that it was too dangerous during daylight, and we had to *sit there all the fucking day listening to them call for help over the radio until the last one died.*"

143

His knee jerked up into the table as he made a hard movement, the crack of the contact sounding through the room. He caught himself and took a deep breath, bending his head. No, it was more than his head. For a moment, he hunched into himself, as if his stomach hurt.

Vi stared at him, beyond words. She felt dizzy, as if she was spinning over vaguely formed mountaintops in another country, trying to peer down through her own fuzzy inability to imagine them to what death and violence looked like in their...snow? Tundra? She handled a lot of dead animal bodies. Did exposed human flesh and bone look the same? Nausea rose up in her.

"Oh, God, I'm so sorry." Her voice puffed out of her harshly, stuffed and strangled. She came off the stool to go kneel across the table from him.

He shoved her words away with a push of his hand, then shoved that same hand across his face and through his hair. Rolled his shoulders. Then shook his head once like a dog shedding water and smiled at her, that easy smile of his. "It was a long time ago," he said, and only a little roughness under his voice belied the relaxed tone. "I'm a civilian now."

"Oh, yeah, what the fuck ever." She put her hand over his, because all words sounded lame, and just held on tight to that callused, scarred hand.

He bent his head and gazed at their joined hands a moment. His eyes closed, and he took a deep breath, his thumb shifting to catch her hand and keep it around his.

"The November attacks," she said, low. "I mean...I went to the Bataclan all the time. It's just a couple of streets over. Nobody even knew what was *happening*, and then...all you can do is leave candles and flowers. When you want to hit someone, to rage. We try not to think about it too much, because...we want to be alive, we want to be Paris still. But...yeah. It's horrible to have nothing you can do. You don't know how many people enlisted in the French military the week after those attacks, in order to try to do something."

"Oh...I have some idea," Chase said with an odd somber wryness.

When had *he* enlisted? He must have been a young teenager for the attacks on New York. Too young to enlist yet, but it would have marked him.

His hand tightened slowly on hers.

"I'll survive this," Vi told him, her tone adamant. "There's no doubt about that."

His eyes opened, and light came back into them as they ran over her. Genuine light, that vivid blue pleasure. "I know you will, honey," he said. "*God*, you're so alive. Life just comes right off you like electricity." He cupped his free hand just shy of her hair, as if he was savoring the buzz. "Damn, you're gorgeous."

"You are, too," she said, and instead of grinning cockily, he flushed a little and gave her a funny, awkward smile.

"In your arrogant, annoying way," she said, and his smile relaxed a little into more genuine humor. "Did you just *one up* my own tragedy?"

"Your tragedies are wussy." But his eyes flickered as he tried to joke, and his attempt at a grand, dismissive gesture came off wooden.

Yeah, so...yeah, she was an idiot, to try humor for that. Some things humor just didn't work for. She squeezed his hand again and settled onto the floor, leaning against the table.

He was quiet for a long time, just gazing at her hand over his and stroking it slowly with his thumb. "Sorry," he said eventually, voice a little rough.

"Seriously, don't make me hit you."

A little smile came back. He squeezed her hand and let it go, picking up the needles again.

She felt stupid now, to have made such a big deal out of her jacket. Even if he should *not* take over her choices and ruin her beautiful jacket. But still...it was only a jacket. It wasn't friends lying dead in the mountains.

But watching him slowly and painstakingly try to heal that unhealable wound in the leather, she didn't stop him.

Maybe healing unhealable wounds was something they both needed to know how to do.

The reality of this big, sexy, hard-willed man who clowned and teased and who...what? He had to be part of a counterterrorism unit. Or working for the CIA in some capacity. That was the only thing she could figure. What the hell else could a military man from Texas whose eyes flickered when she mentioned Navy SEALs be doing in France breaking into restaurants his president might be visiting and then, if she was right, getting them shut down? Bastard.

A laughing bastard who...had spent most of his adult life in Afghanistan and Iraq, maybe? One of those guys who fast-roped into compounds in the middle of the night and took out the enemies of their country and...got shot at. Stepped on mines. Killed people.

That Hindu Kush event that still ate at him...he was upset because his commanders had refused to let him go die, too.

She rested her folded arms on the table as she watched him. Under the table she shifted just enough that her knee tucked against his thigh. Human touch.

He had gotten the needles threaded and was checking the instructions on his iPad. Now he was starting the stitching, which apparently required two needles going at once in opposite directions.

Blue eyes squinted in concentration, so that she could see exactly how they had squinted time and again to leave those lines at their corners. Sun-streaked brown hair a little shaggy for a military man.

"Did you have a beard recently?" she said suddenly, startled.

He glanced at her, then focused on his twin needles again. "What makes you ask?"

"Your skin is paler on your jaw line. Less tanned."

He gave a little nod of acknowledgement and a shrug.

"But...you mean you really are a civilian?" Or had been one long enough to grow a beard, tan around it, and shave it off? Did people in the military get to wear beards these days?

He didn't say anything. She needed to do some Internet research on U.S. special forces.

"You have complete files on me, don't you? And I don't know a thing about you."

"Not a thing?" he asked quietly.

Okay, maybe some things. She knew he was cocky and with good reason. She knew that physically he couldn't conceive of an insurmountable challenge. She knew that a siren-like alarm in the morning threw him into high stress alert, and that in that state of alarm, his first instinct was to cover her body with his own. And that a minute later, he had played the clown as if nothing of any importance had just happened.

She knew he felt bad that she had gotten hurt. She knew that he wanted to save people, but he didn't need her to be weak so that he could satisfy his own superhero complex. He wasn't one of those guys who would try to keep her small to make himself feel strong. No, he'd always give her a wicked grin and a challenge, a *yeah, I know you can do it.*

She knew he loved the way she challenged him, too. He wasn't threatened by her strength at all. If anything, he tried to help her be even stronger.

She knew that he was so incredibly pig-headed that he was almost oblivious to opposition. Like it never even occurred to him that he couldn't stride through any and all obstacles, human or otherwise, and get what he wanted.

Kind of like her.

Which might be why she had an unfortunate tendency to find that characteristic so hot.

But most cocky guys didn't care about anyone their arrogance rode tank-like over. Caring about getting her in their bed and satisfying their own ego was *not* the same as caring about her.

Yet here he was, sitting on her floor, awkwardly and carefully trying to stitch together the sleeve of her favorite jacket. Instead of just buying her a new one, and by doing so dismissing what mattered to her as insignificant.

"If you weren't so annoying, I might like you," she said.

One corner of his lips kicked up. "Too tepid. Who wants to be liked?"

She rested her head on her folded arms, watching him work. His thigh was warm against her knee, under the table. "First time?" She nodded at the sewing without lifting her cheek off her arms.

"I'm a little OCD about my gear. So not entirely. But now that we can use Steri-Strips, I don't get nearly the practice sewing in the field that I used to."

Steri-Strips...for pulling wounds closed instead of setting stitches. She searched his face. "Uh...is that a joke?"

"Dark humor."

Hmm.

Dark humor filled the kitchens. They were, after all, dealing with dead bodies all the time. But...animal bodies.

Flames and burns and knives and tempers but not bullets.

She dropped her splinted hand under the table and let it rest on his thigh, the thumb and fingertip that were mobile stroking his jeans in a soft, repeated motion.

"You ever seen a magician do one of those tricks where he holds up something tiny—his closed fist or whatever—and then starts pulling a scarf out of it?" Chase said suddenly, roughly, focusing hard on the sewing.

What? She nodded against her arm, waiting.

"And the scarf just pulls and pulls and pulls until silk is flooding everywhere? This impossible amount to have fit into that tiny a space?"

"He's got it on him all the time. Hiding it up his sleeve or something. That's the trick."

Chase pushed that comment away with a motion of his hand. "I kind of like to keep the soft, silky, fragile things in a really tiny space."

"Things?"

"Emotions," he said very roughly, trying to push the word away with his hand even as it came out. "Whatever. But it's like you've started pulling. And I'm a little afraid of how much you might pull out."

Yeah, no freaking kidding. What a perfect analogy. She tightened her belly, to prepare for the blow. "So are you going to run away?"

He gave her a look that said he'd never run from danger in his life. "You wish."

Well...sometimes, maybe, she wished he would run. It was scary for her, too. He'd brought so much havoc to her life already. What if he *got* to her? What if she ended up letting soft, fragile things out and he ripped them? Or *then* ran off with them? Took a casual knife to them without even taking the time to find out if they were important?

Came back and tried to mend them.

"See, the first night," he said, "that was easy. Hot blonde in leather throwing knives at me...of *course* I could see you were the woman for me. And trust me, it really was no hardship to go all out after you. But then—"

"I know how hook-ups work," Vi cut him off. The last thing she needed was to hear him spell out his thought process the next morning. *Well, I tapped that and now I'm ready to move on.* "I know all about how easy it is for a guy to fall for me and how hard it is for him to deal with the actual me."

He stopped his work on the leather to look at her a moment. His eyes narrowed. "Pff. You're easy."

Vi sat straight up. "I'm *what*?"

"All I have to do is make you mad. You love being mad. I'm talking about me. *I'm* hard. In fact, right this second, I can't figure out how to deal with me at all. If you keep pulling all those *emotions* out like that, I'm actually"—he dropped his voice dramatically, peering over his shoulder as if to make sure no one could overhear—"deathly afraid I might be *complicated.*" He shuddered.

"You think you're more *complex* than I am?" Vi demanded, outraged.

A tiny smile curved his mouth. "See? I told you you liked to get mad."

Vi folded her arms, her splint getting in the way. "You are harder to deal with than I am," she stated, incredulous. She pretty much defined high-maintenance, damn it!

He slanted a glance at her. The creases showed in his cheeks. "I've got you wrapped around my little finger," he bragged outrageously.

Vi pounced up onto her knees. "*You* have got *me* wrapped around your little finger?"

He held up one pinky and made a twirling gesture, smug.

"Allow me to demonstrate exactly how *simple* and *easy* you are." Vi leaned forward.

Chase gave her a look of polite interest. While struggling to hide those dimples.

She laid her hand flat on his chest, fulminating.

He looked down at it. His mouth curved like the cat that swallowed the canary.

She pushed.

He didn't budge.

She pushed harder.

It didn't even seem to affect him. No yield in his body at all.

She frowned at him.

He smiled at her, and then very slowly let his body curl away from the table, his abs tightening to keep the motion so controlled, until he was resting against the couch behind him.

And instantly heat swept through her, at that yielding. He was, she had to admit, incredibly hot. Broad shoulders, hard chest, a ribbed, flat stomach, all covered right now by nothing but a thin T-shirt. Arrogance and humor and heat, building, focusing on her. She could feel it. See it in his eyes.

See? Easy.

She stroked down his chest over his stomach, just to feel that hard ripple. He took a deep, slow breath. Still smiling a little.

She ran her hand along the line of his jeans, letting the tip of her fingers slide under the band.

His smile slipped away, but then he caught it back. "Shh," he murmured and took her hand, setting it on his shoulders. "You're in too much of a hurry. I don't have to be *that* simple." He stroked her hand down over his arm and flexed a little for her.

Wow. Biceps like that made a woman glad to be alive. She flowed into movement suddenly, straddling him. He tilted his head back against the couch, breathing slow and deep, watching her under short, thick lashes. She was close enough that she could actually see that "kitten scar" on his cheek, so fine that she kept wanting to brush it away because it looked just like a stray hair had gotten caught there.

She touched the scratch left by her own nail, suddenly somber. Then touched the spot on his jaw where her fist had landed.

"Honey," he said suddenly. "You're worried about the wrong thing. My buddies and I try to kick each other's asses all the time, just to keep sharp. In fact, sometimes when we're bored, during some lull in training, we do things like throw rocks at each other's stomachs and whoever flinches first loses."

They had macho contests in the kitchens, too—who could pick up a hot skillet in his bare hand, who kept working through the worst injuries.

Actually, considering that she did the same thing, it was a little annoying to think of that trait as "macho." A woman could be tough and still a woman. Hell, she had some older friends who had been through *labor*.

Without drugs or anything.

"Some people are just idiots," she said.

He smiled.

"This would be your training in hotel security?"

He laughed. And then corrected: "We used to do that. When I was in the military."

"Oh, *purée*," Vi muttered. Her thumb traced over his square, stubborn jaw.

He shifted a little into the caress, like a big cat, his eyes half-closing.

Yeah, see? You're easy. She ran her hand slowly down his throat, caressing the strength of it like something precious and vulnerable. When her thumb came to rest in the hollow, stroking, his eyes closed all the way. A deep breath moved through his body.

So easy. She spread her fingers over his breastbone. A great heat and strength radiated from him, spreading through her body. She wanted to get more of it. Knead it to her and into her, absorb it everywhere.

Her splinted right hand rested chunky and awkward on his left shoulder. It was with her left hand, the hand that was just a little less confident, just a little less capable, that she had to work her wiles.

That was okay. *I can take you left-handed. I can take you with one hand tied behind my back.*

She could feel his arousal, so fast and so hard that he must have been at least partly aroused before she ever made a move. Now he was *definitely* aroused, and she twisted her hips against him in a slow figure eight, savoring how much he wanted her. *And I'm still in control, ha.*

Yeah. Easy.

She ran her hand down his hard biceps, curved her fingers over the defined triceps, trying to get all of him. It frustrated her no end that she couldn't just sink both hands into him, and to make up for it, she bent suddenly and nipped his left shoulder. Mmm. Better. Stroking and rubbing down over his right arm with her unbroken hand, she used lips and teeth and little teasings of her tongue to explore his left arm, too.

God, she loved to savor things with lips and teeth and tongue. That little hint of salt on his skin tasted delicious.

"You have the most incredible *texture*," she breathed involuntarily. All that muscle and heat and resilience, the softness of his hair against the hardness of his thick skull, the silk of his lips, and the bristle of his jaw line. She could touch him *forever*.

His eyes were dilated, already a little dazed. "You have no idea." His hands rubbed over her butt, down her thighs. "About incredible texture. You probably take your own for *granted*."

He probably took his own for granted, too. How odd. When it was so amazing. Her hand stroked down to his strong wrist, and she hooked her splinted hand under his other forearm and bumped that up higher so she could explore that with her mouth, too. She nipped a knuckle and sucked the tip of his index finger into her mouth, curling her tongue around it.

He made a wounded, hungry sound, his hips rocking up into her.

Mmm. Every texture and pressure and pleasure of his body was delicious. She *loved* arousing him. His hand curved against her head, and she nestled her face into it to suckle the base of his palm as she slanted a wicked look up at his face. "You might be right. Slow might be fun."

"Did I say slow?" His voice sounded thick and heavy. "What I must have meant was...honey, you can do anything to me you want."

She grinned and teased the base of his palm with her tongue. "I know."

"God, you are glorious." He sank his fingers into her damp hair and brought her head to his, kissing her. The first kiss grew into another and another, stretched into a long gluttony of kisses that could have been one or could have been a hundred ways of shaping their mouths to each other, tasting and seeking and finding out what they each liked.

They seemed to like everything. Hard and soft, open and closed, teeth and silk, tangling and elusive.

Less and less elusive. Deeper and hungrier until she twisted her face into his throat for breath. God, he smelled good. Just this himness plus vanilla.

Vanilla. Something about that delighted her whole body, that instead of smelling of sand and sun and all the places he must have been, he smelled like someone who carried a homesick scent of cookies with him in his aftershave.

She kissed him for it, kissing down over the hollow of his throat and lingering there, while his hands flexed into her butt and stroked up her back and down her thighs and back to her butt again as if that was their homing place, gripping her, rocking her into him as his hips thrust up to hers.

She nuzzled her face close to his ear to whisper: "How *complicated* are you feeling?"

"Pretty damn simple," he admitted. "And easy." His hips rocked up to hers. "Or hard."

She laughed low into his throat and stroked a heavy hand down his chest.

He drew her hips against him, to and away, to and away. "How about you?" he asked, deep.

She laughed again, into his skin. *Simple. So simple.* Everything falling away, outside this space of him and them. His heat and hers, his skin and hers, the way his hand sank into her hair, the hint of the prickles of his chest hair through his T-shirt as her face rubbed over it.

She pulled at the hem of his T-shirt with her good hand, frustrated that she couldn't just grab it and rip.

He arched up and pulled it off, this long, gorgeous reveal of ripped abs taut with the motion, of heavy shoulders, of the curl of hair across his chest and the fine V of it down to his jeans. She followed it, running her fingers through that hair for the pure pleasure of its texture, following it as it grew finer and softer over hard abs, as those abs sucked in to try to lure her fingers under his waistband.

She toyed there, laughing low in her throat. "*Complicated,* are you?"

He grinned up at her. "Honey, you're making me feel like myself again. As straightforward as a man can be."

155

She kissed under the hollow of his throat and lower, lower, following pleasure, all the pleasure of his body, the tickle of hair, the hardness of muscle, the warmth, the surprising silk smoothness of his skin on his back and ribs.

The way he flinched a little as she lingered over his ribs. "You're ticklish," she said in delight, playing her fingers ever so lightly over the spot that had made him flinch.

He flinched again and grabbed her hand. She brushed his ribs with the two unsplinted fingers on his other side, laughing as he reacted involuntarily.

"All right, now." He rolled them over suddenly, pinning her to the floor between the couch and the coffee table, holding her good hand above her head. "Two can play at that game."

He drew his hand down over her ribs. She held her breath and tightened all her muscles in stern control.

"Seriously?" He tried brushing more lightly, then pressing his fingers into just the most sensitive spots between ribs. She tightened as hard as she could. "Tough girl," he said admiringly and kissed her.

Just kissed her and kissed her, this long, luxurious pinning of her body under his as he savored her mouth as if he never would stop. And then, when all her body was relaxed and pliant under his, when her knees kept bumping against the table as she tried to wrap her legs around him—he dove his fingers into her ribs again.

She yelped and jerked and bumped her elbow.

He grinned in triumph.

"*Aïe.*" She flexed her funny bone.

He bent and opened his mouth over her elbow, kissing and tasting and sucking gently, until that vibrating numbness was lost in erotic sensation.

It made her feel almost...precious. In the weirdest way, as if she could be tough and strong and still be precious to someone, too. It almost made her eyes sting.

Merde, was he pulling emotions out of her? All silky and pretty and fragile?

She tried to catch him and pull his head to her, to kiss all that nonsense back into sex, but he had her good hand pinned, and her splinted hand bumped futilely, unable to grip properly.

He smiled and took her wrist gently, below the splint, then slowly brushed his lips and jaw all the way up the inside of her arm, from elbow to wrist.

The prickles and silk of him shivered through her, over and over, dissolving her into all that mass of magician's scarves, colorful and lovely and helpless before the power of his spell.

Just a trick, not a spell, she tried to tell herself, but she kept getting lost in her own words. They fled away before sensation, as if her mind, too, was only silk and colors and yielding.

Emotion. Hope. Wonder.

Why are you here? Why does being pinned by you like this make me feel safe and wanted and hungry instead of caught in a power struggle?

"Let me go," she whispered, and his hand slid down from her wrist. He freed her with a caress of calluses down sensitive skin, tracing burn marks and spatters near her wrist, then the pale skin that was always protected by her chef's jacket and hadn't seen sun since she spent a week in Réunion after New Year's. His thumb curved over her biceps, tracing the definition of arms that looked so much slimmer than his but were very strong.

She was strong and used her body to its utmost, and he was strong and used his body to its utmost, and here they were—physically, she would always, always be outmatched by his strength. He would always be able to roll her under him and hold her down.

Which was why a woman should keep a good knife and some heavy steel pots to hand, but...

...thoughts of them, of any kind of strength, got lost in silk and colors.

She pushed at him. He shoved the coffee table away to give them more room and rolled them over again, bringing her on top.

Wow, what a fantastic view. That hard body stretched out for her, those gleaming, hungry blue eyes. Even his stubborn chin seemed a little less like something a woman would break herself against, right that second.

She kissed it, to test. No, still hard. But the skin just below that jaw was so soft. His head arched back as she kissed it.

Chase slid his hands under her cami, his palms and fingers rubbing up her ribs and belly as he pushed it up, up, until he came to her breasts. He cupped them through her bra, watching her face, watching his hands, enjoying both views.

She shivered and stretched into his touch. Her half-dry hair slid over her shoulders.

"Incredible," he breathed. "Maybe I'm dead."

She had to pause at that, bracing herself off him with one hand.

"You can break it to me if I am," he said. "I'd be okay with it. I'd actually probably feel a lot safer that way."

"Well, of course you'd be *safer*," she said. "If you're *dead*."

His face relaxed into that grin. "Coward's way out, you're saying?"

"Is there a reason we're having a morbid conversation right now?"

"Well...I figure if some people get angels and some people get ninety-nine virgins or whatever...I'd rather get you. You're perfect."

"You're such an idiot," she said, to fight the upsurge of warmth and, well...honor. She was really his idea of heaven?

"Well, to be honest, the other options always sounded like hell," he confessed. "I'm really relieved someone thought up a special version just for me."

"Just shut up already," she said, because she could feel a tide of color rising up her face, and she ducked down into him to hide it, kissing his chest.

"I talk too much," he confessed into her hair, his hand stroking it. "You make me babble."

He wasn't always like that? Her cheeks heated more, and she kept her face firmly pressed into his chest because that heat just wouldn't die down. It was just that he made her feel so, so...damn *vulnerable* and flattered and special.

No man ever made her feel special. She always had to do it all by herself.

She kissed his chest, very gently, just this little secret thanks, and petted the hard muscle, resting her cheek against him to watch her hand. She liked those springy curls of hair so much. The way his chest felt rising and falling under her hand in a deep breath. The way his abs tightened in response to her palm, the little round hollow of his belly-button—

He covered her hand a moment, pressing it to his belly, and took another long breath. "Honey," he said very softly as he let it out.

And that was all. After a second, his hand slid away, releasing hers to explore again, and he undid the button on his jeans.

How thoughtful.

Her mouth curved a little at this very clear indication of what he wanted, and she nestled her fingers just at the top of his zip, running her thumb under the elastic of his briefs, toying with the tab of the zip.

"Witch," he said.

"But you told me to slow down," she reminded him, biting her lip.

"Damn but you hold a grudge." His hands moved to her butt, and he began to stroke them far too lightly up and down her curves, just grazing, not nearly enough pressure.

She twisted against him.

He laughed, deep and smug.

"Are you *challenging* me?" she asked incredulously.

"Really never saw a gauntlet I could resist picking up."

She slid her fingers under the band of his briefs, to the thicket of curly hair.

His breath hissed. His fingers sank more firmly into her butt, and he pulled her against his thigh, drawing her up and down against that muscle in one long delicious rub.

Challenge and play was so much easier than softness and intimacy.

"Me, neither," she murmured menacingly and trailed just her fingertips to the base of his erection.

"Oh, baby." He pressed toward her hand. She drew it instantly away. He tried to grab her hand.

She laughed and wormed it under his butt, hiding it from him even as she kneaded that hard muscle.

"I'm a poor, lonesome, war-weary soldie—security guard. And you should not be mean to me." He tried for big, pitiful eyes.

"Were you a puppy in another life?" The kind of puppy that grew up to be a wolf.

"Were you a gorgeous siren?" He sank his hands into her hair and pulled her down to kiss her, taking his time, running his hands over her in deep, kneading strokes as he kissed her and kissed her.

In the heat of those kisses, she forgot to tease him, her hand sliding past the loosened denim and under his briefs to cup his bare buttock, hot and smooth and curved against her palm.

"*Mmm.*" A low, hungry-satisfied sound in his throat. "More."

"Greedy," she breathed into his jaw.

His fingers dug into her butt, rocking her against his pelvis as he thrust up. "Oh, yeah, I want it *all*."

Yes. *All.* And that was what he felt like—all. All life, all humor, all energy, all challenge—everything she wanted, right there grinning up at her and daring her to take him.

He made her want to toss those fragile, colorful, silky feelings up in the air and let them rain down around them, beautiful and joyous.

She nipped his shoulder again, expanding into the joy of their bodies tangling and touching, and he got her cami over her head and threw it somewhere, then went to work on her bra.

"Oh, God, *yeah*," he said, as the cups fell away. He clenched his fist around the black lace and kissed it like an Olympic champion might kiss his gold medal, then tossed it away, too.

She laughed, clasped her wrist above her head, and stretched, twisting her hips down into his as she did. Vivid and alive and thrilled to be her.

"You are always trying to kill me," he said, and lifted her suddenly to set her on the couch, coming to his knees between her legs so that he could cup her breasts and bury his face in them, kissing and sucking and squeezing as if he couldn't get enough.

You and me both. She slid her good hand down his back, trying to knead him in closer, trying to use her right arm to squeeze him in, too, since she couldn't use her right hand. *I can't get enough of you either.*

One of his hands slid around her back to hold her to him, the other slid down under her pajama elastic to cup her bare butt. "God, I love you," he said into her breasts, and the words rolled through her, like the roll of land in an earthquake.

Damn him for saying things like that, so easily and so carelessly. Too cocky and too flippant to remember the damage he could wreak. She pushed the words away, into the compartment where she kept all his ridiculous marriage proposals, but it wasn't as easy this time, as if some little part of her wanted to catch the words back out into the open and think about them as if they might be true.

She thrust her good hand down and wrapped her hand around his penis like it was his throat, strangling.

He made a harsh sound into her shoulder, and thrust hard. "Sweetheart...honey...gorgeous..." He really was babbling now, or almost, losing coherence as he yanked her pajama bottoms off. "So pretty, pretty, pretty..." His hands stroked over her bare, spread thighs as if they were a miracle, and then gripped too hard as she tightened her hand again to try to get him to *shut up*.

Pretty and *fine* were one thing. Combining them with *love* was another. A girl could get all messed up that way.

If she was stupid.

If she let him get away with that crap.

So she squeezed her hand down his erection hard, punishingly, trying to force him out of his mind.

He made a sound that could not possibly be deciphered as a word, and slid his hands up her thighs, gripping them wide, thumbs massaging the lips of her sex, sliding down the folds, parting and playing and sliding back up.

She jumped at the intimacy, and then she *loved* it, oh, hell, she loved it, her whole body trying to liquefy in reception. Even the strength of her grip wanted to go, and she fought it, tightening her hold and sliding up and down, because *he* was going to lose his mind this time, she was going to win over *him*.

His head lifted, and his eyes locked with hers, darkened, vivid blue. He stroked his thumbs into her folds, delving into her.

She locked her gaze right back, even though she wanted to toss her head back and close her eyes. Even though she wanted to sink and part and soften. She drew her hand down long, long, and slow, slow back up.

He played with silk-moist insides, with *her*, with all the softened, inner, fragile parts of her.

And she could only get at his hardness, only make it harder and harder, fighting it like an opponent she couldn't beat.

While her breath began to shorten, while her eyes began to tear with the battle, while she wanted nothing, nothing so much as to give in to all that building wanting, let everything about herself yield.

One thumb still sliding and exploring among her folds, he found her clit with his other and began to play. He was watching her still. Almost there might have been the curve of a smile, but she tightened her grip again and that smile disappeared. He made a hungry sound of pleasure.

That sound vibrated into her, gave him still more access, made her still more vulnerable.

"I've got you," he whispered. Damn him, he could still *speak*? "I've got you. It's okay. Come on, baby, come on." One thumb coaxed. The other slid deep into her, and she clutched on the delight of that invasion.

Losing it. She was losing it entirely. Now she was clutching his penis like a drowning person, and she didn't even care if the water was closing over her head because it was so damn beautiful with all those silky colors in it.

"Oh, you're so beautiful," Chase whispered. "Come on, come on, come *on*."

And she did, jerking into it past resistance, hiding her face in her arms, falling back on the couch as her body seized and seized in the overwhelming joy of being her. In his hands.

He milked her down from it slowly. He was steady and patient and thorough, letting her linger in it until finally she pushed his hand away and grabbed his hips. And then he kind of lost his mind. Rolling her under him on the couch. Lifting her and twisting her under him over the arm of the couch. Abandoning the couch all together and carrying her to her bed where he could have this great *feast* of her body, thrusting and taking and turning and taking another way, like he just couldn't get enough.

Until she grabbed him and held on with all her one-handed might, digging her fingers into his butt, lifting to him as she pulled him into her. "God, I love you," he said again hoarsely, that bastard, his face so flushed, his fingers so hard they would have hurt, if she'd been less aroused.

"Shut up," she said, and brought one of his hands around between her legs, pressing his touch to her, because she was desperate again by then, and she came again while he did, crushing her to him with the force of it.

Chapter 15

Careless, arrogant idiot! Vi gripped her head, trying to focus the insult on Chase but feeling as if she was apostrophizing herself.

Of course he was gone this morning. Of course a man said *I love you* when he was in the middle of sex and then panicked at what the hell he had gotten himself into after the arousal faded.

She rolled out of bed and picked up the journal she had knocked to the floor when she woke precisely one minute before her alarm and flung out her hand to make sure it didn't go off.

Aarrgh. What the hell was wrong with her? Why did she keep letting him bring his B.S. into her life? A weakness for cocky guys and a belief that she could handle anything were *not* good excuses. *Just because a woman can handle bullshit doesn't mean she should.*

She slammed the journal onto the nightstand and stood still for a moment with her head bent.

Actually, what the hell was wrong with him? The guy was completely inconsistent. Who showed up to stitch together leather and open his heart and then ran out before dawn?

An emotional coward, maybe. Somebody who scared himself by all the emotions he was pulling out.

Although he had locked his eyes with hers and said, *You wish* in a way that still vibrated in her bones like a challenge.

And she never really had seen a gauntlet thrown down that she could resist picking up.

She frowned at her leather jacket, stroking the sleeve. A worry woke up in her middle and started to stretch. What if there was some *reason* he had disappeared before dawn? Some reason to do with whatever his real reason for being here was?

Oh, shit, he wasn't doing anything else to her restaurant, was he?

She yanked clothes on and hurried over there as fast as blasted public transport would allow, but the place was completely locked up and taped off. Nobody was around, though, so she went ahead and ripped the yellow tape and went in. Darkness and LED lights. Nobody there.

She went through the walk-ins, in deep mourning for all the food spoiling. Damn it, they needed to let her back in here.

The sight just fed her frustration and unreasonable anxiety, and she went out into the street again.

Where two military-looking "health inspectors" were just climbing out of an unmarked car. "*Mademoiselle Lenoir.* We need to ask you to respect our request that you stay off the premises. You could compromise the investigation."

Vi scowled at them. "It's my restaurant!"

"Nevertheless."

She narrowed her eyes at them. "Have you seen Chase this morning?"

"Who?"

She glared at them and stomped off. Getting arrested, she had learned, was a huge hassle.

But she didn't really start to worry until one a.m., when no one had shown up at her door with boxing gloves or leather stitching materials or just a big shit-eating grin on his face.

Also he didn't show up by two a.m.

And by three she knew he really wasn't going to show up that night, and that it was incredibly demeaning that she didn't even have his telephone number, and she was pissed at herself, and she managed to fall asleep.

More or less.

***

"Wow," Célie said five days later. "Wow. I never would have pegged him for someone who would just disappear like that."

"Well, you know how guys are." Vi kicked the pavement. They were waiting in line to get into a favorite comedian's show. Vi could only scout new restaurant locations and fight with bureaucrats so long during the day, and while Au-dessus remained closed, she'd decided to take advantage of the miracle of having evenings free. She'd far rather be going out with friends than waiting in her apartment wondering if Chase would finally show up again. "They say *I love you, I want to marry you* when they want hot sex, but then they scare themselves and run off. Or I scare them," she said sullenly.

"You do scare most men, Vi," Lina agreed. "But...he didn't seem that easy to scare."

Vi shrugged, trying not to think about it. This comedian had better by *really* funny.

"I think you're choosing the wrong men," Célie's boyfriend Joss said. "Maybe you need to select the good guys. Or at least someone with guts."

Vi glared at him. Tall, hot, strong, quiet Joss Castel had come back from five years in the Foreign Legion only a month ago, apparently having been in love with and faithful to Célie all that time. He was pure salt in the wounds of every other woman trying to handle the dating scene. "Maybe the good guys are all gone."

Joss just looked at her with steady, faintly challenging, hazel eyes. "Since you attract essentially every man alive, just by walking by, I'm going to go ahead and insist it's a selection issue."

Vi scowled at him.

"Are you sure nothing is wrong?" Célie asked. "Did you call him?"

Vi's stomach clenched around that worry, that had woken so small and innocent in her only five days before but had long since stretched its cute little tentacles out in her belly, planted them, and started to feed. It was a monster worry now.

She infinitely preferred to believe that she'd been dumped by an emotional coward than to focus on that worry.

If she concentrated really hard on all her past history with men and not Chase himself, that dumped-by-a-coward scenario almost seemed *likely*.

"I don't have his number," she said.

Célie's lips rounded.

Vi flushed. Yes. That made her seem like nothing but a booty call.

"Does he have *yours*?" Lina asked. With her glossy, loose curls and pretty face, Lina looked as sweet and delicate as her desserts, and she'd learned from childhood to have a sure, tough inner core, therefore. Perception, balance, and sense, to Vi's energy and flamboyance. They worked well together at Au-dessus.

"I threw my phone into the river." Vi had ended up getting a disposable phone so she could argue with health inspectors and harass them every hour for results, but she was trying to put off having a new smartphone until the ugliest chatter about her had died down on Twitter.

Chase didn't have the disposable phone's number, though. She'd bought it after he disappeared. She'd called that embassy number yesterday, but they'd acted as if they'd never even heard of a Chase Smith.

She slanted a glance at Lina. "Your cousin hasn't been doing anything weird, has he? Receiving strange guests from Belgium?"

Lina glanced around to make sure no one else in line could overhear them and shook her head. Lina had a cousin who was the despair of their mutual grandparents, a weaselly jerk who had grown more and more weaselly through high school—at seventeen, he'd once grabbed sixteen-year-old Vi's breasts in the stairwell of Lina's building and tried to trap her against the wall, and she'd kneed him and shoved him down the stairs—and who had ended up in gangs, then fallen under the sway of some weirdo imam and started spouting pseudo-religious nonsense that sure as hell didn't correspond to anything Lina or her parents believed, and then run off to Syria and come back fairly soon after, with his tail between his legs.

Everybody in the family worried about him, and Lina personally hated him, but the police did nothing at all. So apparently he was just a misogynist jerk who liked to fantasize about killing people.

Right.

Vi gave her shoulders a flick as if to rid herself of uncleanness just thinking about him and focused on the shrinking line. She would *really* like to be in a dark theater with a very funny comedian making her laugh, already.

Lina's weaselly wannabe cousin is the very last person who would actually know if something was going down right now. Something big enough that American special ops would be involved, inside France.

She couldn't even imagine anything big enough that the French would allow Americans a hand in it, on their soil. The guy responsible for the Christmas flight, maybe. Al-Mofti. She really had no idea whatsoever how countries cooperated on this kind of thing, but she could see them wanting that to be a joint operation. Maybe the Americans would say, *We've got some information, but we want to be in on the kill.*

A vision of Chase, big and easy and grinning and doing his puppy eyes, flashed through her, and all the hair on her arms lifted. She shivered, rubbing her arms.

The wounds of the last attacks in Paris had been immediate. She'd seen with her own eyes the blood on the street only a couple of blocks away, the bullet holes in the walls, she'd laid flowers in memorial. She'd opened her doors to people stranded, fed them in her restaurant for free that night, gone out the next night when so many people were huddling inside, and, along with Célie and Lina and her team and Célie's boyfriend Joss and her boss Dom and his wife and just so many, many people, been part of those Parisians who surged onto the terraces again, saying, *Fuck you. We might be afraid, and we might be wounded, but we won't hide and we won't give in. We're still Paris.*

So she knew plenty of people fighting terrorists emotionally, by refusing to give in to discrimination or by going out into the streets and celebrating life and being together.

But she had never known anyone fighting terrorists with bullets. Well, she knew some police officers, but more everyday riot police and traffic cops. Not RAID.

Not...she pushed her hand through her hair...not American black ops. Not outside of movies.

And a hundred scenes from Hollywood of men in black or camouflage with guns raised, going in, rose in her brain, and she tried to put Chase in the place of one of those men, and...

"You okay?" Célie said.

"Need a jacket?" Joss asked.

"I'm okay," Vi lied. And, as the line shifted forward, "Oh, thank God, we finally get to go in. This guy had better be hilarious."

He was, but not enough to take Vi's mind off the utter bizarreness of receiving a call from the health inspectors right at intermission. It was nine o'clock at night. "We just wanted to inform you as early as possible that the test results came back negative, and the salmonella in your clients was traced to spinach they purchased at the grocery store. Your restaurant is cleared, and you can return to operations."

Vi hung up and went back to her seat, staring at the comedian as he came back out on stage. She needed to call her publicist and try to get the vindication of Au-dessus and Violette Lenoir out as far and wide as possible, even if it would never have the same reach as the story that she had poisoned the president. She needed to call the U.S. embassy and see if the president would still come on his visit the day after tomorrow. She needed to get up early for the market tomorrow and figure out a menu that would absolutely knock everyone's socks off.

But she couldn't shake the conviction that her restaurant had been caught up in the throes of something she knew nothing about, that Chase was at the center of it...and that something might have happened that very day and she had no idea what.

The comedian might have been funny, his second half. But she didn't hear anything he said at all.

Chapter 16

Chase bounced into the kitchens of Au-dessus like he was about to bounce right through the ceiling. He felt like one of those men on the moon—if he wasn't careful, he'd bounce himself into space.

Au-dessus must be busy—what was it, eight p.m.?—because scents and sounds filled the kitchen, heady and clashing and warm. Color splashed across plates in ardent drama. There was motion everywhere and Vi was in full swing, precise and graceful like a whip cracking, pivoting between one station and another, checking food, confirming orders were coming up, calling for waiters.

Aww, look at her in her white coat and with her hair piled up on the back of her head and her skin glowing with perspiration, making everybody do what she wanted. She moved as if this whole kitchen was her orchestra, only they didn't line up in front of her where she could see them, they were all around her, and her whole body was the conductor's wand, jabbing, dancing, lifting, guiding, making sure everyone's note came in at just the right moment, just the right way. Hell, she was hot.

As soon as he saw her, all that energy in him figured out exactly what it wanted to do with itself.

He sprang across the kitchens, so happy to see her and so full of himself he could barely stand it, caught her by the waist just as she pivoted toward him, lifted her up, and swung her around.

All around them, every single motion stopped for five full seconds. Any threat making the gazelles here freeze? No. They were just staring at him and Vi. So he dismissed them from his attention.

"Miss me?" He grinned up at her, set her down, swept her into his arms to squeeze her, and kissed her hard.

Damn that felt good.

He tried to do it again, and Vi shoved him, ducked, squirmed and...wait, what? He loosened his arms, staring at her in confused hurt.

"What do you think you're doing?" she asked between her teeth.

Returning as a conquering hero? Ready to celebrate? Happy to see her? Okay, she didn't know about the conquering hero part because it was really better she not, but...wasn't the rest obvious? "Damn, I missed you," he said, and started to reach for her again.

She shoved him back from her. "I'm *working.*"

Well...yeah, but...he'd been gone for more than a week. And he had ten stitches up his shoulder from a shrapnel wound for *his* job, and he and his team had just taken out one of the most wanted terrorists in the world.

A little kiss might be nice.

"I just got in," he said. "Didn't you miss me?"

Vi stared at him, and a muscle in her jaw flexed. She spun suddenly toward her staff. "Get back to work. I don't need to remind you how perfect everything needs to be today. Adrien." She jerked her chin at a young man and then jerked her chin at Chase in a very similar way but with more disfavor and strode into her office.

He followed after her, starting to get a little indignant, and let the door close behind them. The office was glass-walled. Vi reached up and closed the blinds, then spun on him.

Chase folded his arms. "What a warm welcome."

He'd heard about these kinds of things. *You just shot Bin Laden or something, and you come home and your wife puts your kid in your arms and says his diaper needs changing and it's about time you started pitching in.*

But he'd never actually had to deal with it, that disconnect between his job and the life that went on without him, not on such an intimate scale as the one created by a couple. He didn't like it, he could flat out say that.

"You've been gone for over a week," Vi said, tight and hard. "Without a word. And now you waltz back in during the *service*? And kiss me and manhandle me in front of my *whole team*? The second day we're back open when I've got *everything* to prove to recover my reputation and the reputation of this restaurant from the depths to which you knocked it?"

"I didn't—it—" *It was for a good cause,* he wanted to say. *The salmonella thing. We* caught *Al-Mofti. Didn't you hear it on the news this morning?*

Probably this wasn't a good place for that revelation. Probably she needed a security clearance. Probably no one was going to give him the okay to tell a hot blonde Frenchwoman in leather anything about anything at all. They'd all seen James Bond, too.

He focused on the one thing he could solve. "Didn't you get my message?"

"Oh, I think I got it." Vi folded her arms. "The one where you're full of shit? Where you say all kinds of things when you're horny and then you forget them entirely and go off to live your own life until you're horny again?"

A muscle started to tick in his own jaw. "The one where I told you I was going to be gone for a while. The one where I asked you to get a new phone and give me the number in case I got a chance to call."

Her eyes blazed. "I don't sit by the phone and wait for *anyone* to call."

"Vi." He shoved his hand through his hair, hurt and anger twining inextricably. "Not even for me?"

It was a freaking cell phone, it wasn't as if he was asking her to shut herself into her apartment and not go out with her friends. And even if he was...people had to time calls like that all the time, when they were deployed. Their one chance to Skype with each other that week, to say hi, to touch home. It was *important* when you were deployed. It was important to the people at home, too, right? Important enough for them to sit at home one night if they had to, to catch that call?

Right?

"Just because I had hot sex with a man doesn't mean I have to change my life for him," Vi said coldly.

He almost staggered. "Okay, what the *fuck*, Vi?" The emotions thing they'd talked about. The fragile silky cloths in all their colors? She was *shredding* them, after he'd been so brave about letting them out?

He'd only been away a little over a week. It wasn't as if he'd gone for a golf trip.

"There are more fish in the sea," she said, with her chin up, her eyes hot.

His jaw clenched. A little fuse in his brain just sparked, and the flame started racing down a very short line to the dynamite in the middle of his head. "That goes both ways, honey," he said, even though he didn't mean it, and it was the worst possible thing he could say. She'd just flipped his freaking switch so damn bad.

Her eyes blazed. "Let's just sum it up, shall we? You think what you do is so much more important than me that it's beyond my comprehension and you could *never* tell me what it is. You think *this*," she waved at the blinds and presumably the kitchen beyond them, "my whole life, all my dreams, is casual road kill as you roll your tank over it to some other goal of yours. And you think my own emotions, my *worry* is so irrelevant and so unimportant that you can just disappear for a week and not even think about what I might *feel*. Just show up the first second I'm starting to put the life you destroyed back together and expect me to be thrilled to see you, no harm, no foul."

"I *left you a message!*" Chase roared. "It's in your goddamn journal under your stupid alarm clock with its fucking siren!"

Her eyes glittered. Her fingers flexed into her palms, forming fists and then forcing them apart. He drew a deep breath, trying to un-explode himself. He was pretty sure she was just like him. Once the yelling started, it was much easier to fight than to hear what was being said.

But un-exploding himself was hard to do. He felt as if he was trying to catch jagged shrapnel of his self-control and stuff it back into some semblance of a brain while it was still flying outward from the pressure of the blast. "Look. Vi. My job is really demanding and really important and sometimes—"

"And *mine's not?*" Her own fuse lit. He could see it happen. Just see the explosion as she lost all possibility of hearing him or rational discussion. "You *bastard.* Just get the hell out! I. Am. Working."

She jerked her office door open and strode out, slamming it behind her.

***

The glass walls weren't nearly sound-proof enough, and everyone lifted heads to stare at her as she strode back into the foment of activity.

She cast one fierce glance around, all it took to redouble her staff's activity. Energy radiated off her as if she was a radioactive core. She could not believe that jerk Chase. Disappear for over a week and then show up now, *now* of all times, when they'd just re-opened after a disastrous scandal, when there were at least three influential critics at the tables, and she was still clinging desperately to the increasingly slim possibility that Secret Service would suddenly flood the place and give her a half-hour warning that the American president was about to arrive.

But of course when had Chase ever for one moment really considered that *her* job was important?

She was twenty-eight years old, a Michelin two-star chef, and yet to him, just like to every other man, she was still some cute little woman whose career could never possibly be anything but fluff, easily brushed away when the man's *important* job took precedence.

A man who considered his job so important he couldn't even *tell* her about it. What the hell had he been doing this past week? Had he had anything to do with Al-Mofti's death that had been all over the media that morning? Was it coincidence that the dropping of the salmonella investigation happened at the same time? Could anyone possibly tell her *what the hell was going on* that put her restaurant at the center of this? Was the connection some figment of her imagination?

Lina came by, carrying an open bucket of liquid nitrogen, vapor rising off it as she called, ironically, "*Chaud, chaud, chaud! Chaud devant!*"

Mikhail shaved red tuna with a knife so sharp each slice was transparent.

One of their newer cooks dropped slices of beef into a pan with three centimeters of hot oil, and Vi leaned over him, grabbing the handle. "Not yet. Like this. Watch—"

And a wave ran through the kitchens, a stiffening in shock, like the moment when a lion appears and every member of the herd responds to the reaction of the first gazelle to spot it. In that alert kitchen, reaction time was probably shorter than half a second.

Secret Service? Vi spun and—

Black mask. A man struggling with a machine gun as if something was wrong with it, yelling at everyone to get down, and...

Holy fucking shit.

She swept the pan she was holding around in one hard arc and threw it, oil and all, at his head. Lina heaved that whole bucket of liquid nitrogen straight into the man's chest. Mikhail reversed his knife and threw.

And...oh, shit, there was another man, surging behind this one, and his gun was *not* jammed, and...

Vi leapt across the counter toward him, grabbing more pans as Lina threw herself on the floor and toward his legs and Adrien grabbed a blow torch, lunging in from the side as he squeezed out flame, and...

The second masked man staggered again, again, again, his machine gun giving a little spurt—her brain managed to process that she was seeing the impact of bullets on his body. And then she heard the bullets, in strange delayed echo in her brain, sounds it was finally identifying. She'd never heard bullets except on film. And at a distance that night...that night in November when...

"Vi, get the hell down!" someone was yelling. "Get *down!*"

But she'd already slammed the pot she held as hard as she could into the second man's face.

He went down, and she went down on top of him, her legs going right out from under her as if she'd slipped or something.

She landed in a seated position on his body as it hit the ground, his gun bony and hard under her butt.

"Is he wearing a vest? Vi, get the hell out of the way!" Chase was surging into her view, gun in hand. He grabbed her shoulders and literally threw her over the nearest counter. She bumped and slid and fell hard, and there was a lance of pain up from her side through her whole body.

"Thank Christ." Chase's voice. Then: "Two attackers. Everyone needs to go on full alert. This may not be the only location. Let me know when the streets are cleared and get me back-up as soon as you can. You, lock the door. Everyone else, *get back.*"

Vi dragged herself up—which was *ridiculously* hard to do, anyone would think she was a wimp or something—and managed to get an elbow onto the counter and pull herself upright enough to look over it.

Adrien was the one who had been sent to lock the door. Oh, God, in case there were more attackers. Chase was speaking into something, some kind of communication device she couldn't even see but it was obvious he wasn't talking to them, and he had ripped the second guy's shirt open. There was blood *everywhere.*

Human blood. Vi was used to blood. Most of her best dishes held some kind of meat. She sliced up flesh and caught the blood from roasts all the time. And her brother had a farm these days, had escaped Paris suburbs to seek their grandparents' peasant roots. She'd seen living animals butchered. She knew where her food came from.

But...this was like when a cow was butchered only...human.

"That's not a vest?" Adrien's voice sounded strained.

Vi *felt* strained. First of all, she couldn't seem to stand upright, and second, that looked *exactly* like suicide vests in the movies.

"It's C4." Chase's voice was clipped. "And he didn't detonate it." He yanked something out as he spoke. "If it had been TATP, we wouldn't be here. Will you people *get the fuck clear?*"

He looked up at Lina as if he was about to grab her and throw her after Vi.

Lina reached down suddenly and ripped the mask off the first man.

Vi stiffened. Was that Lina's weaselly, creepy, rapist cousin Abed?

He'd tried to shoot up her kitchens?

He'd tried to hurt her people?

"Vi, stay the hell down!" Chase yelled, but it didn't even penetrate as she threw herself back over the counter—everything hurt like *hell*—and threw herself at Abed.

"You pathetic coward asshole *putain de merde de connard de...*!" Vi kicked him, the nitrogen-fragilized sweatshirt fragmenting under the toe of her stout kitchen shoes, and Lina was kicking the other side of him, yelling at him, and...

A pounding on the door. Chase spoke, not to her team, and then ordered Adrien to let them in. A surge of male military might into the room, several people grabbing her and Lina, pushing and carrying them to safety.

Clearing and securing the room, clearing and securing the bodies—one body and Lina's cousin, who was groaning. Vi struggled, feeling unusually helpless, as a man in a black RAID uniform just hauled her all the way to the opposite side of her own kitchens as if *he* was in charge of them.

"Chase, you're hit," said a crisp, calm voice. A man who looked freckled all over but moved like a mountain lion in a killing mood. "We need an ambulance."

"We've got more injuries here," the man who had hauled Vi to the other side of the room called.

"Triage," someone ordered, while the freckled man sliced Chase's shirt off him with a lethal looking knife.

He was bleeding. Shit.

Vi looked at her fingers, wondering how his blood had gotten there. Had she grabbed him when he threw her?

Merde, she'd done something sloppy. Her chef whites were *all* bloody. She couldn't go around looking like that. A chef worked *clean*.

Damn, her hand hurt. Oh, yeah, the oil from the pan she threw, right. Blisters were already rising. *Merde*, both hands out? She had no luck. Seriously.

"Is everyone okay?" she yelled, and jerked against someone's hold, trying to free herself. "I need to check on my team."

The hand firmed. "Mademoiselle, we need you to lie down," a black-uniformed man said.

Chase's head jerked around.

"It's just the liquid nitrogen," Lina said. "I've had burns before. I'll be okay."

Lina's chef's coat had done its job—any nitrogen that had splashed when she threw the bucket hadn't soaked into the cloth but rolled off it and evaporated. Her hand was cold-burned a bit, probably more from punching Abed's nitrogen-soaked shirt than from the splash of nitrogen, which would have vaporized at the heat of her skin.

Abed, now, was wearing a cotton sweatshirt—he was going to have some serious burns over his torso. Not to mention the knife wound from Mikhail, and the splash of oil over his face from her pan.

Good.

Vi wanted to kick him again. She hoped she'd broken several ribs. She hoped they took him to Guantánamo and interrogated him for *years*. "You fucking asshole!" she shouted at him, just in case he'd been ignoring her the first time. "Adrien, is everyone else okay?"

No one was trying to make *him* lie down. Probably all these military men assumed *he* was the head of the kitchen, damn it, just because he was male.

"No other injuries, chef," Adrien said. "A couple of burns from people grabbing hot pots to throw."

Burns. Vi relaxed in relief. They knew all about burns.

"Mademoiselle. *Please lie down.*" The hand pushed on her shoulder.

"It's my restaurant!" Vi snapped at the hand's hard-jawed owner. *Merde*, any idiot could see this was a situation she needed to take charge of. Even if they were physically unhurt, her staff was going to be devastated by this. And half their diners must be complaining about what was taking their food so long. *Merde*, this was all her reputation needed. She could see the reviews now: *Cold food, melting structures, and no matter how artistic Violette Lenoir imagines herself to be, her dramatic splashes of red across a plate only manage to look like a massacre occurred in the kitchens. Perhaps she's trying to suggest how close all carnivores are to the blood and death of their meals, but this reviewer found his appetite slaughtered in the process.*

"Fuck." A long way across the room, Chase was staring at her from where Jake had sat him on a counter. His face had gone white. "Vi, is that your blood? Jesus, is she hemorrhaging?"

"I feel really sleepy," Vi said, confused. Even her voice sounded fuzzy.

"Here, Vi." Lina, the only person in the entire room who seemed to understand Vi at all, scooted a little closer, proffering her shoulder. "I'll help you up. Lean on me."

So Vi did. Just for a second. Just to help herself get to her feet.

And then she just faded into black.

Chapter 17

"Let me get this straight." Vi's voice. Chase pressed a hand to the hospital wall, taking a deep breath. Dizziness swept over him. A nurse hovered next to him, trying to take his elbow, furious with him for being on his feet at all.

"You had information to suggest someone might try to stage a *ricin* attack in *my* restaurant. Ricin. An odorless, tasteless poison with no possible cure. And you *didn't inform me?*"

Oh, good, she was in fighting form. Chase let his head and shoulder sink against the wall, just breathing for a moment. The last time he'd seen her awake, they'd been loading her into the ambulance, and she'd been trying to fight her way to consciousness enough to argue the EMTs into slowing down and letting her talk to her sous-chef first.

She'd lost the battle. Chase, being bundled into an ambulance himself and arguing about it, had carried with him a horrible, heart-freezing impression of Vi fading, not able to fight her corner. Torso wounds were almost always bad, but, within that context, his had been more minor than hers. They'd managed to keep the infection from the nick in his intestines down, and he'd lost a lot less blood. But Vi's had touched the liver as well as leading to hemorrhaging, and it had required several small surgeries to stabilize and repair the various types of damage done in order of priority. She'd been medicated, mostly out of it, for the first three days, and he'd been going quietly frantic at his inability to talk to her and convince himself she was going to be fine.

A wheelchair appeared beside him, the nurse trying once again to get him to take it. He shook his head. It was only a few steps into the room. It wasn't his wound making him dizzy. It was Vi's wound, and finally hearing her voice again.

"Ma'am, it was imperative we not reveal we were on to them." A male voice. Was that Brandon, the CIA case officer? Be good for him to have to deal with Vi in person. CIA guys always forgot what human flesh and blood was like. "And the information wasn't credible. We were following a lot of threads tracking Al-Mofti, and this one seemed like a red herring."

"It was credible enough for you to shut down my restaurant claiming salmonella!" Vi flared. Vibrant, passionate.

Thank you, Jesus. Chase was not very religious. But there were moments when he just simply did not know what else to do with all the feelings he had.

When her body had gone limp like that, terror had surged up in his, ghastly, clammy. He'd seen too many people die.

Not Vi, not Vi, not Vi.

Vi was *life.*

Passionate, impulsive, risk-loving, overconfident—*insanely* overconfident—hot-tempered, fighting for her space, her paths, her choices...*alive.*

He loved civilians. They were soft-bellied and incomprehensible and sometimes it was like loving his stuffed animals when he was a kid, but he still absolutely loved them. They gave him a reason for being. As a five-year-old, he'd piled those stuffed animals up in a fort made of brush and gone out to fight for them against imagined foes or sometimes his cousins and siblings. He'd made up conversations with them, pretended they could connect.

Vi was a civilian, too. She had that innocence. Or she'd *had* it. But she wasn't soft-bellied. She'd never felt fluffy and made-up. She, too, was a doer, not someone who talked about what other people should do. He'd always felt as if, underneath the battles they had, they understood each other. From the very first moment he'd met her, life force had reached out to life force and just *surged.*

They'd had to tell him over and over and over again that she was okay, as they were loading him and Vi in separate ambulances. But he'd known that all they were really trying to do was get him to calm down enough so that they could follow their best practices for torso wounds and transport the victims to the hospital as fast as they could.

Because torso wounds were shitty. That was why men expecting combat wore body armor, but Chase hadn't, of course, floating on the success of his mission and the assumption that he'd made the world safe again, going to see his girlfriend so she could admire what a hero he was.

"You're an international hero now, Ms. Lenoir," a male voice was saying. "I think you'll find that salmonella story has been buried under a much more fascinating one."

"I'm a hero?" Vi sounded startled. "My whole team brought the first one down. And Chase got the second one."

"Your whole team are heroes. But yes, you and Lina Farah have become the superstars in the world's eyes. We're keeping Mr., ah, Smith's identity secret."

Silence. Wow, Vi must be stymied.

"Once we got Al-Mofti, we found that he *was* producing ricin, so I think we were right to shut down your restaurant until we got a better idea of the threat. Of course, we shut the ricin operation down, and we thought we had stopped any attempts at terrorist attacks coordinated around the U.S. president's visit, but we still had a couple of people staking out your restaurant and every single other possible attack site in the city just in case."

"Hundreds of men," Elias said. "Throughout the city. Some openly, some more discreetly. It's not that we weren't taking seriously the random mention of your restaurant that we had picked up, it was just that it seemed a least likely target among many likely ones, and we thought Al-Mofti's death would disrupt any plans. Plus, with regards to your restaurant, we'd been very focused on the ricin threat and knew we had eliminated that one. I guess we miscalculated the influence of a personal grudge and erratic personality on your pastry chef's cousin's actions, on his willingness to substitute one style of attack for another and avenge Al-Mofti."

"See, if you'd *talked to me* I could have told you all about that jerk," Vi snapped. "*Lina* could have told you about him. I could have told you that if anyone ever gave him a gun and explosives to play with, he'd probably go try to use them on some women he hated."

Chase fought men who hurt civilians all the time. And yet he would never understand them.

He pushed away from the wall and eased himself into the hospital room door.

Since both Elias and the CIA case officer had positioned themselves with a view of the door, they both saw him immediately, of course.

Washed out, hair limp, Vi had the head of the bed elevated enough she could half sit as she argued with Elias and Brandon Miller, and in addition to the expected wrappings around her ribs, she had gauze all over her left hand. Right hand in a splint, left hand in gauze, their motion more limited than usual, but both still gesticulating to make her point.

Until she saw him and her hands dropped in her lap.

"Hey, honey," he said, low. His chest felt so shaky. "Mademoiselle Gorgeous."

Her eyes grew very red. She grabbed a stuffed animal from the huge pile of them filling a chair and threw it at him. High up, far from his wounded side. Where it would sail over his shoulder and not touch him if he didn't catch it.

He caught it. A floppy dark brown bear with silky, curly fur and a big nose. Very huggable. He hugged it and made his way across to her bed. "Room for me on this?"

She eased to the side, trying to control her wincing. He eased onto his share of the narrow bed, trying not to wince, too. Her warm shoulder against his, her thigh brushing his, their calves touching. Alive. Vi was struggling not to cry.

Alive, alive, alive. Thank God.

He gave Elias a beseeching look. He knew Elias was his only hope. Brandon never remembered to be human.

"I need a cup of coffee," Elias said. "Mademoiselle Lenoir, do you mind if we take a break and come back later?"

Vi shook her bent head, looking almost, for a second—and this was really scary—*humble.*

The other two men slipped out.

"Honey," Chase said. He had no idea what else to say. How to encompass it. *You're alive. Thank God.*

187

He wanted to wrap her up in his body and hold on as tight as he could, but neither of them were in any shape for squeezing.

He couldn't even take her hand properly. Both her hands were hurt. He took the wrist of the nearest one, the one with the gauze, and gazed at the tips, calluses peeking out from the gauze. His eyes stung.

Vi said nothing. He could hear her breathing, shaky. She nestled closer into him, turning her head into his body and taking another deep breath. At least their two unwounded sides matched, so they could roll a little toward each other.

"I haven't been able to *see* you," she whispered. "They were always operating on me, or you. I've been in surgery three times, and they kept medicating me, and they said you were okay, but that's not the same as *seeing*."

"I'm so sorry," he said. "I should never, ever have let you get hurt."

She lifted her head. "Was that your job?" The sheen of tears in her eyes turned them very green, but they met his steadily.

Well...no, actually. They'd called the coast clear. Al-Mofti was caught—that *was* his job, and he'd done it—and the threat, they thought, cut off at its primary source. Sure, RAID had kept people in place around the city, including a discreet presence near her restaurant, for a couple of extra days, just on "better safe than sorry" principles. But personal protection of every civilian in Paris had never been his official job. France had a police force for that.

He was a bullet, not a shield. He protected civilians by taking out the villains. And as a bullet, someone always fired him. Called the target, sent him and his team after it.

"It's always my job," he said. "Vi...always."

188

Sometimes dealing with civilians could be frustrating. Even though a part of Chase always loved civilians, there were many encounters with lazy, rude, entitled people that made a man wonder why the hell he was risking his life for them.

But Vi—never. As soon as he first saw her, he knew exactly why a man would risk his life for her.

"They're my kitchens," she said. "I think keeping people safe in them is *my* job."

His mouth tensed. He shook his head. "It's my job."

Her mouth quirked just a little. "That's not what your sexy friend said." She nodded to the door. "He said it was RAID's job. But that they thought the threat had been eliminated."

Sexy? Trust Vi to hand him a lifeline. As if she knew he might drown in all those emotions like regret and anger and pain if she didn't hand him humor. As if she knew him.

He took a breath, focusing on it. Yeah, he could use this. He could find laughter here. "My what friend? Brandon's sixty. Do you have a father figure complex you never told me about? I can dye my hair gray and act bossy."

She smiled a little, that sheen of tears in her eyes warming with more life. "The *sexy* one. You know, black hair, green eyes, an ironic way of looking at you? Looks as if his parents came from Algeria? Why didn't you tell me you had hot friends? I have single girlfriends, you know."

"Are you contemplating an orgy?" Chase considered. "You know, I'm not entirely sure I'd go for that in real life, but..."

Vi touched her splinted hand gently to his shoulder and gave him a feather-light pretend punch. Her gentleness was unsettling. Had this damn wound made him start looking *fragile* or something?

Or did it just matter that much to her that he not get hurt again?

189

He closed his hand around her splint, lifted her hand to his mouth, and kissed her two unsplinted fingers. His eyes closed a moment. *Thank God you're alive.*

"Also, you already act bossy, Chase."

He opened his eyes to find her watching him as if she was glad he was alive, too. God, he couldn't believe he'd ever used fragile silk as a metaphor for his emotions around her. They were so powerful they turned *him* into fragile silk, shredding him ruthlessly, but that wasn't quite the same.

"*You* can talk," he said.

"I don't *act* bossy. I *am* the boss."

He dropped her splint to sink his hand into her hair as one of the few spots on her body it seemed safe to squeeze. "God, I love you."

She closed her eyes a moment. "Chase. You should *really* be more careful about saying that."

"Why?" he asked, baffled. When had he ever been careful about his life? They were lying here both with bullet wounds in them, and she wanted him to be careful about *words*?

"Because I could get hurt!"

He blanked. And then ice slipped over his soul. "You mean, being with me could make you a target? Did they say that was why those two came after Au-dessus?" He'd let hints of who he was slip out to Vi's friends to stir the pot, to maybe shake something loose with some rumors, but had that made Vi the focus of retaliation?

"Not physically hurt! My emotions!"

He stared at her indignantly. "Good God, Vi, I can't protect your *emotions*! How the hell do you expect me to do that?"

"I don't expect you to protect me at all!" she retorted, equally indignant. "*I* fight for *myself*. All I'm saying is—oh, forget it." She stared at the ceiling, exasperated.

Chase's lips parted. "You still think I'm full of shit, don't you?"

An ironic side glance.

"That I'm just some arrogant jock who hits on any woman he sees without thinking too much about the consequences."

No comment. Just that ironic gaze.

He huffed out a breath. "*Fine.* Yes. I pretty much never saw a hot woman I didn't go after. Monogamy is going to be a tiny bit of a switch for me. But Vi...you make me go Wow. Every single cell in my body lights up, every time the thought of you even crosses my mind." He took her splinted hand and rubbed his chest with the two free fingers. "Understand?"

She looked dubious.

"Vi. It's *not* as if you have a confidence problem. You've got to know you can beat out every other woman, as far as I'm concerned."

She tilted her head. Apparently that angle worked quite well on her.

He smiled a little. "*Damn,* I love you."

Her green eyes were skeptical, challenging. Wanting him to pick up the gauntlet and prove her wrong.

Well. He loved picking up gauntlets. He kissed her fingertips again. "I'm surprised I didn't betray the whole mission when we took out Al-Mofti, I was glowing so much. It's amazing your fellow Parisians even let a radioactive man walk around on the street like that. Maybe that explains some of the looks I get. I was beginning to think Parisians were just rude."

She shook her head at him. But her eyes were crinkling with flattered laughter.

"So how could you get hurt?" His eyes flicked involuntarily over her hands and the thick bandages around her torso, and abruptly all the cocky persuasion went out of him. He just flattened, a balloon sucked free of helium.

Vi tried to grip her hair with exasperation and winced away from how much that hurt, pulling her gauzed hand free immediately. Chase winced, too, taking that sign of pain hard in the belly. "Because!" Vi said. "I only just met you and already..." She faltered. "Already, when I imagine you not alive, it's as if this bright, hot power source that warms my whole life gets extinguished. Everything grows cold and dark. And I have a *good* life, Chase. I *made it* good. Nothing about it felt cold and dark before I met you. What's going to happen to me if suddenly I need you as my power source?"

"Oh." Chase could only look at her. "Oh." Yeah, of course. This happened to his buddies all the time. Women just couldn't take the thought of investing their emotions into someone whose job involved so much risk of death. "Oh."

He didn't know what else to say. How did a man respond to his dismissal from someone's heart because he might *die?* That risk of death had always made every single living moment of his life seem that much more valuable to *him.* It was one of the reasons he loved the risk so much—how alive he felt. How valuable his life felt.

"You know I can't *count* on you."

Well, yeah. Yeah. Even if he stayed alive, he'd be deployed and shit, and she'd need help with a plumbing problem or something, and...actually, it was very hard to imagine Vi not able to handle a plumber. Maybe he was going off on the wrong tangent.

"That's a terrible amount of power to give to someone who chases any blonde in leather he sees," Vi tried to explain.

He'd thought she was going to say *to someone who might die.* His eyebrows flicked together. "But I don't do that any more. You blew all the other hot blondes out of the water. Actually, I think you're so hot that you boiled all the rest of the water dry and those other blondes just wilted and died, unable to take the heat."

"You've only known me a few days, Chase! You started chasing me the instant you saw me."

Wait. She was worried about something else entirely from what he had imagined. He could work with this. He couldn't promise not to die, but he could definitely promise not to chase other hot blondes.

"Well, that's true," he allowed. "*I* know the difference in how I feel, but obviously you weren't around for the previous feelings, so you have no basis for comparison. It's probably a lot to take on trust." He nodded briskly. "How much time do you need? I'm on leave, obviously, until I heal, but it sure would be nice to get this straightened out before they ship me off somewhere again."

Green eyes just stared at him. What, did he sound crazy or something?

"It's okay," he said, what he hoped was reassuringly. "The bluebonnets don't bloom until April. And Grandma is healthy as a horse. So we don't have to make any hasty decisions."

Pretty much his entire being reared up in rebellion at the idea of slow patience to get what he wanted. There might have been more than one reason he'd done so lousy at sniper training.

Vi just kept staring at him.

Oh. He probably shouldn't have mentioned... "You forgot I'd be deployed again somewhere else, didn't you? I knew that civilian thing would come back to bite me in the butt. I know I should have warned you before you fell crazy in love with me and all, but you don't have a security clearance, and I guess I was thinking that you seem to have a pretty full life and could probably handle it, when I was away."

"Of course I could handle it!" Vi said indignantly. "I can handle anything!"

His face softened into a smile. "Damn, I love you."

She flushed from her chin right up to her hairline. It was astonishing and fascinating. He'd told her multiple times that he loved her. *Now* she blushed?

What did that mean, exactly? That it had never even occurred to her until this last time that he might be telling the truth?

"I'm supposed to be here five more months," he said. "Of course, now I'm wounded, so I'd normally be shipped home, but I told them I wanted to stay with you. Next tour, maybe I could put in for something longer term with SOCEUR. Something that would at least put me in Europe more. Not to complain or anything, but I am getting really, really sick of the Middle East."

Vi's eyes were so large and intense. They made him feel like he needed to keep floundering to stay afloat.

"That's if I stay in," he said. "I might not forever. You know, long-term, and—"

"Don't get out on my account," Vi said firmly. "Don't you *ever* do less than you want to do on my account. And I won't do less than I want to do on yours."

She warmed his whole middle. "I love you." He just liked saying it. It made him feel whole.

And her flush deepened.

Hunh. "Is this the first time you've actually listened to me when I've said that?" He felt rather indignant.

"It's the blood loss," she said. "It's weakening my brain."

How she almost made him laugh about the fact that she had nearly gotten killed he did not know. His brothers in arms managed that kind of humor all the time, but somehow he hadn't expected it here. "You are so damn perfect for me," he said. "I'm sorry if I'm not perfect for you."

She shrugged. Awkwardly, careful of her wound. "Well, I've only known you a couple of weeks. Even I can't get a man in shape that fast."

Hey. He narrowed his eyes at her.

She gave a little smug smile that showed those dimples.

"I know you think the last thing you need in your life is a cocky, arrogant man who thinks he is the shit," Chase began.

Her dimples deepened. Such an odd, beautiful look on her pale face, surrounded by limp hair. The beauty of courage, of life. "But you really are the shit. So I might have to make an exception."

He blinked a second. "You really think so?"

"Yeah." Even with the dimples, she looked tired. Of course. When her dimples faded, there was a little hint of sadness, or maybe an awareness of the existence of sadness, that she hadn't had before. But there was a softness around her mouth, a curve of...well, it kind of looked like *love*. "Yeah, I really do. I was thinking about it, once I got them to stop drugging me so I could think. How you keep so much laughter in a world where a lot of men would go dark, and how you're still such a damn good guy, too. You sew up my leather jacket. You try to say you're sorry. You know that being a hero is more than facing bullets. In fact, I think you take the facing bullets part for granted, and you work harder on the other stuff. The cuddles."

Now *he* was starting to blush. He rubbed the back of his head, overcome and afraid he would stutter or something if he even tried to open his mouth. "*You're* the one who got wounded," he finally managed.

"You did, too," she pointed out.

Oh, yeah.

"You *forgot?*"

"Only for a second," he said hurriedly.

"Chase." She rested her splinted hand on his chest and closed her eyes a moment. As if *she* was overwhelmed.

"When I said I was the shit, I really only meant I was a badass," he confided in a whisper.

A little smile curled her mouth while her eyes stayed closed. "I'm sure you are," she said soothingly. "I mean *I'm* the one who has to beat terrorists up with pots while you have a gun, but you're not too bad."

That was a little bit of a sore point with him right that second, actually. It had taken years off his life when he came out of that office to realize what was happening. Still, she *had* been magnificent. "God, Vi."

"Lina's squirmy cousin. Do you know I once had to push him down the stairs in their building when I was a teenager?"

"He's the same kind of guy who would throw acid in a little girl's face for going to school in some other part of the world and pretend it was for God, when it was really because he had a putrid soul."

"Is Lina going to have a hard time? Be questioned?"

"She'll certainly be *questioned*, but since she was clearly fighting him and her own parents had several times reached out to the police about their worries about him, I don't think she'll have to deal with any suspicion. Just an attempt to find out as much as they can. You should ask Elias and Brandon. I help gather intel on missions, but I'm not an analyst."

"Who was the other guy? Are there any other attacks planned?"

"I don't do interrogation, honey. But I'm pretty sure they'll find that out. You did good, capturing him alive."

"His gun jammed, didn't it?"

Chase nodded, all the hairs on the back of his neck rising yet again. He couldn't talk about it. His throat and lungs shrank into tiny balls when his brain even ghosted close to what would have happened if Abed's gun hadn't jammed.

He'd stayed behind in the office ten seconds to take a deep breath and calm down, and that might have been two seconds too long.

But even if he had followed her immediately, without that stroke of luck with the gun of the first man in, he might not have been able to make a difference. If Abed's gun hadn't jammed...he couldn't draw a gun faster than bullets sprayed from an AK-47.

Vi's face was very somber. "Damn it. You should have told me."

"Vi. If any of us believed you were still in danger, we would have kept that restaurant shut down."

She glared at him.

"Well, we would have, Vi. I'm sorry. I couldn't tell you, because I was already messing up the *covert* part of my mission enough as it was. We wanted to shake Al-Mofti loose, not scare him into deep hiding. Vi...for as long as I stay in, there will be plenty of times when I can't tell you what I'm doing until long after it's done."

"I understand that. But this was *my* restaurant. *My* people."

He couldn't say anything. He understood exactly why it bothered her so much.

She rested her splinted hand over his, curling the finger and thumb around the edge of his palm insofar as she could. Acceptance. He liked it so much. It just uncurled in him like a flower opening, which was the silliest image for a man in his profession, but he liked it way the hell better than all his death and dying metaphors. *I can disagree with you and be mad at you and still accept and love you and be glad that you're alive,* that touch said.

See? He always felt that Vi went straight to his heart. Or maybe it was that their hearts beat in the same way.

"I know it's stupid that you light up my life so much," Vi said, and those words *light up my life* just kind of shot through him, sparkling, "because I only met you a few days ago and we fight half the time. But...I like fighting with you. It's got zing." She made a wiggling motion of her fingers into the air, apparently indicative of his zing.

He settled his own hand over her wrist, holding that since they couldn't hold hands. "Everything about you has zing, Vi. You make me feel as if I'm going snap-crackle-pop all the time."

"Except sometimes," she said. "Sometimes you're like old pajamas."

Wait, what? "Uh—"

"Like I can be comfortable with you. No matter how tired, or how battered, or how wounded I feel."

He ran his fingers from her shoulder to her wrist. Being so wounded you couldn't even do a proper cuddle was shitty. Maybe he was getting ready for a career that didn't involve so many bullets.

Hard to let go, though. To leave the safety of the world in other hands while he sat on his own.

"It's a powerful combination," she said. "That much zing, and that much peace."

Yeah.

"Hey, Vi?" he said, low.

She angled her head.

He'd noticed that before. When his voice dropped, when he had to say something vulnerable and intimate, she listened to him better.

"Will you marry me?"

God, she had the most beautiful green eyes. They just fixed on a man as if all his worth was held in whether they would blink yes or no.

"I figured out what to do about our grandmothers. I thought maybe we could do two ceremonies, one here and one in Texas. That would work, wouldn't it? I mean, half my family would come to both, so you never know about my grandmother, she might end up coming to both, too. But that way it's not an ultimatum, which it's better not to give my grandma. And—"

Vi put her burned hand over his lips.

He caught himself and slowly sighed, sighed, sighed, trying to sigh out all his need to argue, convince, push, persuade, and just wait. Let her think. Let her answer.

"When are the bluebonnets?" Vi asked. "April?"

He nodded.

"Ten months from now?"

He double-checked on his fingers. "Nine."

"I'll tell you what: if I haven't killed you by January, it's a yes."

His heart leaped. All the blood in his body just seemed to rush to his wounds and *heal* them. He tightened his hold on her wrist, one of the few parts of her body where he could hold her tightly right now. "Do you mean actually kill me or just try to kill me? Because I'm pretty hard to kill."

She started to laugh a little, and it was the way she did it, her eyes shimmering with happiness, that went straight to his heart. "I think your ability to survive me, and stick it out, and keep coming back for more is one of the things I want to make sure you can keep doing long-term. So if I only try to kill you and you survive it, it's still a yes."

She was laughing at him. And laughter leapt in him, too. That glorious *aliveness* that he'd felt from the first moment he saw her. "Damn, I wish I could hug you. Can I tell my grandma?"

She laughed again, as if laughing was easy now, even with a bullet wound through her torso, and a broken hand, and burns, even with terrorists to fight. "Can I *meet* your grandma?"

He beamed. She wanted to meet his family! "Of course. You're going to *love* her. Almost as much as you love me."

He peeked at her hopefully.

She held up her splinted hand and brought the index and thumb so close together paper couldn't pass through them. "You mean this much?"

He frowned at her.

She widened her thumb and forefinger a millimeter. "This much?"

"Violette Lenoir."

She held up both hands, about ten inches apart. "This much?"

He took her wrist and stretched one arm as far out as it could go without pulling on her wound. The other was limited by the bed.

"I don't know," she said judiciously. "Seems a bit much for a man whose real name I don't even know."

"Oh, shit." He'd forgotten about that. He clapped his hand to his face. "My name's going to be on the marriage certificate. Isn't that enough?"

"Or even know for sure what he does for a living." She gave him an assessing glance, and her eyes glinted with mischief. "Rangers, maybe? Delta Force?"

Chase gave her a puzzled look. "Are those soccer teams or something?"

"Probably Delta Force," she decided, her eyes full of mirth. "Those guys are the best, right?"

"They're *what*?"

"Almost as good as the British SAS or the 2e REP commandos."

Chase narrowed his eyes at her, fulminating.

But he didn't really care, because she looked so alive and happy now that she was teasing him, and all that zing was back, but with this underlying solidity, this sense of *hey, we're going to really try to make this work. She's in it to win it with me, too.*

And when Vi was in something to win it, he was pretty sure she didn't lose very often.

She grinned now, so full of herself to have provoked him. "Do you even *remember* you have a small trident tattooed high up on your left shoulder? Are special ops supposed to have identifying tattoos?"

No, but he'd been nineteen and bursting with pride, and so far none of his commanding officers had insisted he have it lasered off.

"You were looking at my naked body?" He clapped his hands to cover his nipples, horrified.

And she giggled so hard. Giggled like a girl, a young girl, who only ever knew happiness.

I love you so damn much, Vi. You don't get it yet. We're lying here, wounded from a terrorist attack, and we can be this happy, just because it's the two of us.

He drew a deep, deep breath and let it out in an exaggerated sigh of defeat. He glanced around to make sure Elias and Brandon hadn't come back. He leaned in close to her ear and ow, that pulled at his wound, but he couldn't risk saying this out loud. "It's...*Chester*," he whispered.

"Chester?" she said out loud, with that erotic precision and rolled R of hers.

"*Shhh.*" He waved his hands frantically.

"What's wrong with that?"

"For God's sake, you people don't know anything about names here in France, do you? I'd better name our kids."

"It does sound a little...presidential, maybe, for you."

"We'll consider it our safe word. If you ever say it out loud, I will instantly stop making love to you and go out for a run or something to rid myself of the horror."

She laughed.

"No, seriously, Vi. I mean it. My name is Chase. I stopped answering to anything else when I was four. Chase Alvarado-Callihan, to be exact. Lenoir is going to be *so* much easier to spell."

"You're so damn cute," she said helplessly.

A little smugness settled in his body. It was good to be cute. "Now you have to love me to the moon and back," he said. "You said the name was all that was stopping you."

She rested her hand against his cheek, splint and touch of callused fingers. Her face softened. The humor slid away, but all the happiness stayed, and it was the most radiant, warming thing. "I'm pretty sure I will."

Chapter 18

Bold, squarish letters:

How about April for a date? The bluebonnets in Texas are beautiful then.

Under it, a drawing of two entwined wedding rings, and the signature, *Chase.*

A cell phone number under his name.

Vi looked up at Chase. Who was actually *blushing* a little bit. "You wrote that the first night?"

They had just been released from the hospital, their first evening back in her apartment. Police security protected the door to the building. Chase's identity had been kept out of the papers, but Vi's was all over the place, and it turned out being a national hero drew an overwhelming amount of attention.

"It was three in the morning," he said defensively. "And you have no idea how hot you are. I was sexually depleted and possibly sappy."

"And right after that, you went and had my restaurant shut down without even warning me?"

His shoulders sank. "To keep you safe," he said.

She glared at him.

"To keep the world safe," he corrected. "And all your staff. And all your guests."

She held up a finger. "You still should have told me about it. Keeping the staff and guests safe is *my* responsibility."

He nodded resolutely. And then added, "Going on top-secret missions that affect multiple lives is mine."

They gazed at each other a long, stubborn moment. Impossible really to tell who was the first one to start to smile just enough to encourage the other to smile, too. "I'm not giving in on this one," Vi warned.

"I know. Of course, I'm not either."

They both broke into bigger smiles. "You know it's really kind of fun to box with someone who is up to your weight," Vi said. "It doesn't happen that often."

Chase grinned at her and flexed one arm to make his biceps pop.

She laughed and returned her gaze to the phone number he had left her from the very first, and the drawing of wedding rings. He had left that note as he left her bed to go take over her career choices with macho conviction, hadn't he? She shook her head at the impossible tangle of emotions he evoked. "It's a good thing you have such good survival skills."

"Five months and seven days left," Chase said brightly.

She gave him a querying look.

"Until January 1. If I survive until then, you said. I was going to do little tally marks on the wall behind your bed like they do in prison movies or ones where people are stranded on a desert island. I get hot sex still, though, right? I mean, you're not going to deny a man basic sustenance."

She laughed and shook her head at him and turned the page in her journal.

Damn, you're beautiful.

XO.

Chase.

She looked back at him.

He arched his head to try to see the page, and blushed some more. "That was the night you fell asleep. I was thinking I should probably go, but then...I didn't."

Her cheeks felt a little heated, too. *Damn, you're beautiful.* She wanted to frame the words, to keep them for years and years and years.

She turned the page.

Got to make a quick trip out of town. Don't mention it to anyone, okay?

A heart symbol this time, and *Chase.*

And:

P.S. Call me maybe?

A funny stick figure holding a phone, giant tears arching out of his eyes and over his head an image of his heart breaking.

A smile trembled on her lips. Funny, demanding, arrogant Chase, who apparently had never once just walked out on her without making sure she knew he'd be back.

"I put it in a very obvious spot!" he said. "Pinned open by your alarm clock. How could you not have seen it?"

She leaned back on the pillows, demonstrating flinging her arm out to fumble and knock an alarm clock to the floor. She still couldn't stretch her arm out far, the movement pulled too much at her torso.

"Fine," he said. "Next time I'll write it in Sharpie on your forehead so you can see it when you look in the bathroom mirror."

"Or, alternatively, if you want to survive, you could try the bathroom mirror itself. Or a note on the door. Pretty nearly impossible for me to leave the apartment without seeing a note on the door."

"I sometimes go out the window," Chase confided. "Just to keep life interesting."

Vi had to grin. "You do keep life interesting, all right."

Chase looked smug, licked his finger, and drew a point in his favor in the air.

She laughed. It was a happy thought, all that life and interest and challenge and a willingness always to answer her own challenges, always to pick up her gauntlets.

"Speaking of keeping life interesting, you know what's terrible about hospitals?"

"Oh, I could make a really long list at this point," Vi said, a little grimly. Pretty much the only good thing she had found about hospitals so far was that hospitals were the reason they were both alive. It turned out survival could be quite a painful, tedious process full of doctors and nurses with no respect for a woman's privacy, absolutely terrible food when Lina and Célie couldn't sneak them some, and a relentless smell of antiseptic.

"The lack of sex." Chase shook his head. "It's insane what they expect a man to live without. Also, French daytime television is terrible, can I just say? There was some exercise show with the woman trying to convince other women to do step exercises in high heels. You people are nuts. Fortunately, it *did* give me some ideas about you and steps and high heels, but I'm saving those for a more-healed rainy day. Now for barely out of the hospital, thank God you're alive, take it very easy sex, I was thinking..."

"That sometimes you talk too much." Vi put her fingers over his lips. "*I* was thinking..." She turned off the light, gave them just that gentle twilight of the July summer evening. "...something like this." She drew her fingertips very, very lightly, as if he was fragile, all the way down his arm to the back of his knuckles, then took his hand and covered her breast.

"Vi." His voice had gone low and rough. "I'm so glad you're alive that I wake up in nightmares about it, over and over."

"I know." And nightmares about everyone in her kitchens being killed, and about terrible, jagged things she couldn't even identify before they woke her in sharp terror. She shifted his hand over her breast, stroking herself with him. The hunger that woke in her was sharp and ferocious, a tantalizing counterpoint to the gentleness with which they touched. "Tonight, let's see if we find a way to get some sleep."

Chapter 19

Healing

"What are you doing?"

"Planning a restaurant. I've got to do something while I'm convalescing. Besides, since I'm forced to learn delegation skills and how to run a restaurant while not being actually in it, I might as well put it to good use to expand to new horizons. And I'm internationally famous now. I've got *backers.* I've got ideas down for four more restaurants, but I'm thinking it's probably better to open one at a time."

"Have I mentioned how crazy I am about you?"

"What did I do this time?"

"You literally take a bullet, turn it into a convenient rung on your ladder, and keep on climbing. Nothing keeps you down."

"Down's not a fun place to be, to be honest. It's pretty boring."

"Let me see if I can keep you entertained."

***

"Hard time sleeping?" Soft voice, in the dark.

"Oh, yeah." Resigned. "I just see it, you know? All the time. See the muzzle start to point toward you, see that blood all over your chef's jacket."

"Yeah." Very soft. "I know. I see things, too."

No other words. Just the shifts of the sheets, the touch of skin, the sounds of holding on.

***

"What are you doing?"

"Oh, I...nothing."

"What does that mean? Why do you look so guilty? Let me see that notebook. Chase, if you're planning another secret mission to destroy my restaurant without telling me..."

"No! Damn it, you have a suspicious mind. I'm thinking about what I would like to do when—if—I get out. I keep having this vision of an adventure sports organization that gets disenfranchised kids out on the slopes or up in the air, gives them a source of physical accomplishment and power and adventure that doesn't come from violence."

A little breath of a pause. A voice gone carefully neutral. "You're thinking about getting out?"

"Well, I...it wears out your body, you know. Bullet wounds and constant joint impacts and all the other stuff. I'll start feeling it in a few years. And I...I mean...if a man had *kids*, you know, he might want to...be there, and not..."

"Are you *blushing*?" A gentle hand in his hair. No splint on it now. The bone had healed faster than the recovery from the bullet.

"I'm a hardened warrior. I eat nails for breakfast. Of *course* I am not *blushing*. It's possible I'm feeling overheated from thinking about pink peekaboo panties."

"You certainly didn't blush the first time you mentioned kids. About two minutes after you met me."

"Yeah, but...Vi...it's starting to become *real*."

***

"Why do you get all the stuffed animals anyway? That's just sexist."

"Chase, they kept your identity secret. How would anyone know to send you stuffed animals? You'll have to be happy with your medal."

"Well, yeah, but...*you* got a medal, too, *and* growly bears from all the kids. It's just not fair."

Vi handed him a pink stuffed unicorn with big eyes.

Chase smiled and tucked against it like a pillow. "That's much better."

***

"Did you just look at that woman's ass?"

"Vi! Of course not! I was just checking for concealed weapons! You know how alert I like to be to my surroundings."

"Alert to your *hot women* surroundings."

"It's the first time we've been out in a while! I'm just trying to see how much fashions have changed."

"In six weeks?"

"Besides, Vi, nobody's ass can compare to yours. I could probably write a poem to your ass. We'll call it 'Ass, a haiku by Chase Smith, alias'."

"*Oh, purée.*"

"Ass

High, firm, round, tempting

Inviting the touch of my hands

Also of my d—"

"Chase!"

"What, doesn't that make five syllables?"

"You know everyone at the other tables can hear you, right?"

"Sorry, honey. I forgot you were so shy."

***

"Tell me a story."

"A story?"

"About you. Anything, really."

"Well…once there was a young man who met this really hot blonde and decided he was going to get her. This woman was so hot that *nobody* could get her. So obviously she had to put him through some tests to make sure he was worthy. She threw knives at him, and he survived. She threw him into a deep river, and he survived. And then she thought, that was way too easy for him. He's going to win too fast if I don't think of something *really* hard. So she thought really evilly, and she figured out the very hardest thing to do for that man, and she said he had to do it: he had to wait. But he was strong-willed, and he was brave, and he was stubborn, and he did that, too. And then she had no choice. She had to keep her word. So…"

Vi buried her head in his side, laughing. There was really maybe nothing quite as perfect as two people stretched out on the same couch, on a quiet evening, tucked together. "But I meant a story I didn't know."

"Oh, so *you* know the ending, too. You're just pretending not to."

She pinched him. But not really enough to sting.

"Okay, what kind of story?"

"Just any story. Maybe a story you like to tell. Or maybe one you never tell, because you wanted to, but you didn't know who to tell it to."

"Comedy, tragedy?"

A little pet of fingers against his chest. "Anything."

He took her hand and ran his thumb up her work-toughened fingers. "We can take turns. You tell me some, too."

She nodded into his side.

He thought and thought. "Well…once there was this young man who saw people fall from tall, tall towers. And it hurt his heart, because he couldn't catch them, and he watched the towers crumble to the ground. And so he tried to make himself into someone who could always *do* something, never just watch a television helpless again. And…I don't think I can tell this."

Vi squeezed his hand. "I'll go for a little bit. You grew up on a ranch, and my grandmother and brother have farms, right? Let's start with that."

***

"Does this package contain what I think it does?"

"Oh, look at that! More fan mail. Now I wonder which of your fans could have sent you pink peekaboo panties?"

***

"Wow, you look happy, even for you. What's going on?"

A big grin. "I'm cleared for action again. You would die of jealousy if you knew the training they've got us on for the next month. It's in Corsica, with your 2e REP, SAS from Britain, and the KSM. They said this time the imperative really was for us to learn how to cooperate and not try to beat all the other forces, but we'll see how that goes."

A faint smile, green eyes watching him very alertly. "This just revs you up, doesn't it? You love your job."

"It's my purpose, Vi."

She came to stand in front of him and rested a loose fist on his chest. "Have fun. Kick ass."

"Will you miss me?"

"Of course I'll *miss* you. But I'll be busy kicking ass, too."

"It will get harder," Chase warned, warily. "I'm with SOCEUR right now, but they don't have to keep me there. The next deployment could be six months in a war zone again."

"Is this the part where you realize you need the kind of woman who can pack up her life and follow yours around?"

"No. This is the point where I know how good it is to be with a woman who has a full, good, happy life without me. So I don't have to feel guilty about my own life choices. But it will still be hard. For both of us."

"Chase. Please try to wrap your mind around what it means to apprentice in a starred kitchen at fifteen and work my way up to my own two stars by twenty-eight. I. Do. Hard. Things."

"Damn, I love you."

"I love you, too, you arrogant idiot. Now go kick ass."

***

"Vi! Vi! Wake up! Guess what day it is?"

"It's...is it *four in the morning? Merde*, Chase, we just got to bed an hour ago."

"It's *January*! I survived!"

"You might be premature on that."

"Too late! I *made it*. Pay up, Gorgeous."

Vi rolled over slowly. In the dim pre-dawn of her brother's farm house, where they'd gone to celebrate New Year's Eve, Chase's big body was propped over hers, his hand shaking her shoulder. He looked as pushy and unstoppable and eager as a kid at Christmas. Which she should know, having been dragged out of bed at this hour only a week before by his nieces and nephews when they spent Christmas in Texas.

Even though she was in that swimmy, queasy space between a night full of dancing and good wine and the hangover that was going to set in soon, she still had to smile.

Chase had fun at New Year's. He danced all night. He carried the kids on his shoulders while he danced and let them put funny hats on him and crouched in a corner coaxing smiles out of a tearful three-year-old who, overstimulated but determined to make it until midnight, was having a harder and harder time handling it when her older cousins ran faster than she did.

He had fun at Christmas, too. He washed dishes and decorated trees and helped cut out cookies—although he mostly ate the dough—and split wood, making sure Vi came to watch him flex while he did it, and kept a fire going. Christmas morning, he got down and built train tracks and robots and even, calmly and with a secret glint of humor in his eyes, played with dolls in princess outfits when his littlest niece begged him, although he tended to have the princesses get in catastrophic situations and then explode into action with flips and derring-do as they surmounted it. His niece loved it.

From what he said, missing Christmas with his family was one of his hardest times downrange, and he was thrilled when, like this year, his tour ended in time for him to enjoy it.

"Pay up what?" she demanded, just to see what he said.

"Your entire life, of course," he said grandly. "Now *mine*. As promised." He held out a small box. "Plus, Grandma says can we quit messing around and pick a date. She's decided she wants to complete a triathlon, and she's worried we'll mess up her training schedule."

Vi had to pause at that. "Seriously?"

"Oh, yeah."

"Won't get on a plane but is considering swimming four kilometers in open ocean? At the age of eighty-six?"

"You met her, right?"

"Yeah, and I think you were exaggerating about the ailing part. If she and my grandmother ever meet, they are going to hit it off so well."

"Maybe *they* can get married." Chase paused as he heard what he'd said, and a grin crossed his face. "Love to see the look on my parents' faces if that happened. Vi!" He nudged the ring box against her hand.

Scarred but healed, that hand.

Resilient. Like them.

"Damn, I love you," she sighed.

A huge smile split his face. He opened the ring box.

And she was a little afraid. Because he hadn't consulted her about the ring choice—she hadn't even known he had bought one already—and when a man chose the engagement ring on his own, it seemed as if he made a statement. Of who he thought the woman he was marrying was, and of who he wanted her to be.

One of those moments when the difference between who a man wanted to have hot sex with and who he wanted to have in his life as his partner and mother of his children really shone through.

What if the ring was fragile and sweet and fancy? What if it had a huge, protruding diamond, to show him off—what a good, generous guy he was who could take care of his little woman—rather than a ring that suited her work and how much she must use her hands?

Chase had such a hopeful look on his face, excited, pushy...exactly like his nieces and nephews on Christmas morning.

Nieces and nephews who had given Chase quite a few handmade presents he didn't quite know what to do with, but which he had exclaimed over enthusiastically anyway, as if they were the greatest treasures he had ever received. He had a bracelet made out of pink yarn and bits of crayon-colored paper stashed carefully in a small treasure box right now, a bracelet he'd worn every day of the rest of the visit and right onto the plane back to France so his niece could see it on his wrist.

She looked down at the ring.

A gorgeous Damascus steel, with the classic ripple pattern, and a tension set diamond held in the wide band like a star caught in strength. Exquisitely simple, the diamond winking in that smooth band.

Her breath caught, and she looked up at him quickly, her eyes stinging.

"I wanted it to be something that showed off your hand," he said cautiously, checking her face, just like his niece had his about that yarn bracelet, to make sure she liked it. "Rather than the other way around."

Her scarred, tough hand. The stinging grew worse.

"I know you'll still have to take it off a lot when you're working, because of hygiene and all that, but I wanted it to be at least *possible* to work in it. Like it...honored what you do, wasn't the opposite of it."

It was very embarrassing, but she was starting to cry.

"A lot of the rings I saw looked like they were really designed for women who liked to imagine themselves as somebody's arm candy, as if the ring was what gave them value, you know? And I wanted the ring to honor the value you already had."

A little tear rolled down her cheek. And she couldn't even remember to fight it. "Chase," she whispered. She stroked the ring.

"When I was in BUD/S, at the start of Hell Week, one of the instructors said they were going to break us open. That we were just pretty clay pots our parents had made, but they would smash us and find out what was inside. And some of us would have nothing inside, and some of us would just have shit. But some of us would have Damascus steel. Like you do, Vi."

And like him. She put her hand on that beautiful pure steel of him, that he cushioned with human muscle and with humor and warmth.

"Will you get me one?" he asked, quiet and deep, almost *shy*. "Because I saw one. A similar style with a broader band and a smaller diamond, as if it was this unbreakable strength that had caught something absolutely brilliant and glowing and precious. I...really liked it." He dipped his head a little. Definitely shy.

She caught his hand, curling her fingertips into his, linking them tight.

Blue eyes met hers, so bright. So full of life and wanting and hope. And full of this certainty, with that strange brush of shyness to it, as if they had reached a point so vulnerable and so trusting that even Chase could not barrel his way brashly through it.

He had to just wait, all open.

Trusting for her to open just as much.

"I never thought I would say this about that *enfoiré* Abed, but he brought me so much luck," Vi whispered, squeezing his fingers. *Brought me you. All the way from Texas.*

"You make your own luck, Vi. Luck's just the world's response to all the energy you put into it."

"Then you, too." She squeezed his hand hard. "You make luck, too."

"Trust me, I know." He looked down at their hands, his expression vulnerable and steady and wondering, and then took the ring out of the box. "I know exactly how lucky I am." He slid the ring onto her finger. "And I'm willing to do everything I can to keep that luck."

And they did.

***

THE END

BUT IT'S REALLY THE BEGINNING

AUTHOR'S NOTE

This started as an ode to Hollywood kind of story—a vision of leather and knives and banter and how much fun it would be to write a knife-wielding heroine like Vi. The counterterrorism plot was essentially a device for what was intended as a lighthearted caper. And then, about three fourths of the way through the writing of it, the November 2015 attacks occurred in Paris. This was a very dark time and, because of the similarities between what the hero in the "lighthearted" plot was working to prevent and the real world devastation, it made it very difficult to return to this book for some time. I think, no matter what, there are elements of darkness in it now that weren't part of my original intention. But I hope that, just like in Paris itself, the life and energy win out. And I like to think Vi makes a good heroine for Paris...no one can keep her down.

LAURA FLORAND

THANK YOU!

Thank you so much for reading! I hope you enjoyed Chase and Vi's story as much as I had fun writing them. And don't miss Lina's story and those of some of Chase's "buddies"! Sign up to my newsletter to be emailed the moment they're released.

Chase Me is the second book in the Paris Nights series. If you enjoyed the Paris setting, you can find Célie and Joss's story in *All For You*. Or head south to a world of sun and flowers with the Vie en Roses series. (Keep reading for glimpses.)

Thank you so much for sharing this world with me! For some behind-the-scenes glimpses of the research with top chefs and chocolatiers, check out my website and Facebook. I hope to meet up with you there!

Thank you and all the best,

Laura Florand

Website: www.lauraflorand.com
Twitter: @LauraFlorand
Facebook: www.facebook.com/LauraFlorandAuthor
Newsletter: http://lauraflorand.com/newsletter

CHASE ME

OTHER BOOKS BY LAURA FLORAND

Paris Nights Series

All For You

Chase Me

La Vie en Roses Series

Turning Up the Heat (a novella prequel)

The Chocolate Rose (also part of the Amour et Chocolat series)

A Rose in Winter, a novella in *No Place Like Home*

Once Upon a Rose

A Wish Upon Jasmine

Amour et Chocolat Series

All's Fair in Love and Chocolate, a novella in *Kiss the Bride*

The Chocolate Thief

The Chocolate Kiss

The Chocolate Rose (also a prequel to La Vie en Roses series)

The Chocolate Touch

The Chocolate Heart

The Chocolate Temptation

LAURA FLORAND

Sun-Kissed (also a sequel to *Snow-Kissed*)

Shadowed Heart (a sequel to *The Chocolate Heart*)

Snow Queen Duology

Snow-Kissed (a novella)

Sun-Kissed (also part of the Amour et Chocolat series)

Memoir

Blame It on Paris

CHASE ME

ONCE UPON A ROSE

Book 1 in La Vie en Roses series: Excerpt

Burlap slid against Matt's shoulder, rough and clinging to the dampness of his skin as he dumped the sack onto the truck bed. The rose scent puffed up thickly, like a silk sheet thrown over his face. He took a step back from the truck, flexing, trying to clear his pounding head and sick stomach.

The sounds of the workers and of his cousins and grandfather rode against his skin, easing him. Raoul was back. That meant they were all here but Lucien, and Pépé was still stubborn and strong enough to insist on overseeing part of the harvest himself before he went to sit under a tree. Meaning Matt still had a few more years before he had to be the family patriarch all by himself, thank God. He'd copied every technique in his grandfather's book, then layered on his own when those failed him, but that whole job of taking charge of his cousins and getting them to listen to him was *still* not working out for him.

But his grandfather was still here for now. His cousins were here, held by Pépé and this valley at their heart, and not scattered to the four winds as they might be one day soon, when Matt became the heart and that heart just couldn't hold them.

All that loss was for later. Today was a good day. It could be. Matt had a hangover, and he had made an utter fool of himself the night before, but this could still be a good day. The rose harvest. The valley spreading around him.

J'y suis. J'y reste.

I am here and here I'll stay.

He stretched, easing his body into the good of this day, and even though it wasn't that hot yet, went ahead and reached for the hem of his shirt, so he could feel the scent of roses all over his skin.

"Show-off," Allegra's voice said, teasingly, and he grinned into the shirt as it passed his head, flexing his muscles a little more, because it would be pretty damn fun if Allegra was ogling him enough to piss Raoul off.

He turned so he could see the expression on Raoul's face as he bundled the T-shirt, half-tempted to toss it to Allegra and see what Raoul did—

And looked straight into the leaf-green eyes of Bouclettes.

Oh, shit. He jerked the T-shirt back over his head, tangling himself in the bundle of it as the holes proved impossible to find, and then he stuck his arm through the neck hole and his head didn't fit and he wrenched it around and tried to get himself straight and dressed somehow and—oh, *fuck*.

He stared at her, all the blood cells in his body rushing to his cheeks.

Damn you, stop, stop, stop, he tried to tell the blood cells, but as usual they ignored him. Thank God for dark Mediterranean skin. It had to help hide some of the color, right? Right? As he remembered carrying her around the party the night before, heat beat in his cheeks until he felt sunburned from the inside out.

Bouclettes was staring at him, mouth open as if he had punched her. Or as if he needed to kiss her again and—*behave!* She was probably thinking what a total jerk he was, first slobbering all over her drunk and now so full of himself he was stripping for her. And getting stuck in his own damn T-shirt.

Somewhere beyond her, between the rows of pink, Raoul had a fist stuffed into his mouth and was trying so hard not to laugh out loud that his body was bending into it, going into convulsions. Tristan was grinning, all right with his world. And Damien had his eyebrows up, making him look all controlled and princely, like someone who would *never* make a fool of himself in front of a woman.

Damn T-shirt. Matt yanked it off his head and threw it. But, of course, the air friction stopped it, so that instead of sailing gloriously across the field, it fell across the rose bush not too far from Bouclettes, a humiliated flag of surrender.

Could his introduction to this woman conceivably get any worse?

He glared at her, about ready to hit one of his damn cousins.

She stared back, her eyes enormous.

"Well, *what*?" he growled. "What do you want now? Why are you still here?" *I was drunk. I'm sorry. Just shoot me now, all right?*

She blinked and took a step back, frowning.

"Matt," Allegra said reproachfully, but with a ripple disturbing his name, as if she was trying not to laugh. "She was curious about the rose harvest. And she needs directions."

Directions. Hey, really? He was *good* with directions. He could get an ant across this valley and tell it the best route, too. He could crouch down with bunnies and have conversations about the best way to get their *petits* through the hills for a little day at the beach.

Of course, all his cousins could, too. He got ready to leap in first before his cousins grabbed the moment from him, like they were always trying to do. "Where do you need to go?" His voice came out rougher than the damn burlap. He struggled to smooth it without audibly clearing his throat. God, he felt naked. Would it look too stupid if he sidled up to that T-shirt and tried getting it over his head again?

"It's this house I inherited here," Bouclettes said. She had the cutest little accent. It made him want to squoosh all her curls in his big fists again and kiss that accent straight on her mouth, as if it was his, when he had so ruined that chance. "113, rue des Rosiers."

The valley did one great beat, a giant heart that had just faltered in its rhythm, and every Rosier in earshot focused on her. His grandfather barely moved, but then he'd probably barely moved back in the war when he'd spotted a swastika up in the *maquis* either. Just gently squeezed the trigger.

That finger-on-the-trigger alertness ran through every one of his cousins now.

Matt was the one who felt clumsy.

"Rue des Rosiers?" he said dumbly. Another beat, harder this time, adrenaline surging. "113, *rue des Rosiers?*" He looked up at a stone house, on the fourth terrace rising into the hills, where it got too steep to be practical to grow roses for harvest at their current market value. "Wait, *inherited?*"

Bouclettes looked at him warily.

"How could you *inherit* it?"

"I don't know exactly," she said slowly. "I had a letter from Antoine Vallier."

Tante Colette's lawyer. Oh, hell. An ominous feeling grew in the pit of Matt's stomach.

"On behalf of a Colette Delatour. He said he was tracking down the descendants of Élise Dubois."

What? Matt twisted toward his grandfather. Pépé stood very still, with this strange, tense blazing look of a fighter who'd just been struck on the face and couldn't strike back without drawing retaliation down on his entire village.

Matt turned back to the curly-haired enemy invader who had sprung up out of the blue. Looking so damn cute and innocent like that, too. He'd *kissed* her. "You can't—Tante Colette gave that house to *you*?"

Bouclettes took a step back.

Had he roared that last word? His voice echoed back at him, as if the valley held it, would squeeze it in a tight fist and never let it free. The air constricted, merciless bands around his sick head and stomach.

"After all that?" He'd just spent the last five months working on that house. Five months. *Oh, could you fix the plumbing, Matthieu? Matthieu, that garden wall needs mending. Matthieu, I think the septic tank might need to be replaced.* Because she was ninety-six and putting her life in order, and she was planning to pass it on to him, right? Because she understood that it was part of his valley and meant to leave this valley whole. Wasn't that the tacit promise there, when she asked him to take care of it? "*You?* Colette gave it to *you*?"

Bouclettes stared at him, a flash of hurt across her face, and then her arms tightened, and her chin went up. "Look, I don't know much more than you. My grandfather didn't stick around for my father's childhood, apparently. All we knew was that he came from France. We never knew we had any heritage here."

Could Tante Colette have had a child they didn't even know about? He twisted to look at his grandfather again, the one man still alive today who would surely have noticed a burgeoning belly on his stepsister. Pépé was frowning, not saying a word.

So—"To *you*?" Tante Colette knew it was his valley. You didn't just rip a chunk out of a man's heart and give it to, to...to whom exactly?

"To *you*?" Definitely he had roared that, he could hear his own voice booming back at him, see the way she braced herself. But—who the hell was she? And what the *hell* was he supposed to do about this? Fight a girl half his size? Strangle his ninety-six-year-old aunt? How did he crush his enemies and defend this valley? His enemy was...she was so *cute*. He didn't want her for an enemy, he wanted to figure out how to overcome last night's handicap and get her to think he was cute, too. Damn it, he hadn't even found out yet what those curls felt like against his palms.

And it was *his valley*.

Bouclettes' chin angled high, her arms tight. "You seemed to like me last night."

Oh, God. Embarrassment, a hangover, and being knifed in the back by his own aunt made for a perfectly horrible combination. "I was *drunk*."

Her mouth set, this stubborn, defiant rosebud. "I never thought I'd say this to a man, but I think I actually liked you better drunk." Turning on her heel, she stalked back to her car.

Matt stared after her, trying desperately not to be sick in the nearest rose bush. Family patriarchs didn't get to do that in front of the members of their family.

"I told my father he should never let my stepsister have some of this valley," his grandfather said tightly. "I told him she couldn't be trusted with it. It takes proper family to understand how important it is to keep it intact. Colette *never* respected that."

His cousins glanced at his grandfather and away, out over the valley, their faces gone neutral. They all knew this about the valley: It couldn't be broken up. It was their *patrimoine*, a world heritage really, in their hearts they knew it even if the world didn't, and so, no matter how much they, too, loved it, they could never really have any of it. It had to be kept intact. It had to go to Matt.

The others could have the company. They could have one hell of a lot more money, when it came down to liquid assets, they could have the right to run off to Africa and have adventures. But the valley was his.

He knew the way their jaws set. He knew the way his cousins looked without comment over the valley, full of roses they had come to help harvest because all their lives they had harvested these roses, grown up playing among them and working for them, in the service of them. He knew the way they didn't look at him again.

So he didn't look at them again, either. It *was* his valley, damn it. He'd tried last year to spend some time at their Paris office, to change who he was, to test out just one of all those many other dreams he had had as a kid, dreams his role as heir had never allowed him to pursue. His glamorous Paris girlfriend hadn't been able to stand the way the valley still held him, even in Paris. How fast he would catch a train back if something happened that he had to take care of. And in the end, he hadn't been able to stand how appalled she would get at the state of his hands when he came back, dramatically calling her manicurist and shoving him in that direction. Because he'd always liked his hands before then—they were strong and they were capable, and wasn't that a good thing for hands to be? A little dirt ground in sometimes—didn't that just prove their worth?

In the end, that one effort to be someone else had made his identity the clearest: The valley was who he was.

He stared after Bouclettes, as she slammed her car door and then pressed her forehead into her steering wheel.

"Who the hell is Élise Dubois?" Damien asked finally, a slice of a question. Damien did not like to be taken by surprise. "Why should Tante Colette be seeking out her heirs *over her own*?"

Matt looked again at Pépé, but Pépé's mouth was a thin line, and he wasn't talking.

Matt's head throbbed in great hard pulses. How could Tante Colette do this?

Without even warning him. Without giving him one single chance to argue her out of it or at least go strangle Antoine Vallier before that idiot even thought about sending that letter. Matt should have known something was up when she'd hired such an inexperienced, fresh-out-of-school lawyer. She wanted someone stupid enough to piss off the Rosiers.

Except—unlike his grandfather—he'd always trusted Tante Colette. She was the one who stitched up his wounds, fed him tea and soups, let him come take refuge in her gardens when all the pressures of his family got to be too much.

She'd loved him, he thought. Enough not to give a chunk of his valley to a stranger.

"It's that house," Raoul told Allegra, pointing to it, there a little up the hillside, only a couple of hundred yards from Matt's own house. If Matt knew Raoul, his cousin was probably already seeing a window—a way he could end up owning a part of this valley. If Raoul could negotiate with rebel warlords with a bullet hole in him, he could probably negotiate a curly-haired stranger into selling an unexpected inheritance.

Especially with Allegra on his side to make friends with her. While Matt alienated her irreparably.

Allegra ran after Bouclettes and knocked on her window, then bent down to speak to her when Bouclettes rolled it down. They were too far away for Matt to hear what they said. "Pépé." Matt struggled to speak. The valley thumped in his chest in one giant, echoing beat. It hurt his head, it was so big. It banged against the inside of his skull.

Possibly the presence of the valley inside him was being exacerbated by a hangover. Damn it. He pressed the heels of his palms into his pounding skull. What the hell had just happened?

Pépé just stood there, lips still pressed tight, a bleak, intense look on his face.

Allegra straightened from the car, and Bouclettes pulled away, heading up the dirt road that cut through the field of roses toward the house that Tante Colette had just torn out of Matt's valley and handed to a stranger.

Allegra came back and planted herself in front of him, fists on her hips. "Way to charm the girls, Matt," she said very dryly.

"F—" He caught himself, horrified. He could not possibly tell a woman to fuck off, no matter how bad his hangover and the shock of the moment. Plus, the last thing his skull needed right now was a jolt from Raoul's fist. So he just made a low, growling sound.

"She thinks you're hot, you know," Allegra said, in that friendly conversational tone torturers used in movies as they did something horrible to the hero.

"I...she...what?" The valley packed inside him fled in confusion before the *man* who wanted to take its place, surging up. Matt flushed dark again, even as his entire will scrambled after that flush, trying to get the color to die down.

"She said so." Allegra's sweet torturer's tone. "One of the first things she asked me after she got up this morning: 'Who's the hot one?'"

Damn blood cells, stay away from my cheeks. The boss did not flush. Pépé never flushed. You held your own in this crowd by being the roughest and the toughest. A man who blushed might as well paint a target on his chest and hand his cousins bows and arrows to practice their aim. "No, she did not."

"Probably talking about me." Amusement curled under Tristan's voice as he made himself the conversation's red herring. Was his youngest cousin taking pity on him? How had Tristan turned out so nice like that? After they made him use the purple paint when they used to pretend to be aliens, too.

"*And* she said you had a great body." Allegra drove another needle in, watching Matt squirm. He couldn't even stand himself now. His body felt too big for him. As if all his muscles were trying to get his attention, figure out if they were actually *great*.

"And she was definitely talking about Matt, Tristan," Allegra added. "You guys are impossible."

"I'm sorry, but I can hardly assume the phrase 'the hot one' means Matt," Tristan said cheerfully. "Be my last choice, really. I mean, there's me. Then there's— well, me, again, I really don't see how she would look at any of the other choices." He widened his teasing to Damien and Raoul, spreading the joking and provocation around to dissipate the focus on Matt.

"I was there, Tristan. She was talking about Matt," said Allegra, who either didn't get it, about letting the focus shift off Matt, or wasn't nearly as sweet as Raoul thought she was. "She thinks you're hot," she repeated to Matt, while his flush climbed back up into his cheeks and *beat* there.

Not in front of my cousins, Allegra! Oh, wow, really? Does she really?

Because his valley invader had hair like a wild bramble brush, and an absurdly princess-like face, all piquant chin and rosebud mouth and wary green eyes, and it made him want to surge through all those brambles and wake up the princess. And he so could not admit that he had thoughts like those in front of his cousins and his grandfather.

He was thirty years old, for God's sake. He worked in dirt and rose petals, in burlap and machinery and rough men he had to control. He wasn't supposed to fantasize about being a prince, as if he were still twelve.

Hadn't he made the determination, when he came back from Paris, to stay *grounded* from now on, real? Not to get lost in some ridiculous fantasy about a woman, a fantasy that had no relationship to reality?

"Or she *did*," Allegra said, ripping the last fingernail off. "Before you yelled at her because of something that is hardly her fault."

See, that was why a man needed to keep his feet on the ground. You'd think, as close a relationship as he had with the earth, he would know by now how much it hurt when he crashed into it. Yeah, did. Past tense.

But she'd stolen his land from him. How was he supposed to have taken that calmly? He stared up at the house, at the small figure in the distance climbing out of her car.

Pépé came to stand beside him, eyeing the little house up on the terraces as if it was a German supply depot he was about to take out. "I want that land back in the family," he said, in that crisp, firm way that meant, *explosives it is and tough luck for anyone who might be caught in them.* "This land is yours to defend for this family, Matthieu. What are you going to do about this threat?"

Available now!

ALL FOR YOU, EXCERPT

Paris, near République

Célie worked in heaven. Every day she ran up the stairs to it, into the light that reached down to her, shining through the great casement windows as she came into the *laboratoire*, gleaming in soft dark tones off the marble counters. She hung up her helmet and black leather jacket and pulled on her black chef's jacket instead and ran her fingers through her hair to perk it back out into its current wild pixie cut. She washed her hands and stroked one palm all down the length of one long marble counter as she headed to check on her chocolates from the day before.

Oh, the beauties. There they were, the flat, perfect squares with their little prints, subtle but adamant, the way her boss liked them. Perfect. There were the ganaches and the pralinés setting up in their metal frames. Day three on the mint ganache. Time to slice it into squares with the *guitare* and send them to the enrober.

She called teasing hellos to everyone. "What, you here already, Amand? I didn't expect you until noon." Totally unfair to the hardworking caramellier, but he had slept in once, after a birthday bash, arriving to work so late and so horrified at himself that no one had ever let him forget it.

"Dom, when's the wedding again?" Dominique Richard, their boss, was diligently trying to resist marrying his girlfriend until he had given her enough time to figure out what a bad bet he was, and the only way to handle that was tease him. Otherwise Célie's heart might squeeze too much in this warm, fuzzy, mushy urge to give the man a big hug—and then a very hard shove into the arms of his happiness.

Guys who screwed over a woman's chance at happiness because they were so convinced they weren't good enough did *not* earn any points in her book.

"Can somebody work around here besides me?" Dom asked in complete exasperation, totally unmerited, just because the guy had no idea how to deal with all the teasing that came his way. It was why they couldn't resist. He was so big, and he got all ruffled and grouchy and adorable.

"I want to have time to pick out my dress!" Célie protested, hauling down the *guitare*. "I know exactly what you two are going to do. You'll put it off until all of a sudden you wander in some Monday with a stunned, scared look on your face, and we'll find out you eloped over the weekend to some village in Papua New Guinea. And we'll have missed the whole thing!"

Dom growled desperately, like a persecuted bear, and bent his head over his éclairs.

Célie grinned and started slicing her mint ganache into squares, the guitar wires cutting through it effortlessly. *There you go.* She tasted one. Soft, dissolving in her mouth, delicately infused with fresh mint. *Mmm. Perfect. Time to get it all dressed up.* Enrobing time.

She got to spend her days like this. In one of the top chocolate *laboratoires* in Paris. Okay, *the* top, but some people over in the Sixth like a certain Sylvain Marquis persisted in disputing that point. What*ever*. He was such a classicist. *Boring.* And *everyone* knew that cinnamon did not marry well with dark chocolate, so that latest Cade Marquis bar of his was just ridiculous.

And she didn't even want to think about Simon Casset with his stupid sculptures. So he could do fancy sculptures. Was that real chocolate? Did people eat that stuff? No. So. *She* did important chocolate. Chocolate that adventured. Chocolate people wanted to sink their teeth into. Chocolate that opened a whole world up in front of a person, right there in her mouth.

Chocolate that was so much beyond anything she had ever dreamed her life would be as a teenager. *God*, she loved her day. She stretched out her arms, nearly bopped their apprentice Zoe, who was carrying a bowl of chocolate to the scale, grinned at her in apology, and carried her mint ganaches over to the enrober.

She'd been loving her day for a little over three hours and was getting kind of ready to take a little break from doing so and let her back muscles relax for fifteen minutes when Guillemette showed up at the top of the stairs. Célie cocked her eyebrows at the other woman hopefully. Time for a little not-smoke break, perhaps? Were things quiet enough downstairs? Célie didn't smoke anymore, not since some stupid guy she once knew made her quit and she found out how many *flavors* there were out there when they weren't being hidden by tobacco. But sometimes she'd give just about anything to be able to hold a cigarette between her fingers and blow smoke out with a sexy purse of her lips and truly believe that was all it took to make her cool.

Because the double ear piercings and the spiky pixie hair were a lot less expensive over the long-term, but they could be misinterpreted as bravado, whereas—

A teenager slouching against a wall and blowing smoke from her mouth was *always* clearly genuine coolness, no bravado about it, of course. Célie rolled her eyes at herself, and Guillemette, instead of gesturing for her to come join her for the not-smoke break, instead came up to her counter where she was working and stole a little chocolate. "There's a guy here to see you," Guillemette said a little doubtfully. "And we're getting low on the Arabica."

Célie glanced at the trolley full of trays where the Arabica chocolates had finished and were ready to be transferred to metal flats. "I'll bring some down with me. Who's the guy?" Maybe that guy she had met Saturday, Danny and Tiare's friend? She tried to figure out if she felt any excitement about that, but adrenaline ran pretty high in her on a normal day in the *laboratoire*, so it was hard to tell.

"He didn't say."

And Guillemette hadn't asked? Maybe there had been several customers at once or something.

"I'll be down in a second," Célie said, and Guillemette headed back while Célie loaded up a couple of the metal flats they used in the display cases with the Arabica, with its subtle texture, no prints on this one. Dark and exotic and touched with coffee.

She ran down the spiral metal stairs with her usual happy energy, and halfway down, the face of the big man waiting with his hands in his pockets by the pastry display counter came into view, and she—

Tripped.

The trays flew out of her hands as her foot caught on one of the metal steps, and she grabbed after them even as they sailed away. Her knuckles knocked against one tray, and chocolates shot off it, raining down everywhere just as she started to realize she was falling, too.

Oh, *fuck*, that instant flashing realization of how much this was going to hurt and how much too late it was to save herself, even as she tried to grab the banister, and—

Hard hands caught her, and she *oofed* into them and right up against a big body, caught like a rugby ball, except it was raining chocolates during this game, and—

She gasped for breath, post impact, and pulled herself upright, staring up at the person who still held her in steadying hands.

Wary, hard, intense hazel green eyes stared back down at her. He looked caught, instead of her, his lips parted, as if maybe he had meant to say something. But, looking down at her, he didn't say anything at all.

Strong eyebrows, strong stubborn forehead and cheekbones and chin—every single damn bone in his body stubborn—and skin so much more tanned and weathered than when she had last seen it. Brown hair cropped military-close to his head and sanded by sun.

Célie wrenched back out of his hands, her own flying to her face as she burst into tears.

Just—burst. Right there in public, with all her colleagues and their customers around her. She backed up a step and then another, tears flooding down her cheeks, chocolate crushing under her feet.

"Célie," he said, and even his voice sounded rougher and tougher. And wary.

She turned and ran back up the staircase, dashing at her eyes to try to see the steps through the tears, and burst back up through the glass doors into the *laboratoire*. Dom looked up immediately, and then straightened. "Célie? *What's wrong?*"

Big, bad Dom, yeah, right, with the heart of gold. He came forward while she shook her head, having nothing she could tell him, scrubbing at her eyes in vain.

The glass door behind her opened. "Célie," that rough, half-familiar voice said. "I—"

She darted toward the other end of the *laboratoire* and her ganache cooling room.

"Get the fuck out of my kitchen," Dom said behind her, flat, and she paused, half turning.

Dom Richard, big and dark, stood blocking the other man in the glass doorway. Joss locked eyes with him, these two big dangerous men, one who wanted in and one who wasn't about to let him. Célie bit a finger, on sudden fear, and started back toward them.

Joss Castel looked past Dom to her. Their eyes held.

"Célie, go in the other room," Dom said without turning around. And to Joss: "You. *Get out.*"

Joss thrust his hands in his pockets. Out of combat. Sheathing his weapons. He nodded once, a jerk of his head at Célie, and turned and made his way down the stairs.

Dom followed. Célie went to the casement window above the store's entrance and watched as Joss left the store, crossed the street, and turned to look up at the window. She started crying again, just at that look, and when she lifted her hand to swipe her eyes, he must have caught the movement through the reflection off the glass, because his gaze focused on her.

"What was that all about?" Dom asked behind her. She turned, but she couldn't quite get herself to leave the window. She couldn't quite get herself to walk out of sight. "Célie, who is that guy and what did he do?"

She shook her head.

"Célie."

She slashed a hand through the air, wishing she could shut things down like a *man* could, make her hand say, *This subject is closed.* When *Dom* slashed a subject closed with one move of his hand like that, no one messed with *him.* Well, except for her, of course. "Just someone I knew before. Years ago. Before I worked here."

"When you lived in Tarterets?" Their old, bad *banlieue.* "And he was bad? Did he hit you? Was he dealing? What was it?"

She gazed at Dom uneasily. For all that he was so big and bad and dark, always seeming to have that threat of violence in him, it was the first time she had ever seen him about to commit violence.

"No," she said quickly. "No. He didn't."

"Célie."

"No, he really didn't, damn it, Dom! *Merde.* Do you think I would *let* him?"

"You couldn't have been over eighteen."

"Yeah, well—he didn't."

Dom's teeth showed, like a man who didn't believe her and was about to reach out and rip the truth out of her. "Then *what*—"

"He left me! That's all. He fucking left me there, so that he could go make himself into a better person. Yeah. So *fuck you*, Dom. Go marry your girlfriend instead of playing around with this *I-need-to-be-good-enough* shit and leave me alone!"

And she sank down on her butt, right there in the cooling room, between the trolleys full of chocolate and the marble island, in the slanting light from the casement window, and cried.

Just cried and cried and cried.

It sure as hell put a damper on chocolate production for a while, but for as long as she needed it, people did leave her alone.

Available now!

CHASE ME

ACKNOWLEDGEMENTS

First of all, I want to offer a huge thank you to Mercy and Dale Anderson, a wonderful editing team whose support and encouragement and insight into story has meant so much to me. And many, many thanks also to readers Lisa Chinn and Lynn Latimer for all their early feedback. And of course my thanks would not be complete without heaping praises on authors Virginia Kantra and Stephanie Burgis for their feedback.

And a huge thank you, of course, to all my readers, as always, for all your support which has kept me motivated to write more books! Thank you all so much.

ABOUT LAURA FLORAND

Laura Florand burst on the contemporary romance scene in 2012 with her award-winning Amour et Chocolat series. Since then, her international bestselling books have appeared in ten languages, been named among the Best Books of the Year by *Library Journal, Romantic Times,* and Barnes & Noble; received the RT Seal of Excellence and numerous starred reviews from *Publishers Weekly, Library Journal,* and *Booklist;* and been recommended by NPR, *USA Today,* and *The Wall Street Journal,* among others.

After a Fulbright year in Tahiti and backpacking everywhere from New Zealand to Greece, and several years living in Madrid and Paris, Laura now teaches Romance Studies at Duke University. Contrary to what the "Romance Studies" may imply, this means she primarily teaches French language and culture and does a great deal of research on French gastronomy, particularly chocolate.

CHASE ME

COPYRIGHT

CPSIA information can be obtained
at www.ICGtesting.com
Printed in the USA
LVOW03s0538231217
560621LV00004B/713/P